THE PURSUIT OF CHANCE:
ENERGY HISTORIES BOOK ONE

C.M. Walker

GREEN IVY
PUBLISHING

Green Ivy Publishing
1 Lincoln Centre
18W140 Butterfield Road
Suite 1500
Oakbrook Terrace IL 60181-4843
www.greenivybooks.com

The Pursuit of Chance-Energy Histories Book One/C.M. Walker

ISBN: 978-1-946446-97-8
Ebook: 978-1-946446-98-5

For my loving wife

Without you these characters would still just be living
in my head

Safe Houses

"Safe Houses." That's what they were supposed to be. Chance knew he had two weeks at best before the Hunters caught up to him. When that happened the running would start all over. Chance had barely evaded them last time. The trap they had set was very good. It was only dumb luck that a security guard had walked into the warehouse where he was hiding on a routine check. The fifteen-year-old boy had been on the run for almost three years. In the meantime, he would lay low and enjoy this particular safe house's amenities. It had been weeks since he had a good meal and a hot bath. He walked around his temporary home, a multiple story house that had once been the seat of power in his world.

The house itself was bone white. Large columns could have been Greek or Roman. Inside, across from the large double door entrance, was a huge staircase that spiraled both left and right. The stairs were made of oak or teak. Chance really did not know the difference, but they were beautiful. Carvings of horses on the bottom of the banisters made them look regal. Murals of Greek mythological figures adorned the walls. The third floor rooms were large. At one time they were reserved for leaders and special guests. Chance took the stairs to the second floor to look for a dorm room. Each one had a nice bed, closet and a small bathroom. Chance chose a room a near the west end of the second floor. He made sure that there was no one inhabiting the rooms around him. He liked to be ready to leave at a moment's notice and people tripping him up in the halls did not help.

He looked out the window of his temporary room at the vast lands surrounding the house. From where he stood, he could see the stables bustling with activity. A young man rode out on a pale horse, presumably to explore the lands. Farther out he could see cattle grazing and what looked like a chicken coup. Wheat and corn crops were growing out in the open, and there was also a greenhouse the size of a small manufacturing facility. He could not see them from his room but on his way in he had passed by an apple orchard and the vineyards that lined the sides of the road. Chance could see pumps for natural gas on this land that the house used for heat. He imagined there was a cistern out there somewhere providing water, maybe filled by an underground river. He knew that the house was built totally off the grid on purpose when the Queen ruled from there. Eventually the gaslights had been replaced with electric. A small power generator was installed that could use the natural gas to spin the turbines and make electricity. Small teardrop shaped chandeliers lit the hallways in a dim light. The Queen could have stayed here forever if she wished. Not even the council contradicted the Queen's decisions although they were supposed to run Chance's world. He know she wasn't really a Queen. She was not related to royalty or anything, people just called her that.

Chance stepped into the bathroom and looked in the mirror hanging above the marble sink. The frame on the mirror was pure silver of course. He looked at himself for a minute and was startled. Did he always have those bags under his deep blue eyes? Was his chestnut colored hair always so dirty and unkempt? He sighed heavily and turned on the shower. For some reason there was a mask on all the handles of the sink and shower. He could not remember ever seeing that at any of the other houses he had stayed in. Then again some of those had been in the heart of a city and looked more like hotels or apartment complexes. Chance found it funny in a way that the people who lived all around those buildings had no clue of the danger that lurked just next door. He stepped out of his clothes and into the steaming shower. As the water ran over him he closed his eyes and tried to remember how he got here.

Chance was a Crèche kid and like a lot of the children in his world he didn't know who his parents were. When he was old enough he had asked one of his teachers and was told, "When your father dropped you off he said, 'I care little what happens to him. I just never want to see him again.'" He didn't know anything about his mother. Growing up in a Crèche was not all bad; he even liked some of the kids who were there with him. Jim was always cracking jokes and Eliza could be counted on for a challenging chess match. Chance absently wondered what happened to them. All the kids he knew learned the same lessons, school was only a few hours a day however practice was constant. Traditional school was not really important. Everyone was taught to read and write, and the basics of math. History, science, and other subjects were left up to the student to study or not at his or her own discretion. Combat skills, survival skills, and special disciplines were the rule of the day. Be the best, the strongest and never fail at what you learned.

Chance was ok with it all until he started noticing other students disappearing, usually around age thirteen or so. When Chance asked about it he was told, so and so had moved on, or so and so was not good enough. "Just hope when you come of age you will be." That was it, he never saw them again. Of course all the kids talked among themselves about it. What happens when you come of age? What were we being trained for? Why is it such a big secret? Why did the teachers concentrate on certain students? Chance also noticed how much attention the teachers paid to him. "You have great potential," they would say. "Look at how much control he has," they would comment to each other.

When he turned twelve he decided he was not going to wait for the teachers to decide he was ready. Chance knew that soon he would be taken to the upper classmen to be prepared for whatever came at thirteen. He had the strong suspicion based on all his training that it was some sort of fight. In the middle of the night on a spring morning just as the weather was getting nice, Chance fled. That was almost three years ago, he had been running ever since. Somehow the Hunters always found him.

The longest period of rest he had was when he met a young boy named Marcus in the park. Chance told Marcus he was on a road trip with his mom and they got separated in a mall. They didn't have cell phones so she and he created a system where they would retrace their steps and meet back at the park. Marcus's family took him in for a short time while he "searched" for his missing mom. If Chance had not been trained in persuasive techniques he was certain they would have called the police. When the Hunters finally caught up to him, Marcus and his family were killed in the attempt to capture Chance. He vowed then to never put innocent people in harm's way again.

Chance went down to the mess hall. He was surprised at how few people were around. Like all safe houses, this one was fully staffed, but the staff must have been bored out of their minds here. In Chance's world everyone had a job as house staff, cook, stable keeper, or something else. Now and again a leader would take a position of a cook or a maid, not only to escape the chaos that surrounded them but to show others that everyone was equal. This usually only happened for a few months at a time, but it was enough.

Chance didn't know where he fit in the scheme of things. Right now he was a transient refugee he supposed. Always keeping one step ahead of the Hunters, he still did not know why they chased him or how they found him. They had to have better things to do with their time then chase one young boy who obviously did not want to be found. Chance ordered a couple of burgers and some fries. He could have ordered anything, from lobster tails to a peanut butter sandwich. He sat down to eat and looked around the room again. While on the run Chance almost always found someone to teach him new skills. He wondered if any of the men and women here would be willing to show him something new. Chance decided to check out the training area in the morning. Tonight, he would eat and sleep.

In the morning Chance took a jog around the property. Despite being on the run, he kept to a training schedule of sorts. He had not met the head of the house yet, whoever was in charge here was so far content to let him settle in. After his run he went back to the house and took the stairs down to the training area. Chance was not certain what he would find here. Some places only had a single open basement, while others had more elaborate training equipment.

He was surprised to see the house had at least three sublevels. The first level turned out to be a shopping area. There were two large rooms split down the middle by a hallway. The right side back wall was lined with shoes, boots, and even slippers. Row upon row of jeans, shirts, suits, coats, even socks and underwear filled the room. The survival gear was here as well. Tents, lamps, cooking and camping gear were all categorized neatly. In the other room was an armory; swords, daggers, shields, whips, even an assortment of axes.

What is with this place, he thought. He knew that safe houses were places to restock; however, he had never seen such a large assortment of items to be taken.

Following the hallway, he went down to the next level. This was a huge training area. It had to be far wider than the house above it. The training floor was split off into several small combat rooms. Each of them had training dummies and the floors were covered in one inch thick mats designed to minimize the impact of a fall from a throw or a takedown. There was a large aquatic area as well with several pools of various sizes and depths. Some were for lap swimming, while others were obviously just for aquatic training. He could see a few people in various stages of their workouts in some of the rooms.

• •

Looking around Chance saw three elevators. These were the only doors in the entire house that had guards around them. Two of the guards were talking in low voices just within ear shot, being on the run for so long had taught him to listen for any information he could gather.

"I hear Lord Cyrus is going to oversee the fight," the first guard said quietly. "Word is he is really angry about leaving the construction of Sanctuary to be here too," he added with a laugh. The second man laughed as well and they both resumed their silent posts. The guards looked bored.

Walking over to the closest elevator, he saw the word "Challenger" written above it. The first guard was a man in about his thirties. He was dressed in casual clothes and had shoulder length hair tied off in a ponytail by a piece of what looked like rawhide. He did not appear to be armed but

Chance did not let that fool him into thinking the man was not dangerous.

"Where does that lead?" Chance asked.

Dark eyes looked at Chance and the guard answered, "The arena of course," as if the answer was obvious.

"Oh, I didn't realize there was one here," Chance responded. He knew that there were battle arena's all over the world in different locations. Having missed his debut at thirteen, Chance had never seen the inside of a battle arena.

"Do I know you kid?" asked the guard. He was looking at Chance like he should be seeing something he didn't.

"Nope, first time here," Chance replied, holding his hand out. "I'm Chance, and you are?"

"They call me Hector." The guard took Chances hand. "Why do they call you Chance?"

"Not sure. Have been called that for most of my life."

"You didn't get a combat name?" Hector asked. "Most people do after a few battles."

"How did you get yours?" Chance asked, changing the subject.

"I fight well with a sword and shield, old Greek style, so I earned the name," he said with a smile. "I don't usually guard the elevator, but there is a challenge tonight that will be fought in this arena. Typhoonus asked us to make sure no one was messing around down there. If you want to watch the fight you will need to use the spectator's elevator. Caster is guarding it until fight time." He pointed to the other man he had been talking to.

Chance looked over to see a rather large man with dark hair, a large sword hanging from this hip. *Great* he thought *I choose the one safe house in the area with not only a battle arena but one where there is a fight tonight.*

Looking back at Hector he asked, "Do you know who the opponents are?"

"Someone named Talon challenged Lord Gerrod. He must be awfully confident."

"Thanks for the info Hector. I'll have to get down here before the crowed to make sure I get a seat," Chance said with a smile. He was beginning to wonder if he should just raid the clothes area for what he needed and leave immediately. Hector was dropping names as if they were important but years on the road in hiding kept him out of the loop. He had heard the name Gerrod before; supposedly he was given his name from a book written by an author named Knack or something like that.

Chance knew that fighting names were given to fighters by their group members or earned for some reason. It was considered bad form to pick one's own. Most of the time once earned, a combat name stuck with a fighter for life. There were always exceptions. Chance knew of a woman named Flare who was renamed Wind Walker when she awoke a year after a fight in which no one thought she would live. Something about the way she won the fight earned her a new name. The funny thing about combat names is they could come from anywhere. Some, like Hector, came from mythology; some people's names came from books, ancient and modern; still some came from popular movies and even animation. Chance had heard of people named after stars, and elements. All he knew was that he avoided arena combat at all costs. It's not to say he has not had to fight. Over the last three years there were several times he had to fight to keep alive and it was not always the Hunters who he fought.

He decided to pick up the items he needed just in case he had to take off quick. Chance didn't think the Hunters would be at the fight tonight but he wasn't taking any chances. Maybe that's where he got his name. Looking around the clothing area he decided on a couple pairs of blue jeans, some t-shirts, a new pair of Nike running shoes and a light leather jacket. He figured that if it was cold the jacket would provide enough warmth till he could get another from a safe house or steal one. It would not be the first time he was forced to steal to live. Chance was about to take the items back to his room when he was met by a stunning tall blond woman with amazing blue eyes. They were the palest color blue he had ever seen; almost white they were so blue.

"Hello young man," she said. "I am Clotho. I oversee the Manor, and you are?"

For a moment Chance lost his powers of speech, but he finally stuttered, "Ch- Chance. My name is Chance."

She laughed a beautiful musical laugh and said, "Chance and Fate, well met," and extended her hand.

"N-n-nice to meet you," he replied shaking her hand. "I was wondering who was in charge of this place. It's called the Manor? I'll work off the clothes and food. I was going to pick apples in the orchard tomorrow," he added quickly.

"No need to worry about that," she said. "I was just curious about the young man who was brave enough to stay in Phantom's old room. That one and the surrounding rooms have been vacant for years."

Good grief, Chance thought. *It's no wonder no one was around!* Looking at the beautiful woman before him he said, "Well I just figured it was a room like any other. No reason not to use it since it was available." He smiled. "What did you mean by Chance and Fate?" he asked trying to change the subject.

"My name," she said studying the young man in front of her. "Clotho is one of the aspects of Fate. So here we are, Chance," she said pointing to him, "and Fate," pointing to herself with a smile.

"Oh...well...um...I didn't know that," he stammered.

"That's ok, few people really do."

"Um, if there is not anything else you need I guess I'll be heading back to my room now. Don't want to be a burden to you and I want to pick out something nice to wear to the battle tonight. Will you be in the leadership box with Cyrus?" he asked.

"You're well informed Chance. Yes, I'll be in the box with Lord Cyrus. If you need anything while you are here just let one of the staff know and I will see to it."

"Thank you Lady Clotho," he said bowing and slightly flushed, wondering why she was spending this much time talking to him but too flustered to ask.

"No need to call me Lady. Clotho is just fine," she said with that musical laugher again. "Enjoy your stay with us." With that, she left without looking back.

As she walked back up the stairs Chance had the opportunity to admire her figure, paying particular attention to the way her slacks hugged her posterior. Blushing, he waited until she was gone to make his way back to his room.

After returning to his room Chance took another look around and realized he was in fact in Phantom's room. That explained the masks on the handles and why people seemed to avoid this part of the hall. When Phantom was a teen around Chance's age this had been his room! How stupid could he get not recognizing the signs? Even someone as out of the loop as Chance knew the name of the man who took down the Queen, it was part of his studies growing up. He decided not to worry about it and play it off just like he told Clotho. This was a room like any other.

He changed into a new pair of jeans and t-shirt and packed the rest of his new clothes in his backpack. Looking at the roughed up item he decided to keep it. After all it had been with him since almost the beginning of his journey and felt like an old friend at this point. Chance thought he might add one of the camping kits to his traveling attire. It was a smallish bundle with a two-man tent, sleeping bag, cooking gear, and a lantern. The last time he had to hide in the woods he had to build his own lean-to and only had a ratty old blanket; it was a disaster. Seven miserable cold days in the forest trying to lose the Hunters, he thought a travel kit would be a good idea. Now the question at hand was to stay or to run. Clotho seemed ok. He had been there less than twenty-four hours, not enough time for the Hunters to know where he was yet. He lay down on the bed, closed his eyes and went over his options.

After looking at it objectively he decided that going to the fight that night might be a good thing after all. He would see if he was being followed and might learn a thing or two from watching. He had never seen a sanctioned fight before. Chance didn't know anything about Talon but he had heard Gerrod was a cunning warrior from Mercer, one of the teachers he had found on the road. He had not found anyone here so far that struck him as a potential short term teacher. Trying to spend more time with Clotho had his young mind going in all sorts of wrong directions and he knew she was much too old for him. Besides, she kept making him forget how to speak properly.

Realizing how much of the day had gotten away from him and taking his pack out of habit he went back to the mess hall to get some lunch. Clotho had told him not to worry about working in the orchards which was different; however, this entire safe house was different. He should have known it would be when he realized this was the Queens house. Clotho had called it a Manor. The Queen was an evil tyrant. Chance was not sure how she had gotten the Council to do her bidding but she did, until Phantom put a dagger in her heart. The story was legendary. Phantom, young and powerful had hero worshiped the Queen. When he was nineteen he killed the Queen for unknown reasons, then he disappeared and here Chance was sleeping in the same bed. Maybe the future had great things in store for him too!

Pizza for lunch! Chance loved pizza, he tried the pizza in every city he went to. Chicago had had some great pizza, however the safe house there was a dump compared to the Manor. It was a small apartment building sitting in an area surrounded by gang violence, not that anyone in the building cared about that sort of thing. Here at the Manor the mess hall had a few more people in it then when he was here last night for dinner. Chance assumed it was people arriving early to get good seats for the fight. He wondered if Caster would let him in early enough to grab a glass side seat.

Chance grabbed a drink and made his way down to the arena after stopping in the clothing area to snag a camping pack and a hoodie to be safe in case someone in the audience was a Hunter. Caster was still at his post in front of the elevator. Chance could see he had let several people in already.

The arena was roughly half the size of a professional football field. The seats were raised eighteen feet from the floor and protected by glass. Looking down into the arena for the first time Chance was intimidated by the sheer size and magnitude of what was before him. He realized at one point in time he was supposed to have fought someone in a similar setting. This had to be what was supposed to be waiting for him when he turned thirteen. Deep in his thoughts, he was unaware that Clotho had walked up behind him.

"Quite frightening to behold for the first time isn't it?" she said, startling Chance.

"Jesus, you scared me." He tried to settle his heart rate while looking at the woman before him. She had changed into a rather revealing black dress with a plunging neckline.

"Have you never seen an arena before Chance?" She asked not at all oblivious to the slightly askew jaw and the eyes checking out her body.

"Well, um, no. I have seen one, just not an arena like this one," Chance replied, his face turning red as he tried to concentrate on Clotho's eyebrows.

"Well then let me educate you," she said with a knowing smile. "This arena was the first of its kind, designed by the late Lord Apollo to allow for a full range of combat from its occupants." She sat down in one of the open seats. "The interior as you see is designed to be both beautiful and functional. The floor is oak planks and the walls are just simple drywall with acrylic paint and murals retouched for each fight. We can also change the composition of the floor from sand to ice depending on the groups whims." She pointed to the glass.

"The glass that separates us from the combatants is bullet proof and supposed to be shatter proof as well. The lighting in the ceiling is a full thirty feet away so it is assumed it is mostly safe." She added a wry smile to this comment.

"The major design is however what you don't see. Behind the walls, including the walls behind the audience, there is two feet of concrete, with an inch of steel on the backside. Then there is a layer of water three foot thick. This goes for above and below as well. Finally, there is another layer of steel and concrete on the outside of the water barriers." She paused in her speech and looked at Chance. "Quite impressive, isn't it?"

"What is the reason for all of that protection?" Chance asked.

"Until Apollo designed this room all fights had to be outdoors as far away from civilization as possible," explained Clotho. "Now however, an arena such as this could be in the heart of downtown DC and no one would know what goes on there. Enjoy the fight, I must go greet Lord Cyrus." With that she was off again. Chance took his seat near the protective glass, still close to the elevator and waited for the combatants to arrive.

The Battle

The stands filled up quickly as the hour of the fight approached. One o'clock in the morning, eastern standard time, was the traditional hour for a challenge to begin. No one could remember why that time was chosen, only that is was chosen in the time of the Queen. Some traditions were followed no matter who set them. Weapons of all sorts were used with the exception of guns. E-worlders considered them to be cheap and beneath them, no art or skill involved in simply pulling a trigger. Only the most evil of them would consider using a firearm under any circumstance. Chance wondered how the elevators played into the design of the building. How did they bypass the water system? What did the system serve?

A young woman around his age sat in the seat next to him but paid him no notice. She was pretty from what he could see, with dirty blond hair, blue eyes, a cute nose, and a nice figure. He was thinking of Clotho again. *Stop that*, he thought to himself.

Turning his eyes to the arena he noticed that Gerrod was already standing at his side of the arena. He was dressed in a black poet shirt and jeans. Chance was surprised to see he was barefoot. Then he remembered that when a combatant is unsure of what his terrain would be it was best to be barefoot. Gerrod looked to be wearing a rapier and main-gauche combo for weapons. The combination of weapons also known as Florentine style used the long thin Rapier in your main hand. The main-gauche which is a medium length dagger was held in your off hand, usually the left. In fact, the name main-gauche is literally French meaning left hand. Chance wondered what his skill level was with the pair, knowing that his own best style was long sword. He had tried to use long sword and short sword together but had not yet gotten the hang of it. Chance began to feel that watching Gerrod fight with these two weapons would not be of much help. He looked to the other door to see when Talon would arrive and wondered what weapons he would be using.

"Is this your first fight?" the blond girl next to him asked out of nowhere.

"Why do you ask that?" Chance replied startled.

"Well you're really tense. It's coming off you in waves."

"I have been to a lot of fights," he lied. "Just not this high profile"

"You need to work on that," she told him with a grin.

"Need to work on what?"

"Lying." She winked. "If I can read it like a book, imagine what people better trained can do."

"Do you always start out conversations with new people by insulting them?" His mind immediately went to Clotho and how she had spoken to him. Did she know he was lying?

"Sorry, I'm Athena. I have been told I'm too blunt sometimes."

"Hello Athena, I am Chance." He offered his hand to her, agreeing mentally that she was too blunt.

"Nice to meet you Chance," she replied taking his hand. "So how many fights have you actually been to?"

"Wow you are blunt!" he exclaimed. "This will be my third."

"Oh, you're in for a treat then. My leader tells me Lord Gerrod is awesome!"

Her leader? thought Chance. With that they both looked to the arena as the challenger entered the ring. Talon was dressed in a red leather vest with small metal plates on it. He was also wearing tall red greaves, a piece of armor designed to protect the shins and sometimes knees over his black jeans and boots. Over all he looked far better protected than Gerrod. He was carrying a hand and a half long sword in his right hand.

Challenges have changed over the years. Originally the challenger issued and set terms. The recipient of the challenge either accepted or was considered a coward and forfeited his or her position. Considering most challenges were for position in the hierarchy, ambitious people used this to their advantage. As time grew on the nature of a challenge altered. It went from position to possessions. Greedy or less then moral people would challenge someone they knew was better than them overall, but set the terms to a certain skill. The Council who made all laws and rules decided to step in and make some changes to how challenges were issued. Individuals who accepted a challenge could name at least the terms of the fight. So, if a person challenged another for his position in their group, the challenged person got to name how they fought. This eliminated opportunistic combatants from taking advantage of a vastly superior opponent by using their weakness. Oddly enough most combat took place within a person's own group by people vying for a coveted leadership role.

As time wore on, the Council decided that when a challenge was issued there were only three rules to be agreed upon. The first one: Is the fight to submission or death? In the time of the Queen all fights were to the death. The second: Is it single purpose (position, title, or weapon) or is it for everything the other person has? The last: is combat limited or unlimited? In limited fights fighters agreed on the weapon and specialties. In unlimited combat, fighters could use anything.

"Do you know the terms of this fight?" Chance asked Athena suddenly.

"I heard it's to the death, for everything including positions and unlimited combat."

"That's about as bad as it gets,"

"Talon doesn't like Gerrod," Athena explained. "Gerrod married a woman Talon wanted. It started a stupid feud several years back. Now shh, Cyrus is about to speak."

In the leadership box a mountain of a man stood up. Chance could not get over the size of him. He must have been close to eight feet tall and as wide as a truck. Clotho looked like a child standing next to him and Chance knew she was at least five foot six. Cyrus had olive colored skin, black hair, and from what Chance could see deep brown eyes.

• •

"Ladies and gentlemen," Cyrus said in a deep clear voice. "Talon of the Arclights has challenged Lord Gerrod of the Forum to combat." Cyrus paused and looked over the crowd. No one missed the title given to Gerrod. "The terms are last man standing, for everything the other has, no limits. Let the best man win. Fight!"

When Cyrus sat he leaned over to Clotho and asked, "Why is Athena here? And who is the young man next to her?"

Looking over to where Cyrus gestured, "Oh, that's the young man I was telling you about, Chance. He seems a little lost. He had a very difficult time speaking around me." She laughed.

"Most young men do, but what is he doing with Athena?"

"I don't know Cyrus. I don't think they know each other though. Perhaps Horatius is here somewhere. Remember he's on vacation right now so we can't contact him. I'll have Cassiel check it out." Looking over her shoulder she motioned for a tall thin man. He had shoulder length brown hair and green eyes.

"Yes, My Lady?" Cassiel said taking a knee.

"See if Horatius is with us tonight, and find out why his daughter Athena is here please. And stop calling me My Lady."

"Certainly Clotho," he said with a smile and left the box on his assigned task.

• •

Talon and Gerrod approached each other cautiously, each man sizing the other up as best they could. Talon looked to Gerrod's bare feet and his choice of weapon which looked weaker than his own long sword. Chance noticed how calm Gerrod seemed. He was already sweating and he was not even in the fight. Looking at Talon with his armor, boots, and superior weapon, Chance knew he would have been terrified. Gerrod shifted his stance slightly and moved his position to be more on Talon's left side. Judging by his right-hand grip he would be more vulnerable on that side.

"Gerrod is looking to create an opening," Athena said enthusiastically.

Suddenly Talon jumped forward and swung his sword down in a strong attack to Gerrod's shoulder. Gerrod parried the strike with his rapier, catching the blade all the way on the basket hilt before pushing it away and trying to connect a quick strike with his offhand weapon. Talon rolled out of the way and tried to slash Gerrod on his now exposed stomach. Gerrod, expecting the move, was not there as he had already stepped back out of reach of the long sword. The two men started circling each other once again.

"What style is that?" asked Chance. "I know long sword and that was not a typical long sword attack."

"That was Chinese broadsword," Athena answered. "Talon is trying to throw off Gerrod's concentration by attacking with a style that does not exactly meet the look of his weapon. Twenty bucks says Talon had his hand and a half designed to look like an English weapon but it is balanced like a Chinese sword."

"Why?"

"Chinese broad swords are lighter, faster and more flexible than a European hand and a half, but they have about the same length," said Athena. "If Talon was trying to trick Gerrod with the look of the weapon, it may have backfired. A rapier is also light and flexible. A true long sword would have been a better weapon for this fight as it could break a rapier." They continued to watch the fight.

Gerrod attacked Talon with a number of quick thrusts followed by a low slash to Talon's forearm. Talon stepped back after blocking the attacks, with only a small cursory nick on his left arm. Pressing his attack Talon, unleashed a flurry of quick fluid slashes at Gerrod. The blade of Talon's sword was bending slightly.

"Told you," said Athena. "Did you see the way Talons blade flexed? No way a European long sword would do that!"

"Long sword is my main style Athena. I think I know what it looks like in use!" Chance hissed.

"Yours too?" Athena responded with a smile.

Gerrod, having seen through the charade, attacked in a series of decisive blows with both rapier and main-gauche. Each attack was designed to push Talon closer to a wall. The look on Talon's face made the spectators realize that he knew Gerrod had outmatched him in swordplay. The hoax of the long sword had been exposed by both style and flexibility of his blade. Talon knew that in a sword fight of masters, the first to make a mistake loses and he had made a mistake. It was time to change tactics. Soon enough Gerrod had him up against the wall with a sword almost at his throat.

"Give it up Talon," Gerrod said to him. "I don't want to kill you but I will if I have too."

Talon realized that Gerrod had him cornered. He responded with two words, "Combat unlimited."

Gerrod had just enough time to put up a shield before the telekinetic energy blast knocked him fifteen feet across the room. Moving almost faster than the eye can see Talon shot across the room hoping to capitalize on his attack. He slashed downward at the prone position of Gerrod his sword hit the floor as the man was no longer there. Turning his head, he had just enough time to dodge the bolt of electricity coming towards him from Gerrod's outstretched hand. Throwing a quick diversionary ball of energy at Gerrod, Talon again accelerated his body to a blur hoping to use speed to his advantage.

"Did you see how Talon is using hyper acceleration to attack?" Athena asked Chance.

"Yes, but I can barely follow him he is moving so fast."

"Do you know the limits?"

"What do you mean the limits?"

Athena smiled and said, "When you use hyper acceleration it speeds up everything from your physical speed to your cellular level. So, you age much faster than normal and burn out your body's fuel and energy much sooner."

Chance, not wanting to seem like he did not know, asked a question in return "I often wondered why people used that ability when it can be so harmful if you're not careful. What do you think?"

"Usually it is used in short bursts to finish your opponent quickly," she explained. "Better to lose a year of your life than the entire thing."

Gerrod dodged another energy blast and sheathed his sword. Talon could not seem to get past Gerrod's defenses. Accelerating around the room, he fired off two more bursts of energy and moved in for a strike. He was beginning to feel hot. Gerrod saw the attack coming and put up a barrier of energy that made Talon feel like he was moving through water. With his left arm extended he showed Gerrod why he was called Talon. Two hidden talon-like spikes shot out from his left wrist catching Gerrod in the right shoulder. The audience reacted in shock as it looked like Talon was about to win an upset victory.

Chance was so engrossed in the fight he didn't notice the three men carefully making their way to him and Athena. Cassiel who had been searching for Athena's father did. He was immediately concerned for the young woman. Unfortunately, he was on the other side of the arena and was trying to intercept one of the men without alerting them to his presence.

Gerrod opened his eyes wide in shock and pain. He had been one step ahead of Talon from the beginning of the entire fight, despite the tricks, and he was not expecting this. Talon opened his right hand and charged up an attack to finish the battle. The audience watched, preparing themselves for Gerrod's defeat when Talon burst into flames. Gerrod stepped back and fed the energy from his combustion attack. Realizing too late that the heat he felt was not from the acceleration exertion, but from Gerrod building up the temperature in his own body, Talon screamed in pain. Gerrod quickly pulled his sword and decapitated his foe not wanting him to suffer any longer. The crowd went crazy chanting Gerrod's name and stomping their feat in time with his name "Lord Gerrod, Lord Gerrod!".

The Hunter nearest Chance and Athena was knocked over by a man jumping to his feet to cheer. The commotion caused Chance to look over and he recognized the man. Standing quickly, he looked around and saw he was surrounded.

"What's wrong?" Athena asked him.

"I have to go," Chance said grabbing his pack.

"Take me with you!" Athena pleaded.

Chance looked down at the girl, her eyes like steel looking at him and made a snap decision. "Take my hand." When they clasped hands, he teleported.

Athena

Athena had a good life, a father who loved her, friends, and good trainers. Life in the Argonauts was everything you could want. E-worlders or energy users lived next door to but outside of society. Well not every energy user, after all many of them lived in normal society, had jobs, friends and mortgages. These so-called Peripheral members only had to worry about challenges and keeping a low profile, you could not use energy in public. People like Athena and her family were full inclusion E-worlders. They lived in groups like the Forum, Argonauts, or Seraphs. Most energy users spent their entire lives living in the e-world, training, using, and learning to channel energy. Once energy is tapped it can be harnessed and shaped to do amazing things. Human bodies being just large chemical electrical batteries when it comes down to it are filled with energy.

The e-world is roughly one percent of the population. In a world of six billion people that meant at any given time there were sixty-million e-worlders, give or take. Athena was one of the people who had learned to tap and manipulate her body's energy, or draw energy from other sources.

Over the millennia, e-worlders had faced many hardships at the hands of Non's, those people who could not use it. They have always existed but were misunderstood, hunted and burned at the stake for being witches or abominations. They don't need books or special words for things like spells although Non's always think they do. They just had the ability or talent to see how energy flows and shape it. Like athletic aptitude or musical talent, some people have it and some people don't. However, it does run in families. It wasn't until the discovery of genes that energy users even realized although not a mutation like in comic books, it was simply a gene that was active in them that was dormant in others that allowed them to do what they do. Most genes are the same in all people, but a small number of genes (about one percent of the total) are slightly different giving different talents and so it was with energy users, their one percent allowed them to harness energy. E-worlders have been forced to hide their abilities from Non's for centuries. The Council degreed that people who could not use energy would never understand or trust those who can and persecution would happen again. The most recent evidence of this was the Salem Witch hunts. Not everyone who is an energy user knows they are. People in the normal world hear stories all the time about things they can't explain. The boy that survives the plane crash unharmed, the girl in Russia who has x-ray vision, the grandmother who lifts a truck off her grandchild, the mother who finds herself on the other side of them room just as her child falls. Non's call these events miracles, but in each case, the individuals involved were energy users who didn't know what they were. They just unconsciously drew on the ability.

Because of the persecution and misunderstandings over the centuries, groups were formed. Groups usually had five leaders. The odd number was to ensure a majority for large decisions like raiding another group. Athena's father, Horatius, was one of the leaders of the Argonauts. He had been chosen for the position by Hera when another leader was killed in combat by Darthus. Hera thought Darthus would bring evil into her group, so she challenged and defeated him herself, which gave her the option of appointing a leader since she now held two seats. The Argonauts, or Argos as they called themselves for short, traditionally named themselves after Greek and Roman gods and warriors. Horatius was a good, fair and just leader who treated the group well.

Argonauts teachers taught by specialty rather than age, so classes consisted of students of all ages at once. Group members learned to harness fire, electricity, wind, kinetic energy and even manipulate cells to close wounds faster. Like anything, people had a natural affinity for a particular type or form of energy, so as they progressed, they would take advanced classes in their specialty. Horatius was a teacher before he became a leader so he continued to check in on the classes from time to time.

Athena was an excellent student. She excelled at martial combat as well as fire energy. It made her a formidable opponent during her debut at thirteen. The challenge was a submission battle with terms for an ancient long sword, unlimited combat. Her opponent was a fifteen-year-old boy who was very skilled at manipulating earth energy. She superheated the earth barrier he had erected around himself and trapped him in it. There were no hard feelings. An older member was always chosen to fight a younger member's first fight. Good practice for when someone received a real challenge. Athena was on the fast track to becoming a powerful influential member of the Argos when disaster struck a month shy of her fourteenth birthday. Her mother, Andromeda, was defeated in a challenge that was supposed to be to submission, but she died from her injuries.

Athena's father changed drastically after that and became overprotective out of love. Her training became less intense as her teachers were afraid of accidentally hurting her. The few challenges she had received (all for the sword she won in her debut) were championed by her father. Injured, pregnant or members under the age of sixteen were allowed a champion to fight in their place. This prevented less than moral e-worlders from taking out enemies in a weakened state. There was also a Leaders' Right rule that allowed a leader to champion any fight if they wished. Because Horatius was so concerned about losing his daughter he kept using Leaders' Right. Athena was beginning to feel both stifled and humiliated. She tried talking to her father about it but he only became more protective. She was not allowed to date, she had an escort when she went horseback riding, and she was no longer allowed to attend arena battles.

Athena decided she had enough. She convinced her best friend Caval to cover for her and she slipped out taking a car. The fifteen-year-old girl drove all night till she arrived at the Manor. She was well aware of all the groups that had nonaggression pacts with the Argos as well as those directly affiliated. When she arrived at the Manor she took a room on the first floor and slept what felt like her first free night in close to two years. When she heard a battle was to take place she knew that she could be recognized but decided that she could slip out afterwards and head to the Dual Hearts further east if she was seen.

What she did not count on was meeting the strange boy named Chance at the fight. He seemed wild, almost feral. She knew that there was more to his story by the way his eyes darted around the room. Athena was enjoying their conversation and her anonymity and was taken by surprise when he said he had to go. She didn't know what possessed her to ask him to take her with him, or what she expected when Chance said, "Take my hand." She certainly did not expect to wake up in the middle of a forest not knowing where she was or how long she had been unconscious.

Athena looked around and noticed that she was covered in a warm blanket and had a jacket tucked under her head. There was a two-man tent close by and a small camp fire was lit. A tripod hung over the fire a small pot hanging from the middle. She could smell something cooking and although she did not know what it was, it smelled wonderful. Athena saw no sign of Chance. Getting up she looked around trying to recall how she got here.

Her eyes opened wide when she remembered. She had grabbed Chance's hand and they teleported! She didn't even know how to teleport. How did Chance, who she was sure was not as skilled as her, know how to teleport? Time and space energy was heavy stuff, and difficult to use. *I must have passed out from the pain*, she thought.

Chance must have set up camp then went off for food or something. As she looked around the campsite, she noted that the two-man tent was kind of small. *How did he have all this stuff? We were in the arena. He saw he didn't like, and they we were gone. Did he leave me here and go back and get this stuff? What is he running from? Where did he take them?* Too many questions were running around her head. Athena walked over to the tent, there was a note pinned on it.

Athena, you were out when we arrived. I assume you have never ported before. Covered you up for comfort, and then set up camp. I had to find you some clothes. Rabbit stew is cooking - help yourself. When I get back we can talk about what to do next.

Chance

P.S. you can use the tent; I am used to sleeping outdoors.

Well at least he doesn't expect us to sleep in the tent together she thought. *Father must be going out of his mind right now.* It was one thing to take off, and another to be seen by Cyrus and Clotho and then poof out with an unknown person. She hoped they didn't think Chance kidnapped her. Athena looked inside the tent and saw a comfortable looking sleeping bag and a small lantern. She thought this could work if they had to stay here a few days although she didn't know where here is. She looked at her watch and saw it was three o'clock in the morning. She had been out for over an hour. She gathered the blankets Chance had covered her with and threw them in the tent with the hoodie. Then she took the sleeping bag out of the tent and placed it on the ground near the fire. She scooped out a bowl of stew and slowly ate. After the events of the night and the catnap she was not ready for sleep.

Will Chance be able to find his way back here? Who is he anyway? She was busy with her own thoughts when she felt the displacement of air that indicated someone teleporting in.

Chance stood by the campfire with an armful of clothes and what looked like a heavy fuzzy blanket. "Oh, you're awake," he said putting the clothes in the tent and setting the fuzzy blanket down by the fire. "I was hoping you would be. I see you found my note."

"Thanks for covering me up. The stew is good"

"Why did you take out the sleeping bag?" he asked, noticing it on the ground. "I put that in the tent for you."

"Well I figured if you were giving me the tent, the least I could do is give you the sleeping bag. I'll use the blankets."

"Oh, well, ok. I just was trying to make you comfortable is all."

Athena smiled at him. "So, you can teleport." She let the statement hang in the air, and waited for him to answer.

"Yeah, I learned to port when I was eleven." He went on to explain, "I didn't tell my teachers at the Crèche. Whenever we asked about it the teachers told us that some people just don't have a natural aptitude for it and it takes extensive training to make it work. They promised they would teach it to us when we got older."

"You were eleven?" she said. *That's pretty advanced for eleven,* she thought. *You were raised in a Crèche, but just who are you Chance?*

"My teachers always said things like 'what great potential he has blah blah blah.' It doesn't even hurt me anymore so I forgot about that part. Sorry, it must be why you passed out huh? If this was your first time, you might feel a little weak and tired for the next twelve to eighteen hours."

Athena laughed and said, "Let's just say that was the last thing I was expecting when you told me to take your hand. So where exactly are we anyway? It's a bit warmer here so I am assuming you took us south a ways."

"You're not wrong. We're somewhere in the Pisgah National Forrest in North Carolina. It's about five hundred acres or more so I figured it would be a safe bet to come here."

Athena thought about that. The Manor was in northeast Ohio, and now they were in western North Carolina.

Chance read the look of concentration on her face as a look of worry.

"It's only like six hundred miles. I can take you back if you want. I just need to drop you off in the orchard or something in case the Hunters are still there."

"No, it's fine Chance. I am just surprised is all. My father told me that teleporting is very difficult and it takes practice for someone to be able to teleport more than a few miles."

"Oh, I think that's a myth. Teleporting is all in your head. I could take us to Europe if you like," he said with a grin.

"Ok, now you're just showing off!" Athena said laughing.

"You're just getting back at me because of all the things I knew at the arena aren't you?"

"Maybe a little," he said sheepishly. "But porting isn't that hard, you just need to concentrate on your destination and make sure you get things like elevation right."

"Elevation?" She yawned, beginning to feel drained after all.

"Yeah, because you know land is all at different elevations. So if you want to teleport to say the Rockies, but you teleport too low, you could wind up inside a mountain."

Athena shuddered at the thought. Maybe that's why her teachers told her it was so hard. If someone rushed out too confident and taught themselves to teleport they could kill themselves. Once again she wondered who this guy was. *Why would they teach him a skill so potentially dangerous at such a young age?* She finished up her stew and said, "In the morning you and I need to talk some more, but right now I need some sleep."

"Sure thing. It will be a little different having company. I don't know if I snore or anything so if I keep you up sorry about that." Chance took the sleeping bag and rolled it out on the other side of the fire opposite the tent. He gave Athena the fuzzy blanket and said, "Good night Athena. It was really nice to meet you. Sleep well."

Athena crawled inside the tent and fixed her blankets. She looked out one last time and said, "Goodnight Chance," and zipped up the tent. She thought he was asleep before she even said it.

Missing

"What do you mean she disappeared?" Horatius yelled at Cyrus and Clotho. Horatius was furious. The six foot two man with the same dirty blond hair and blue eyes as his daughter could not believe she was missing. He had returned from a three-day vacation where all communication, even mental, was blocked to find his daughter gone.

Cyrus who was not accustomed to being yelled at by anyone stood up. At seven feet six inches it was clear why he stayed out of the normal world at all costs. He did not like to use his size to intimidate people because his mind was twice as sharp as most people he knew.

"We told you Horatius, she was at the fight sitting with a young man who called himself Chance. We had Cassiel look for you as we could not contact you. When the men attacked Chance, he teleported out of the arena with her. We do not know why they were together or what this means, but we will find out. Isn't that right Cassiel?"

Cassiel who had been silent and standing back away from the conversation spoke up, "I could not get an accurate read on Chance's energy signature. However, I did manage to capture one of the three men. I don't know who they were after yet."

"They were after her of course!" said Horatius. "The last year there have been threats and assassination attempts. I had to have her guarded at all times! And now you tell me she just teleported away with some kid?" He ran his hand across his face, obviously tired and frustrated.

"We don't really know anything about Chance," said Clotho. "But when I spoke to him I did not feel anything negative. He is running, that much was obvious. So it is a distinct possibility that these men were after him and have no connection to the people threatening your daughter. How on earth did she get here anyway?"

Sighing Horatius explained, "She convinced Caval to cover for her for twenty-four hours. I noticed when I got back because she took the Camaro. I taught her to drive in that car when she was thirteen as a reward for doing so well in her classes."

"So when you noticed both her and the car gone you put two and to together; however, you chose not to contact anyone and let them know. Why?" asked Cyrus. "Had we been informed that she was missing or you opened up again, we would have informed you when she arrived yesterday. So don't sit here and yell at Clotho and me over your mistake."

"Don't worry," said Cassiel. "I contacted Uriel. She will be here soon to work on our prisoner. She is the best at breaking mental barriers. It won't be long until we at least know who he is, who he works for, and why he was here."

Horatius looked at the three people in the room. "I'm sorry, I let my emotions control me. I just can't lose my daughter. I have been trying so hard to protect her. I knew I shouldn't have gone on a short vacation."

Cyrus set a hand on his shoulder. "No worries old friend. Just keep calm and we will find Athena. You have our full support behind you."

"You're sure it was Chance who teleported?" asked Clotho.

"It had to have been. We don't start teaching Teleporting till their sixteenth birthday in the Argonauts," Horatius replied.

"It was him," Cassiel said. "I know Athena's energy signature too well. Had it been her I could have at least tracked their rough location."

Thinking this over Cyrus asked, "The other two men who were trying to capture them, did anyone recognize them?"

"I checked with some people in the audience before they left. No one seems to know who they are. Could be a group we know nothing about or some rouges," Clotho answered.

"Well someone had to have trained Chance. You don't just accidentally teleport," Horatius said.

As they were talking a small displacement of air appeared in the room. Uriel walked towards them with a smile. She was a small woman, about five foot two, with pixie cut black hair and dark brown eyes.

"Hello everyone," she said in a voice far stronger than her petite frame looked capable of producing.

"Uri," said Clotho giving the smaller woman a hug. "Thanks for coming so quickly."

"I would have been here sooner but I was sleeping," she said with a pointed look at Cassiel.

"Thank you, Uriel. We would not have woken you if it was not so important," Cassiel replied.

"So, where is this man who tried to kidnap little Athy?"

"We don't know that for certain Uriel," Cyrus explained. "They might have been after the other kid."

"Well I suppose I should get to work. Take me to him," Uriel said in a stern voice.

The holding cells for energy users are special. There are always at least three guards on duty who specialize in dampening fields which block the use of any other energy user in the area. The down side of a dampening files is that they cannot be keyed to an individual, so anyone who enters the area is rendered powerless. Gyro, their head scientist is working on a machine that can generate the field, but until he is successful in creating one, guards are needed. The cells themselves vary from house to house and group to group. The cells at the Manor were designed to be very uncomfortable. They are cold, dank, and almost medieval with heavy oak doors that have only a small window to look in on the prisoner. Clotho had been considering renovating this area, after all, she was not a sadist like the Queen.

Currently the Manor had only two prisoners. The first was a man called Scourge who was caught using energy in the non-energy world. He was a twisted soul who enjoyed hurting people who could not defend themselves. Before he was captured he had tortured eleven people to death. Men, women and teenagers, he had no pattern other than who he happened to see first. At one point in time he worked for the Queen. Death by execution or combat was considered too soft of a punishment by the Council and he had been sentenced to live the rest of his life in a cell with no energy.

The second prisoner was walking around looking for ways to escape. The beds were welded to the floor, and there was only a small toilet and sink. Nothing could be used to try to smash the door down. After Cassiel tossed him in the cell without the use of his energy he knew he was in trouble. Cassiel had asked him some questions but he refused to answer. The widow to his cell opened.

"Hello in there," a stern sounding woman's voice said. "Do you wish to talk or do we have to do things the unpleasant way?"

"You have no right to keep me here," he said. "I have done nothing wrong and the Council will hear of this!"

"If you have done nothing wrong," the voice said while unlocking the door, "then you will have no problem telling me who you are and why you were here." Uriel walked into the cell.

"Who are you?" the man asked looking at the small woman that entered his cell. She didn't look like a threat but looks were deceiving in his world.

"I am Uriel and you and I are going to talk about why you were here tonight. Ok?" She smiled. The man before her had hair almost as black as her own. His hazel eyes were steady but she could still read the fear in them. He was roughly six feet tall from what she could see and by his toned arms he had been well trained.

"Who I am is not important. The fact that you are keeping me here illegally is," he said trying to muster bravado. Something about the small woman unnerved him.

"Well it's considered rude and poor manners to not tell someone your name when they introduce themselves," she said with a frown on her face. "Were you raised with poor manners?"

"It-it's also considered rude to keep a man locked up who does not deserve it," he stammered.

"We know you were working with the other two men who escaped. We just don't know who you were after, the boy or the girl. You can make this very easy on yourself by cooperating." She raised an eyebrow. "Or do I have to start getting unpleasant?"

He was already feeling like she was unpleasant, even with her energy dampened. He almost spilled then fearing what she could do with energy, but thought he could port out as soon as they lifted the field for her. "You have no right to keep me here. I will not answer your questions. Let me free."

Uriel sighed heavily, "Very well then, we will do it the hard way." Looking to the door she called out, "Cyrus, would you be so kind as to take this man to the interrogation room?"

Cyrus walked in looking angry. For some reason the prisoner was more afraid of the woman called Uriel than the giant of a man in front of him.

"Well son," Cyrus said shaking his head, "we tried to do this the nice way."

Walking out of the cell, the prisoner prepared to teleport as soon as he crossed the dampening field. Whoever was holding him would be pulled along but his group would take care of them in short order. It may cost him his life but his secret would be safe. His mind was focused on that single thought, as he waited for his energy return to pop out. Except that when he felt his energy return, he was not able to teleport. He was so shocked that he did not try to use any other powers at his disposal. Cyrus had the prisoner's arms in an iron grip as he sat him down on a chair. They did not even bother to strap him down.

Uriel looked the prisoner in the eye and said, "You noticed that you cannot port out didn't you? That is our newest power, a teleport lock. It stops any form instantaneous movement from happening."

The prisoner panicked and tried to attack with energy, but then the mental assault started.

Runaways

In the morning Athena found that Chance was already awake. He was making breakfast over the fire. The pot of stew from last night was sitting half in a hole he had dug and eggs were frying in a pan. Her body still felt weak and heavy.

"Good morning," Chance said, looking over his shoulder. "There is a stream about half a mile to the north if you want to get cleaned up."

"Good morning Chance," she replied. "Did you sleep at all?"

"Yeah, I got a couple hours," he explained. "I don't sleep much anyway."

"I think I'll eat before I get cleaned up. I'm still feeling run down."

"I thought that might happen, sorry about that. I didn't realize you had never teleported before. We'll stay here till you feel up to traveling again." After a pause, Chance said, "Unless you want me to take you home?"

"No, I'm fine. I think my dad will be furious at me right now but I don't want to go back just yet. Breakfast smells good. Where did you get the eggs?"

"Popped out while you were asleep, snagged them from a Chinese market I know. They always have fresh eggs and produce. I usually just scavenge or hunt for food like I did with the stew but I thought you needed something a little more normal for breakfast." He smiled.

"When you say snagged them you mean..."

"Stole them. Yeah, sorry about that, but I don't have money. Stole those clothes in there for you as well. I don't trust the safe houses right now."

"Who are you Chance?" Athena asked "You're so many contradictions I can't keep up!"

"What do you mean?" he asked a little confused.

"You're obviously an e-worlder. You know about things like safe houses but you had never seen a fight. You're what, sixteen? And yet you have never been in an arena fight! I could tell last night while we watched. You have powers that you shouldn't have, like teleporting. You're so casual with thievery and yet I can tell you're a good person by how you've treated me since we arrived here."

"I'm just a kid trying to keep out of the hands of those Hunters." He explained, "I don't like stealing but I don't have any money. I tried to go straight and even stayed in one of those shelters they have in the common world but the Hunters found me."

"Who are these Hunters?"

He put a plate of eggs in front of her and a cup of coffee. "Hope you like coffee," he said. "I'll tell you what, I'll tell you about me if you tell me about you. When I ran, you asked me to take you with me so you're obviously running too." He picked up the pot of stew and added more hot coals to the hole, then set the pot back down.

Clever, she thought. *"He's keeping the stew hot for later with coals under it. How does he know how to do all this?"*

"Ok, it's a deal. Thanks for the coffee, not my favorite but I think I need the caffeine," she replied.

"Caffeine helps with the effects of the teleport. It should help you feel more like yourself sooner. And for the record I am fifteen."

Athena laughed, "That's what I am talking about. I had no idea that caffeine would help, but you do."

Chance smiled at her. "Ok spill. Who are you Athena? Why are you running? Twice now you have rejected my offer to take you home."

She looked at Chance for a long moment. She was nervous being here with him alone. Up until the point he had teleported, she was certain she could defeat him if she had to. Her father had taught her to always size people up just in case. Now however he was a complete unknown. Chance just sat back, eating his eggs and drinking coffee looking at her expectantly.

"What do you know about the groups in the e-world?" Athena asked suddenly.

Chance laughed. "You're supposed to be telling me about you! But ok, I'll bite. I don't know all that much. I was told growing up to avoid them because they would want to use me."

"Only evil groups would do that!" she exclaimed. Calming down a bit she got back on track. "First off, groups very in size from as small as thirty to as large as a few thousand. Groups all over the world form permanent alliances, or at least have nonaggression pacts. Lastly there are good, evil, and neutral groups."

"Ok, go on."

"The largest group, you could even call it the controlling group, is the Forum. They have been around the longest too, the Manor belongs to them. When energy users started getting persecuted millennia ago the Forum was formed by a group of people with energy who literally held a meeting or a 'forum' about what to do about the problem."

"Very original way of coming up with your name," Chance laughed.

"Don't make fun," Athena said as she also laughed. "Cyrus is the leader of that group, and the Queen was for a very very long time before him. You have heard of the Queen I hope?" she asked.

"Yes I have heard of the Queen. Also Phantom, the guy who took her down then disappeared."

"Well he didn't really disappear," Athena explained. "He just became a permanent Peripheral member, although he is still heard from, from time to time. Still most people think he's dead."

"Ok, let's get back to the part where this has to do with you."

"I grew up in a group called the Argonauts," she smiled. "We're a good group. The people are friendly and I have some really good teachers." Her smile faded a bit. "You mentioned you were raised in a Crèche?"

"Yes. There were about fifteen of us around my age," Chance said, "and forty or so total."

"So many..." Athena looked a little troubled. "In the Argos we have a Crèche as well, but it's used more for a daycare and a place for orphaned kids before they get adopted. In fact, most of the Crèche's I have ever heard of are used in that way. You know the old saying, 'Takes a village to raise a child.'"

Chance looked puzzled by this and encouraged her to continue. "Please, go on."

"Well, like any group, we have a debut fight at thirteen. Until then we are trained to the best of our ability by our teachers. They gave us aptitude tests to see what form of energy we were most proficient with and help us with energies we had more trouble controlling." Athena explained. "For example, I had trouble with water manipulation so I would never be a good healer. My teacher Dionysus worked with me until I had enough of a handle on it to manipulate it properly. I'm not proficient so it takes more energy from me but I am able to use it if I have to."

"They didn't just push you into what you had the best control of?" Chance asked.

"No, they wanted us to have a fighting chance against whatever was thrown at us, so learning to use even what we're weak in was a great help."

"Ok, go on."

"Well, battles give you prestige, and even wealth. The better you are the more you can achieve. I won my debut battle against an older boy and was really looking forward to increasing my name and making the Argos proud. I was given the name Athena because I was both clever and strong in a fight."

Chance collected their plates and poured more coffee. Shaking his head, a little he asked Athena to continue.

"I loved my life and then I lost my mother Andromeda in a fight..." She paused and frowned. "After that my father became unbearable. He would not let me fight, date, go out on my own. It was like I was living in a prison. So I stole a car and left. I was only at the Manor a couple of days when I ran into you. I knew that Clotho and Cyrus had seen me. I liked talking to you. You were funny and unsure so when you looked panicked and said you had to go I wanted to go with you."

"Correct me if I am wrong, but you decided that because your father loved you too much and wanted to protect you the answer was running away?" Chance said in a voice that trembled.

"It sounds really bad when you put it like that."

"So that's it then? Your 'group' loved you, protected you, trained you as best they could and you felt like you were in a prison. Sorry if I sound a little confused."

"Look Chance, you don't understand what it was like ok!"

"You're right. I don't," he said calmly. "I was dumped in a Crèche with tons of other apparently unwanted children and told my father who was alive did not care if I lived or died."

Athena looked horrified. Chance stood and paced to avoid looking at her and continued, "My whole life was train, train, train, excel, be better than the next kid and never ever fail. They didn't really tell us anything. I did figure out something happened when you were thirteen because my friends would disappear and never come back. So when I was twelve I ran away. I just teleported right out one day with the clothes on my back and the skills in my head." He clapped his hands together loudly "A few weeks later the Hunters caught up to me the first time so I have been running ever since." Chance sounded bitter. "Forgive me if I can't empathize with your situation."

"Look Chance, you asked me about my life and I told you. Maybe it didn't fit into your neat little idea of what a person running away is like," she yelled.

"We all feel the need to run for different reasons, you bailed on your Crèche and the kids you knew because it was too hard for you. I left because it wasn't hard enough! Does that mean you're somehow better than me? How dare you pass judgment on me!" she exclaimed.

The angrier Athena got the higher the flames in the small campfire leapt. Chance had to take a step back. He could see that it was her energy feeding the fire. Chance knew she was not doing it on purpose, but the emotional outburst was physically manifesting in the flames before them. For the first time since sitting next to each other in the arena he realized just how strong the young woman in front of him might be. Athena was certainly not some damsel in distress to be rescued.

"Athena," Chance said in a soft voice, "you might want to calm down before you set the forest on fire."

Athena looked at the flames then at Chance and said, "I am going to go get cleaned up now. Thanks for bringing me a towel." She stalked off due north to the creek and left Chance looking after her.

Chance sat at the campsite stoking the fire trying to calm down. He did not normally lose his temper like that and wondered if she did. The situation just drove him crazy. Athena's unconscious display of power was impressive. He knew he should probably take her back home where she belonged. He also knew he had pretty much demanded she tell her story, so it was wrong to be angry about it. Part of him wanted to keep her around; he was tired of being alone.

When Athena returned to camp, her hair was wrapped in the towel he had given her. She didn't say a word, just climbed in the tent to change clothes. She was surprised at how well they fit her. Chance did a nice job guessing her size. Athena was still hurt and angry about his words though. Not only because they ring a little true, but because they were unexpected. People did not normally talk to her that way. She was still feeling the effects of the teleport and with her emotional outburst she felt run down. Athena lay down in the tent and drifted off.

While Athena slept Chance thought more about what had happened. Was he wrong to judge her? He still felt they were not fit companions. Chance spent his life running from battles. He didn't want to take part in the carnage he was afraid was waiting for him. She seemed to revel in it. Athena wanted to increase her fame by fighting more. But more bothersome was that she thought he had basically abandoned the others. As much as he liked her company, he felt it was time to go their separate ways before they hurt one another.

"Athena?" Chance called out quietly after several hours had passed.

"What do you want?" she replied waking up, still feeling angry and hurt.

"Can we talk?"

"We're talking now aren't we?" she snapped.

"I'm sorry for going off on you like that," Chance replied, "but I think you and I both know that this partnership is not going to work."

Athena sat up quickly. "What do you mean?"

"I may have been born into the energy world but I don't think I belong here. I don't want to fight! I did leave people behind. I don't want to gain fame or money from being stronger then someone else in the arena."

Athena sat quietly taking it in. Finally, she asked, "Is that all you took from what I said? Maybe you're right, maybe I do want to be known, but that's not all I am. I just need to prove that I can make it without protection."

"If you want, you can keep the camp," Chance offered. "The road is about twenty miles to the west. I'll wait till you're recovered then take off."

Unzipping the tent Athena looked out at Chance who was poking the fire with a stick. He had the pot of stew on the tripod over the flames again. "Tell me the rest," she whispered.

"What?"

"Tell me the rest of your story," she said. "I can tell you more about what I know, but I really would like to hear the rest of your story."

Chance sighed and threw what looked like a handful of herbs in the pot. Taking a deep breath, he began, "Because I can teleport, I was always able to get away. The first few months were the hardest because I didn't know much about the outside world. I was unsure how to get along. The people around me all felt…" He paused. "Empty. That was when I realized they didn't have energy. I tried to eat in a restaurant and they called the police when I didn't pay."

"You didn't know anything about the normal world?" Athena asked.

"No, we were only told at the Crèche not to use energy around non energy users. At the restaurant, all I knew was there was a menu and food. The Hunters caught up to me again in a few weeks. I ported out because I recognized one of the men from the Crèche. I knew it was dangerous because I was doing blind ports but I didn't have a choice. I reminded myself a dozen times I could end up in a tree or worse, but I didn't to want to be caught.

"That's when by dumb luck I met a man called Sabre. He was the first person to ever give me any real knowledge of the outside world. We spent a few days together and he even gave me a book with pictures of where safe houses could be found by location and elevation. Sabre explained that he didn't need it anymore so he was passing it on to another 'lost soul' who needed to survive. We parted ways when the Hunters caught up to me again but I was able to use the book to teleport to safe house."

"Did Sabre tell you about energy signatures or soul signatures?" Athena interrupted.

"No. What are those?" asked Chance.

"They're like a fingerprint. Everyone has one and they're very unique. They're called energy signatures or soul signatures because there are theories that we pull energy from our souls. It would explain why some people are naturally stronger than others. Their soul is older so they have more natural energy to draw from."

"How would that help the Hunters track me?"

"If they know your signature they can pinpoint your location even after a teleport. They can track the residual energy left behind."

"So, you mean to tell me, the last few years I have been running, the reason I can never seem to escape is because they can always track where I went?!" Chance exclaimed!

"Well, some people can block the tracking or mask their signatures but it is really hard. I think you might have a natural ability at it though. That's why they can never pinpoint your exact location. I can teach to you to see them. I am not really good at it yet. So far my dad has only taught me the basics." Athena said.

Chance sighed, "Well that explains why I am constantly on the run. I memorized as much of the book as I could. I also started hanging out in parks and just listening to the people around me to learn about things in the world I didn't understand. Libraries were a god send as I could just sit in them and read for hours. I lost the book of safe houses when I was nearly captured at my friend Marcus's place. That was the last time I attempted to have a friend."

"Chance," Athena said. "We may come from different backgrounds, but I think there are things we can teach each other. I have skills from many years of training that can help you. At the same time, I can see you have many skills that can help me as well."

Chance looked over at the young woman who had just scooped a bowl of stew out of the pot. She seemed sincere, but she also seemed similar to the people who wanted to fight. He knew that she had skills that he could use. Reading these so called signatures would be a huge help. Even just knowing more about these other groups could be helpful. He took a bowl of stew for himself and looked at Athena again trying to decide if he should just leave, drop her at a safe house or continue to travel with her.

"I know you're thinking of leaving me here," Athena said suddenly. "Teach me to teleport and I'll teach you what I know in the meantime. It's a fair exchange. I can't go back yet."

"If I teach you to teleport, you teach me how to see signatures as best you can and tell me more about your type of groups." Chance counter-offered. "If not, I'll just port you back to the Manor and you can take that car you mentioned and go off on your own."

"It's a deal." She extended her hand across the flames, making them part.

"Deal," Chance said, taking her hand.

Broken

Uriel left the interrogation room with an unconscious man sitting in the chair. Guards took the man down to the prison area. After the information she pulled out of his mind there was no way to let him go. She always felt a little sickened when she broke a prisoner's mind. Uriel naturally excelled at working with brainwaves. Like any other energy, brainwaves could be controlled, manipulated and of course read. Any energy user could learn the basics of the skill, but it took a specialist to break minds that had been trained in defense. She walked into the room where Cyrus, Clotho and Cassiel were waiting. *Three C's,* she thought. *I wonder if they noticed.*

"Are you ok Uriel?" Cassiel asked. Being a Seraph like Uriel his first thought was not of the mission but his friend.

"I'm fine Cassiel. I just want to get this ugliness out of my head," she replied. It had taken twelve hours of concentrated effort and concentration to break into Verock's mind. He had been well trained and almost lost his life in the process.

Clotho placed a hand on Uriel's shoulder and asked, "What did you learn my friend?"

"His name is Verock. It's some variation on a Samarium name or something; I didn't look that deep once

I had it. He works for a group calling itself the Overlords. I have never heard of them. Have you?"

"No," Cyrus replied. "I'll check with the Council and see if one of the Overlords is in their ranks."

"The man he reports to, Harbinger, has Hunter groups out with the express mission to bring Chance back alive," she continued. "I don't know who they work for or who runs the group, but I did see unspeakable acts being committed on children. They're raised as weapons, nothing more, taught to harness their strongest ability for some war that is supposed to be coming. I think whoever this Harbinger is has far more information. Even the Hunters have not been told everything, just where and when to meet Harbinger with Chance. Some of the Hunters like Verock were a part of this group of kids being trained."

"Then I'll track Verock's signature back to where this Harbinger is waiting and capture him," said Cassiel. Before anyone could even speak he was gone.

"I hate to say it but I think Cassiel put himself on a wild goose chase," Cyrus said. "Two of his men escaped. They would have warned Harbinger that the location was comprised."

You're probably right," Clotho agreed, "but Cassiel has to try. He feels it's his fault that Athena fled with Chance. Besides, he is the best at feeling energy traces. If anyone can track the origin he can."

"It's too bad we don't know Chance's soul signature. We could go get him and Athena. It seems the young man is in need of protection." Cyrus sighed

"Why did my daughter leave with him?" Horatius asked. "She had to have seen the two of you."

"Maybe that's why she did," Clotho suggested. "If she is running for some reason she probably assumed you had told us and we would detain her for you."

"I'm beginning to realize how wrong I was for not contacting everyone when I got back and realized she was gone," said Horatius. "I just don't understand why she left."

"She's young Horatius. What's important now is finding her and Chance. I don't think either one of them realize how much danger they're in." Uriel explained., "You never told her about the assignation attempts and Chance may not understand how hunted he actually is."

"Maybe we should talk to Caval. He might be able to shed some light on what she is thinking," suggested Clotho. "The two are very close."

"That's a good idea I'll get him," Cyrus said. "I was watching her more than the fight. After all, I knew Gerrod would win this one and I was a little bored."

Cyrus arrived with Caval about five minutes later. The boy was sweaty from the training session he was just pulled from. The fourteen-year-old stood close to six foot already. He had sandy blond hair and eyes so dark blue they almost looked purple. Those eyes were currently radiating an undercurrent of energy. "Did you all finally decide to let me have my first sanctioned fight?" Caval asked. "I am sure I could take Talon for Lord Gerrod," he smiled eagerly.

"That's not why we asked you here," Cyrus relied.

"Come on, I am over a year past debut age!" Caval exclaimed.

"And your teacher wants you to wait! We have been through this Caval. Horatius and I have some questions for you." Cyrus was firm.

"Honey," Clotho said, "you know it took almost a year for us to convince him to teach you. Listen to him he knows best."

"Fine. What do you want to know?" Caval asked a bit put out.

"For starters," Horatius began, "we want to know why Athena left."

"Oh, that." Caval said with a smile. "She left because she wants to prove to you she can take care of herself. She said you constantly baby and protect her and she will never amount to anything that way. She's right you know. You do protect her too much. What happens if you lose a fight and die? She needs to be able to handle things on her own."

Horatius looked about ready to explode when Cyrus cut in. "Caval, I want to show you what she was doing at the Gerrod's fight. Perhaps you will see something I did not."

"She was here?" Caval asked. "She told me she was heading west, maybe to stay at the Wave Runners for a bit. Wait, who won the fight? I thought it was tonight, not last night."

"Well for some reason she changed her mind and wound up here. When Gerrod accepted Talon's challenge night before last, the fight was set here and Gerrod won of course." Clotho explained.

"Tough luck for Athy. She should have gone west like she said," Caval laughed. "Ok show me this memory of the fight."

Cyrus and Caval connected mentally and he began to replay the memory from the previous night. The process did not take too long, only about five minutes. By the time they were done Caval was not only smiling but laughing.

"Who's the kid?" Caval asked first.

"We don't really know, only what you heard Clotho say in the memory. He calls himself Chance," Cyrus explained.

"Well Athena was really into him. Did you see the way she was leaning in? And that little smirk she had, she must have been explaining something to him and enjoying correcting him." He laughed again.

"That might explain why she left with him. What else did you notice?" Horatius asked.

"Well, aside from Athena thinking he was something, did you notice his stuff? Whoever he is he has been running for a while and is used to running."

"I thought that too," Clotho said. "But why do you think that? What else did you see?"

"Well for starters did you see that haircut? New jeans and a shirt are not going to cover up self-cut hair like that. Also, while you were all looking at Athena you totally missed the bags he snagged before he ported out. He's used to running on a moment's notice. The last thing is, did you see how effortless that teleport was? It was like he was not even trying. The only one I've ever seen port like that was my teacher."

Cyrus laughed. "Fourteen years old and schooling us. You're right. We were all looking at her at that point not him."

"Well we know one thing for sure," Horatius said. "They're going to need to rest up. Athena has never teleported before so she will need recovery time."

"Did you need anything else?" Caval asked? "I might have time to get back and finish my training session."

"We're good Caval. Thanks for telling us your thoughts." Cyrus said. And before he could say another word Caval disappeared. "Show off," Cyrus laughed, "He must have just been taught that." Looking at Uriel he said, "Tell us more about these kids you said Verock was a part of.".

"Ok, but I want you three to listen very carefully. I fully intend to purge these memories as soon as possible," Uriel pleaded.

"It's ok Uri. We understand that it's not pleasant seeing them. Just tell us what you can," Clotho said softly.

"The place Verock is from is nothing like what we are used to. The kids there are clueless about what is really out here. They're given a twisted view of the world. Taught from a young age that people outside of their small world will only use and abuse them. What they can't see, because they're so young, is that the people where they are, are actually doing to them what they're warning them about. It's brilliant in its reverse psychological standpoint." Uriel shuddered.

"Bastards," Cyrus whispered under his breath.

"They seem to target the kids who are lost, the ones who need something to hold on to. Orphans and runaways make the best marks, but I get the feeling there are kids much younger than what I was able to see in Verock's mind, possibly kids born there. He was an orphan, found around eleven maybe twelve years old, he isn't certain.

"The teachers are very good at manipulating those feelings. They teach to a child's strengths which gives them a sense of purpose, but it creates a distinct caste system. They still give them their debut battles at thirteen; however, they pick kids that were raised together for the fight. Only those who are ruthless enough, or scared enough to kill someone they know move on to the next level of training. Those that do it viciously are rewarded. These 'Overlords' are creating an army of fanatics. Most like Verock are so broken they don't know there is another way and follow orders blindly."

When she was finished Uriel was crying. Having a young son of her own, she could not imagine having him grow up in such a place.

Clotho took Uriel in her arms. "We will stop them Uri, I promise. It's time to let go of these memories now." She started pouring soothing energy into the younger woman and soon Uriel was asleep in her embrace. She looked at Cyrus and said, "We need to find this group and save these kids. Chance is running from them but I don't think he understands how bad it can get."

Cyrus just nodded. He hoped Clotho was right about the goodness in Chance. He did not want to have to kill the young man who took Athena when he teleported from the arena just fifteen hours ago. For now, he would wait for Cassiel to return and hope he found something at the rendezvous point.

"Contact Shifter we may need his help," Cyrus said to Clotho. Then, looking at Horatius, he said, "We will get your daughter back. If we have to go to war with these so called Overlords to do it, we will get her back." The look in the elder man's eyes frightened Horatius.

Friendship

Chance and Athena both agreed that they needed to move from camp soon. He had a good idea of where to take her to learn to port, but he did not know if he would have enough time before they were found. He expressed this concern to Athena.

"So we need to cover our tracks is all," Athena explained.

"I have been running for over two years and the Hunters always find me," Chance said exasperated.

"Yes, but now you know how. They tracked your signature. Even though you seem to mask pretty well naturally we need to set up false trails," she said calmly.

"That's a great idea!" Chance exclaimed. "I can port to like fifty different places and they would have to track down each one."

"Yes and no," Athena said with a frown. "Because I lost control a little bit and used energy on the fire, and because they saw you take me they are going to be looking for two traces not one."

"That means I need to take you with me. This could be rougher than I thought."

"If we make four or five jumps a day together and let me sleep we can leave to where you want to actually train in three days. It still takes hours or days to pinpoint a destination from a signature trail. That should leave enough trails to keep them busy." Athena smiled.

"You do realize how much that will take out of you, right?" Chance asked.

"Yes," she said, "but it's necessary and my body will be that much more ready to handle teleporting when you teach me."

"Well, if that's our plan then there is no time like the present. You forgot one detail though. We can't just port out. We have to port back as well."

Athena looked a little sick but reached out and took Chance's hand. They only managed three separate locations the first day. While Athena was resting Chance was thinking about the things she had told him. He couldn't imagine a world the way she described it. He teleported into a sports store in the middle of the night and stole a bow and several arrows with broad head tips. He remembered he had a good hunting knife in his pack and thought about hunting a deer for venison. He knew the meal would be good for Athena as well.

When Athena awoke she once again smelled food and though, *He's always cooking something! Probably a good thing since I can't cook.*

She looked outside the tent at Chance who was sitting by the fire flipping what looked like steaks. He had plates and steak knives sitting by a couple of small benches that were not there before. Leaning on a nearby tree, under the hanging carcass of an eight-point buck, was a composite bow and a quiver of arrows. "Where did you get all this stuff?" It fell out of her mouth before she could help it.

"Uh...stole it."

"Do you steal everything?"

"Well, I'm like Aladdin. I steal only what I can't afford." Chance laughed. "And since I have no cash, that's pretty much everything."

"Ok, if you burst into song, I am leaving," she laughed. "But seriously, you need to be careful. The next time you want to get something just ask me. I have money."

"What?" he asked, surprised.

"I told you I drove a car halfway across the country. I needed money for things like gas and food so I took a money belt from emergency stores." Athena explained. She lifted up her shirt slightly and unstrapped the money belt around her waist and tossed it to Chance.

"There must be three thousand dollars in here!" he exclaimed looking in the belt.

"Well, yeah. The Argos always keep several of them on hand for when we need to venture out into the normal world. If you don't have money you can find yourself in trouble. I couldn't get a fake ID made because I was running so I don't have a driver's license or anything." Athena shrugged.

"I'm trying to wrap my head around a world where you can just take three thousand dollars." Chance said.

"Well I don't like to steal ok, so I would rather you bought things when you're porting out ok?" She leaned over the steaks. "These smell great, but if you want to eat both of those I would prefer if you bought me something."

"Oh, well, these are venison steaks. I shot the buck over there and carved us out some dinner. But if you don't want to eat them because I stole the bow..."

Athena grabbed the plate from Chance's hands and started cutting into the food. "Well, you went to all the trouble of catching it," she said before shoving a fork in her mouth. She closed her eyes as she chewed, enjoying the taste., "It would be rude not to eat it. Just buy food next time is all," she said around a mouthful of venison.

Chance laughed, "Sure thing. Enjoy your steak".

• •

The next few days were hell on Athena. She had no idea that it was going to be so rough. She pretended to be ok so they could squeeze out five locations a day but when they were packing up camp in preparations for departure she practically fell over.

"Just one more port today," Chance said. "Then we can rest all day tomorrow and start training the day after. You're recovering faster and faster each time. Just a lot of ports in a short timeframe have taken their toll."

"You seem fine," she mumbled.

"Well, I have been porting for quite a while. The first few months on the run I felt like you do quite a lot. Don't worry, you're doing great." With that he put his arm around her waist and teleported to their next camp, hoping to start training each other.

• •

The area that Chance chose was the large plains between Kansas and Colorado. From time to time herds of wild horses could still be found roaming there. When training started Athena tutored Chance on the basics of reading an energy or soul, signature.

Everyone in the e-world believes in souls. Astral projection is an advanced power that allows you to leave your body with your soul and travel anywhere. The energy signature in your body resonates with your soul, so in essence they are the same thing. Whenever a person uses energy they leave behind a signature, like a fingerprint. If someone knows your signature, friends or family for instance, they can read the signature you leave behind and know if you have used energy in a particular place. There are advanced energy techniques that can mask your signature. There are some specialists though, Cassiel is one, that can detect someone even with a masked signature.

Athena started channeling some heat energy into her palms. "Ok Chance. Look at me, but not just me. Use your energy sense, just like seeing power flow through your arms."

Chance looked at the young woman before him and saw the energy flow to her hands. He analyzed the pattern being used and stored it in his head for later use. "Ok," he said. "Now what?"

"Don't let the energy in my hands distract you. Look at my body, and look at the source of the energy flow." She blushed a little, realizing she had just told the young man to stare at her body.

Chance did as he was told. He followed the flow of energy back until he saw what he realized was the source, swirling energy in various colors. "I see a cloud. Not really a cloud but it's the nearest description I can think of. It's linked to the energy in your hands."

Athena cut off the flow of energy to her hands. "And now what do you see?"

"Even when the energy flow is cut off, I still see the cloud. It's a little calmer, but it's still there. I never really looked that hard before, but now that I see it I can't un-see it." Chance blushed to his ears and looked down, embarrassed as he realized how intensely he was staring at her body.

Wow! How did he pick that up so fast! Athena looked at Chance and tried to get a read on his signature. She was not very good at it herself but had been taught the basics. Chance had described exactly what her father saw when he looked at her. "Great job. Now try to turn it off and then back on."

Looking at Athena, Chance did as he was told. Now that he knew what to look for it was easy. He chastised himself for not noticing before. He was always able to sense and feel energy from others. He should have known to look deeper.

"Ok, let's work on porting for you," Chance said suddenly. "I can practice seeing signatures while we work on that."

"Ok," Athena said. "How do I begin?"

"I am going to do some short jumps back and forth in front of you. Watch how the energy gathers in my body."

"Ok, but what energy am I using?" Athena asked. "I assume you manipulate time and space in order to move from one place to another in an instant."

"Maybe. I never gave it much thought. I watched one of my teachers do it. I watched her energy flow when she teleported away. We didn't really have classes in this at the Crèche."

"So when did you practice?" Athena asked interested.

"I didn't, my first teleport was my only test. The second one I used to escape."

Athena's eyes opened wide. She wanted to say something about how crazy that was but let it pass. "I am not used to learning only by energy flow. I usually know what type I am looking for but I'll do my best."

Chance purposefully slowed down his process to an almost physical painful pace. When he had the flow of energy going in the correct pattern, Chance teleported three feet to the left. Athena stared at him in concentration, then shook her head. Chance began the process again, this time teleporting three feet to the right.

"I had to watch it the second time on a deeper level. The particles in your body seemed to accelerate the instant before you were teleported!" Athena exclaimed. "That's not time and space energy at all! It's like you shattered your body into billions of particles and reassembled them on the other side!"

"That's basically how I do it, so you can see how the energy flows," Chance said with a smile.

"But how does it work? I mean it's like you destroy and rebuild yourself!"

"No, not at all," Chance said. "I don't destroy my body although it does flow apart, that's why it hurts so badly. I simply tell my body with energy to move one molecule at a time from point A to point B very quickly. Eliza was convinced there were other ways to do it, but I knew this would work for me."

"Who's Eliza?" Athena asked stalling for time; she still didn't completely understand the process. Maybe that's why it was left to more experience people. She was also surprised she felt a little jealous.

"She was a friend I had in the Crèche. I didn't have that many left. When I told her I was thinking of using it to escape she was certain the process would kill me."

"What IS your main?" Athena asked out of the blue.

"Hmm, well the teachers had me concentrating on kinetic energy. They always claimed I was really good with it and it was usually hard for people to master." Chance explained.

"I'm fire," Athena said. "Kinetic energy is not a strong point for me. I think you're using it to teleport."

"I saw how your energy pattern looked earlier when we were working on signatures. Is that how you utilize energy to make fire?"

"Yes. Fire energy is destructive; we who are most proficient in it learn to harness how the waves of fire work at its core. From there we channel our energy into that shape, but I am sure you know that much already," Athena speculated. "That's why I am weak to water, it's not natural to me."

"I can use fire, but I do it different. I use the motion of particles inside the object to set it on fire." Chance explained.

"That's impossible!" Athena challenged.

Chance shook his head. "Seriously, I think Gerrod did the same thing to Talon. Here, watch." He picked up a stick and stared at it intensely. The end burst into flames.

Athena was astounded. "That was completely different from how I use fire."

Chance shrugged. "I can freeze things the same way."

Athena knew Chance was not being arrogant, he was just explaining what he knew and how he manipulated energy. It was totally foreign to her. He may have been correct about Lord Gerrod; however, she was still shocked that he seemed to do things so effortlessly. While she was thinking about this, Chance froze the stick in his hand solid. He then shattered it on the ground like an icicle.

"It's not that hard," he said. "I can teach you if you want."

"I think I know why these guys want you back so bad Chance."

"What? Why? What do you see that I don't?"

"I have only seen one other person learn so quickly and effortlessly, and that's my friend Caval. Because of that, he has had private tutors his whole life. They don't even want him to have a battle because they don't want him to get a reputation this young and become a target. I don't know if you're as strong as he is, but really you control energy so easily and you look at it in a different way. Maybe well trained adults do the same, but I have never heard them talk like you do. You also use the same type of energy to manipulate other elements. It's intense."

"It's just the way I see energy," he explained. "I even found I can change the weather with it if I try."

Athena shook her head and laughed in amazement. "Anything else I should know?" she said with a smile.

"Well," Chance lifted off the ground with telekinetic energy. "I can fly." he said with a grin.

"Now you *are* just showing off!" she said laughing.

Chance returned to the ground, laughing as well and the two new friends started working on the problem at hand. How could he teach Athena to teleport using an energy she was not good at?

Several days passed and Athena was still having trouble gathering the necessary energy pattern to teleport. In the meantime, she had been teaching Chance about mental communication or telepathy which e-worlders used all the time to keep in contact with each other. This was another talent she was new at, but the two of them quickly mastered communicating with each other. Athena didn't know if it was because of Chance's natural ability or her own teachings but chose to think it was her doing.

"Ok, stop," Chance said after several hours of training on the fourth day. "We're looking at this wrong."

"How so?" Athena sat down on the ground, frustrated.

"We've been working under the assumption that what I do is different from what you do," Chance said.

"It is different!" she exclaimed.

"Yes it is, on the surface, but we need to tackle this from a different angle. You're a main fire. You heat things utilizing waves. Those waves make the particles in the object move faster and poof," Chance pushed his arms out in a circle. "I use kinetic energy to speed up the particles and create fire. It does the same thing but in different ways."

Suddenly a light bulb went off in Athena's head. "Maybe I should be focusing on utilizing waves like the waves that come from the sun creating heat! As a main fire I can do that easily. It's second nature."

"Ok, so use these waves, like light waves transferring heat, but instead of making fire just try to flow with them" Chance said, excited. "By doing that you should be able to teleport in a light wave or heat wave instead of a particle stream!"

Athena stood on her side of the prairie, concentrated on her location, and tried to use the changes she and Chance just discussed. After feeling like she had hit a wall for so long, Athena saw the opening she was missing. She transferred her essence into a wave, and for the first time, ported.

• •

After a day of practice and coming close to losing consciousness, Athena was still thrilled she was able to teleport on her own. She found her version of porting was not as painful as Chances which made her happy. She was also slowly becoming addicted to coffee. They had planned to work on increasing distance. Athena was looking forward to it. Chance was proud of her progress. They knew this camp was not going to be safe for much longer but they both wanted Athena more comfortable with her new ability before moving on.

Chance suggested a game of hide and seek. "You teleport and I'll try to track your energy." He should have listened to his instincts.

When the Hunter's came Athena had just performed her fourth teleport of the day. She was still nervous about teleporting long distances but was feeling more comfortable with the power in general. They had partially packed, and Athena was wearing her money belt. She was already beginning to understand Chance's lifestyle from the way he spoke and always looked ready to bolt. She was just about to port back to camp when Chance told her in her mind, *"Run, they're here."* She knew she should have listened but she did not want to be separated from him so she focused on the camp site instead and leapt.

There were four Hunters surrounding Chance. She had teleported to the north of camp and was directly behind one of them. Athena reacted by sending a quick fireball at his back. The stunned Hunter screamed as his clothes caught fire. He dropped to the ground rolling.

Chance was trying unsuccessfully to teleport and realized he was being blocked. When Athena arrived and attacked the Hunter he was shocked, angry and grateful that she did not listen. The Hunter to his left caught fire and the one in front of him fired a pulse of energy at Athena. The blast picked her up and tossed her. She was holding her ears as she hit the ground. Chance lost his head seeing his friend attacked. He had promised himself that he would not allow anyone else to get hurt for him when Marcus and his family were killed. Almost without thinking he picked up three stones about half the size of a golf ball. Charging them up with kinetic energy he shot them at the three men still standing like a bullet from a rifle. Two of the men collapsed, but the third, the one who had hurt Athena, sent that same pulse of energy at the projectile shattering it before it got to him. Chance sprinted over to Athena, picked her up while gathering kinetic energy around his body, and took to the air. The Hunter on the ground fired a pulse at the now airborne Chance just as he felt his teleport ability return.

By the time the concussion wave passed his location, Chance and Athena were gone. The Hunter looked around the prairie. Two of his companions were dead and the third was badly burnt. He walked over to the man lying on the ground, and blasted him with a slicing cut of energy comprised of air. No sense in listening to those screams while he checked out the campsite. They had underestimated the kids. Chance had never attacked so brutally and efficiently before. His little fire wielding girlfriend was probably to blame.

The teleport lock power recently acquired by spies should have contained them. Their spy informed them that the girl was the daughter of an Argonauts leader. He would have to be careful. He found a tent, a bow, camp gear, and clothes. Despite the setback it was still a good day. Chance would have to resupply, and they had his book of safe house locations. He had left it at that brat's house when they killed the family looking after him.

The Hunter contacted the others telepathically. *"Put people at all the safe houses. Chance and his girlfriend should be showing up. She is unconscious and hurt. They will need to rest and resupply, now is the time to catch them."*

Looking around camp one last time the Hunter said to himself, "You're not the only one who can play with fire little girl." He incinerated all traces that people had been here including his fallen companions remains, then calmly teleported out.

Recovery

Florida was nice in the offseason. Chance had taken them to a small open area near Disney Springs Marketplace. He looked Athena over and saw blood coming out of her ears. He was just about to teleport back to the Manor when her eyes fluttered opened.

"Please tell me that we are not captured," she moaned.

"No, we escaped, but you're hurt. I think I should take you back."

"Don't," she said taking his hand. "They'll be expecting that. Also I look worse than I am. That Hunter was attacking with non-lethal power. It was a sound wave or something. It just really hurt my ears. You sound like you're under water."

Skeptical, he frowned and said, "Athena, I don't know."

"I managed to get a partial shield up. My father used to drill me with a game he called power ball. At random he would shoot little balls of energy at me. Not enough to hurt, just enough so I would feel it. I had to learn to block them quick. Great game but this time it failed me actually. I only put up a weak shield to block the type of ball he would shoot." She smiled and sat up.

"So you accidently conditioned yourself for a weakened energy shield." Chance laughed in spite of himself. "Wait till you tell your dad that power ball practice could have gotten you killed." He was laughing pretty hard now and Athena joined him laughing.

"Where are we?" she asked suddenly.

"I wanted somewhere crowded so we could rest without using energy. If we're not porting around or using too much energy they should have trouble tracking us, correct?"

"Yeah, but again, where are we?"

Chance handed her a strip of his shirt to clean the blood off her ears. He stood up and held his hand out to her. "Come on. I'll show you."

They walked closer to the lights of the marketplace, checking to make sure they were not getting too many stares. "We're in Florida," Chance said guiding her to a bus top.

"Florida? Near Disney World?" she asked in a whisper.

Chance laughed, "Trust me there are some good places to rest around here. With all the people around, as long as we don't use energy and draw attention to ourselves, we can just relax a bit."

"Ok. I am in your world after all Aladdin," she said with a smirk.

Chance laughed at the reference. Athena noticed her hearing was returning and that now and again Chance would shudder. She was so focused on where they were she realized she forgot to ask him how they had escaped. The bus pulled up to what looked like a luxury hotel. Athena gave Chance a quizzical look since they were too young to check into a hotel. Chance just shook his head slightly and they exited with the rest of the passengers. He took her hand once again to seem more casual and he walked them out away from the hotel and towards what looked like a construction zone of new luxury condominiums or apartments. As they approached, Chance looked around a bit and pulled Athena behind the construction fence. He lifted a couple of construction helmets off the rack and handed her one, then walked purposefully into the rising structure.

"What are we doing here?" Athena whispered furiously.

Looking around again he said, "These are timeshares. People pay to live in them for like two weeks at a time or something. Marcus' family had one and they told me all about it. They used them when they came here on vacation." He motioned with his arm, "This timeshare is still under construction. I learned about it from Marcus's father. He was thinking of upgrading theirs. The great thing is, when they finish a side of the building they move the furniture and everything in so they can open as soon as the place is one hundred percent completed."

"So, what are we doing here?" she asked again.

"We are going to go up to the third or fourth floor on the finished side and commandeer a suite for ourselves," he said as if that were perfectly obvious. "We lost our trace by teleporting to downtown Disney and took a bus to an unknown location. They will be looking all over Florida for us."

Athena opened her mouth to retort, then closed it, thinking over the merits of this plan. "Where did you come up with this idea?" she asked, "Because it's brilliant really. But how do we explain leaving and entering here?" She was smiling again knowing he would probably have an answer.

"Well I sort of did something like this before. The worker's families are allowed to stay here as a kind of bonus while they finish construction. As long as we don't draw attention to ourselves we can come and go as we please. People will think we are one of the worker's kids enjoying a free vacation. We could probably even use the pool."

Timeshares it seemed were as awesome as a resort. Athena thought the room was even better than some of the leadership quarters she had seen. The unit had two identical mirror image suites connected by a common area. Chance must have known this as he asked if Athena wanted left or right when they walked in. While Athena walked around looking at the rather large kitchen, living room with big screen TV and master bedrooms that had king-sized beds and private bathrooms with walk in tubs. Chance tested all the electric, water, and gas. Once he was certain they everything was in fact on as he thought it would be he sat down on the plush couch and smiled. After Athena had finished her own private tour she sat in the armchair across from Chance.

"This place is great," she said. "What do we do now?"

"Well first, we get cleaned up in a real shower or tub," Chance said laughing, "Because we both need it. Then we get some rest. Tomorrow we can decide how long we want to stay here."

"First shower, then talk about how we escaped, then rest. Ok?" she countered firmly.

Chance looked shaken. "Alright. You do need to know what happened after you were blasted." He got up from the couch. "Thanks for coming back for me. If you hadn't set that Hunter on fire, I would have been caught." Then he made his way to the bedroom on the left to take a long hot shower.

Athena really wanted to try the bathtub, but she assumed if she tried to take a long bath Chance would sneak off to bed before he provided her with answers. So she took a quick shower instead. Feeling glad that her hearing was almost back to normal and oddly safe, she wrapped herself in the robes provided for guests, dried her hair and walked out to the common room. She looked around the room thinking about the crazy week she had just had.

When she went down to watch Lord Gerrod's fight she had no idea that she would meet a strange boy and that it would change her life possibly forever. She knew it was a close call and she should be more frightened, but she was exhilarated. Tired, but exhilarated. Chance walked out a few minutes later. He looked more run down then she had seen him, and almost sad.

"Nice room?" he asked.

"Yeah, the shower was great. You stayed in one of these places before?"

"Once, about a year ago. I made the mistake of staying in a timeshare that was already opened. A family of four walked in while I was in the shower. I had just enough time to grab my pants before teleporting out. It took two days before I could sneak back in and get my pack where I hid it."

Athena laughed at the image of Chance almost naked soaking wet trying to escape a vacationing family. "Why did you choose a place that was occupied?"

"Well, I was still a little new to all this. I met Marcus and his family after that fiasco. I just thought it was a big open hotel in Vegas. Who was going to notice an extra guest?" Chance said with a little smile. "In any case, if I had not run into Marcus I would not have known about the construction and such. His dad was pretty cool."

"Chance how did we escape?" she asked gently. "You seem to be avoiding it."

"Well," he began slowly. "When they attacked, I wasn't able to teleport. I was so surprised; I thought they were blocking all energy with one of those dampening fields. I was taught about those. Kids who were being punished would have to live in an area without energy for a couple weeks or so."

"Ok, go on," she said encouraging.

"I should have realized when I sent you the mental message that at least some energy was working." He looked down and frowned to himself. "The Hunters started surrounding me when you arrived and blasted one of them. After you were hit, I realized I could still fight. I sort of lost it. I charged three rocks with kinetic energy and basically shot the three men still standing." He shook his head. "I killed two of them instantly...there was so much blood.

"The Hunter who attacked you blocked the rock with another wave like the one that hit you. You're probably right it was sound waves or a shockwave. When he was doing that I ran over picked you up and took to the air. When I was about twenty feet off the ground I felt my teleport link come back and took us to the field outside the Disney Market." He looked at her hard before saying, "I thought you were dead."

Chance looked on the verge of tears and Athena did not understand why until it hit her. "You have never had to kill before have you?" she whispered.

"No, I haven't. I ran because I feared that's what was in store for me." He sighed, "And now I have anyway."

"You had to do it. Your life was in danger--"

"I did it for you Athena," Chance cut in. "I saw you fall and there was no hesitation. I killed them." With that he got up and went to bed leaving a stunned Athena on the couch to ponder what she just heard.

In the morning Athena felt as well rested as she ever had. She was concerned about Chance, and still confused by his sudden confession that he had killed for her. Did that mean that if she was not there he would have let himself get taken? She knew that she needed to take his mind off it and try to get him to smile. The question was how? Also, they needed some clothes. Everything they had was left at camp. She was going to miss the tent, and the fuzzy blanket. Chance was cooking breakfast already; she could smell coffee, eggs and bacon. She wondered if he had slept at all. She was still in her robe when she walked out to meet him.

"Good morning," he said brightly. "Don't worry, I didn't steal the food. I took some money from your belt. There is a change of clothes in a bag around here somewhere."

"Morning," she replied. "Smells good." She noticed he was wearing a new shirt and saw the bag he pointed at. "Where did you get the clothes?" she asked.

"Wal-Mart. They're open twenty-four hours."

Athena laughed to herself. "I am supposed to be teaching you, but it seems you're always teaching me." Shaking her head, she asked," What should we do today?"

"I don't know," he replied. "We could always just hang here and let you get some strength back." He handed her a plate of breakfast.

"Thanks," she said. She thought about his offer and rejected it immediately. Chance needed to get out, not brood about the house all day after yesterday's events. Smiling to herself she said, "Chance, I have never been to Disney World. My father was always so protective about things; he never took me. Can we go?"

Chance looked at her for a minute seeing the bright smile on her face. "Sure. I know a great place to port in." He smiled back at her.

Athena laughed again. "We are keeping a low profile remember! This will be my treat," she said walking over to her money belt. "We can even get those park hopper passes and the fast past options!"

"How do you know about Disney World and not know about Wal-Mart?" Chance laughed.

"Everyone knows about Disney World. Come on Aladdin," she teased, "show me a whole new world."

"Alright," he said smiling back genuinely. "But I have to warn you, I may burst into song."

"I'll take my chances." When she finished her breakfast she grabbed her bag of clothes on the way back to her bedroom to get ready.

• •

Sitting on a bus on their way to Disney World, Athena had to laugh about the fact Chance bought her a Minnie Mouse T-shirt. She looked cute in it she had to admit, but she wondered if he was already thinking about going before she mentioned it. He admitted that he had been here a couple times. Athena had to confess she was excited to see the park. The young woman had seen amazing things in her time from people in flight to Cyrus using fire, ice, lighting, water, and wind energy all at the same time at a party. However, she was still thrilled about seeing the castle and rides at the park.

Chance figured that the Hunters would not try to corner him in the Magic Kingdom. Because he only ever teleported in and out there was no chance of finding his trace outside of here until his last port to the Marketplace. Chance picked up on Athena's mood and smiled as well. He wore a Mickey Mouse T-shirt that matched the one he had purchased for Athena. He had not actually planned to go, but bought them as souvenirs.

When they arrived at the gates, Athena purchased three-day park hopping passes with all the extras from food credits to fast passes to get on rides quicker. She took his hand when they put the bands on their wrists and made straight for the first ride on their list - Splash Mountain.

"This is awesome," Athena yelled as they went zooming down the first hill. Both of them grinning and laughing, they stopped by the ride shop when it was to make fun of their picture on the ride. The walked the park smiling and waving at the characters, for the entire world to see just a couple of normal kids enjoying a day of fun. When it was time for lunch, they ate at the *Be Our Guest Restaurant*, while Athena joked about finally having a meal that was not Chance's cooking.

"You look like you're having a great time," Chance said over lunch.

"You do too," she commented. "Have you ever eaten here before?"

"No. First time, I didn't have money when I was here. This is great."

After lunch they rode the Seven Dwarfs Mine Train, enjoying it so much they hopped back in line and waited thirty minutes as they had already used their fast pass. Athena wanted to shop so they bought ice-cream off a silly looking truck and checked out some of the shops.

Chance began to feel better and better as the day went on. He could not forget about what happened at camp, but he felt he could live with it if he had good memories to help balance out the bad. He didn't let Athena know he'd had nightmares all night about the incident. Once again he was grateful to have the young woman with him. Without her, he knew he would have gone crazy in their borrowed timeshare. As the sun began to set they got good seats for the Light Parade and enjoyed the spectacle in front of them. Following the parade back to the Castle to watch the Fireworks show, the two sat hand in hand. Athena rested her head on Chance's shoulder. Both teens though that maybe everything would be ok after all.

Tracking

Cassiel felt desperate. He had to locate this Harbinger. Athena was in trouble and he had missed saving her by such a thin margin he could scarcely believe it. *If Gerrod had taken thirty seconds longer...* he thought to himself. When he arrived at Verock's point of origin, he was fully shielded and ready for combat. The trouble was the place was empty. It had been hastily cleared out and Harbinger was gone. "Damnit," he said out loud. "I knew I should have just left once I had the trace."

Angry and displeased with himself Cassiel began feeling for energy signatures and traces. He picked up Verock's quickly, sensing the man had been in and out of this place so often, faint echoes of past teleports were still there, like a ghost spider web. He took note of other signatures but could not get a solid read. The smudged energy fingerprints were like a blurry photo. Cassiel had already read Athena's companion Chance's signature at his teleport spot. He had the same blurred effect from the boy.

I can't go back empty handed. I have a lot of work to do if I am going to find them. The question is, can I find them before they catch Athena and Chance?

He picked the trace with the second strongest echo of energy from Verock and teleported. He was disappointed to find it must have been his favorite restaurant. Cassiel knew this was going to be a long day. The next few locations were also duds, parks and such places where they were obviously searching. Interesting enough there were also two safe houses on the list. After an exhausting eighteen hours of tracing without sleep, Cassiel had a lead. He wound up in a warehouse. The place was teaming with energy that had been used there less than a week ago if his senses were correct.

Cassiel, in addition to being a strong fighter, was highly skilled in tracking energy traces. He picked up a faint trace of Chance and spent four hours examining the residual energy and echoes left behind to fill in some of the gaps in the signature he had for the young man. Soon the blurry photo would become a crystal-clear image.

Eventually he went back to the Harbingers meeting point to get some sleep. The place was abandoned and he knew his prey would not be back. After several hours of sleep, Cassiel traced another of Verock's echoes and landed in the middle of a crime scene in a nice suburban house. The pictures on the walls and over the fireplace showed a nice looking young family, from the looks of it, a husband, wife and a tween son. The blood on the walls and outlines on the floor painted an ugly picture of what happened here. Walking up the stairs he saw scorch marks and a blood trail. In the hallway on the second floor was another tape outline, smaller, from a child. Cassiel swore under his breath and walked through an open door into a bedroom that had clearly belonged to the boy in the picture. It had been tossed and searched. The sky blue paint seamed too innocent for the carnage that had happened there.

Cassiel once again got the hint of Chance's signature. He crouched down and reached out with his senses. An hour later he had another piece to the puzzle of Chance's soul signature. It was then that he decided to use the jumps Verock took to complete his picture of Chance. All the places aside from the dining hall he saw must have been places Chance had been, or they thought he would be. If he went to these places and was able to build the entire signature, he could track Chance directly from the arena. Feeling hopeful he jumped back to the hideout.

"Lady Clotho," he said, contacting her mentally.

"How goes the search Cassiel? You have been gone almost two days."

"I have an idea how to possibly track the boy," he told her. *"How is Uriel doing?"*

"She is fine," Clotho said. *"She had to purge the memories quickly. There was a lot of ugliness in that man's mind."*

"If the crime scene I just came from is any indication I am not surprised."

"Crime scene?" Clotho sounded alarmed.

"Looks like Chance was staying with a young family of non-energy users. They were killed, and from what I can see, he barely made it out," Cassiel explained. *"I am going to get back to work. Just don't use the arena at the Manor for any sanctioned battles. I don't want Chances port trace corrupted."*

"Alright Cassiel, but be careful. I'll have the arena sealed until your return. Contact us if you need anything."

"Will do," and he cut off communication. Heading back to the safe houses he traced, Cassiel sought out the Heads of House. He asked them both a few questions giving them a description of Chance. Mulbrook, who ran the safe house in Chicago, remembered him immediately. He thought Chance was a nice kid and he took Cassiel to the room he stayed in. Cassiel picked up a strong echo from a past teleport and

spent the next few hours adding pieces to his Chance puzzle. Thanking Mulbrook he took his leave and went back to the hideout. As Cassiel ported away, Mulbrook called out, "Let me know if the kid's ok. Alright?"

The trails left behind were getting harder to read as they got older, but Cassiel was determined to not miss anything. He spent as much as eleven hours on an echo that lead to a port location under a bridge. There were several people milling about and Cassiel realized they must be homeless. *What kind of life did you lead Chance* he thought? He was able to extract another small piece of the signature and left after giving the people under the bridge the few hundred dollars he had on him.

The following days where a hellish cycle of traces and little sleep. He found pieces at another safe house, and a boy's home in queens. Cassiel was so close, he knew he just needed one more strong port echo and he would have the entire signature. He was also scared he was running out of time. Cassiel had run out of viable trails from Verock and was not able to track anyone else at this point.

"Uri, are you up?" he asked through a mental link.

"Yes I am up, Caz. What can I do for you?" she responded.

"Did Clotho tell you what I am working on?"

"Yes. Clo said you were getting a stronger picture of Chance's soul sig to track him. How can I help? I can feel you need it."

"I am so close but I need just a little more. I have run out of places Verock has been. I can't complete his signature without it." He sighed, *"I know you did a memory purge, but is there anything else you can remember about where Verock may have been?"*

Uriel apologized. *"Sorry my friend, I don't remember what I wanted to forget, but I know I am glad I did. There is nothing left. You may want to ask Clotho about Chance's point of origin though. There should be a trace there if I am not mistaken."*

"Uri, you're a genius. Of course there will be!" Cassiel exclaimed.

"You have been working too hard or you would have thought of that yourself," she laughed. *"Swing by the manor and talk to Clotho. I am certain she knows where he showed up. You know after what happened in the arena she was searching the Manor grounds to find how those men got in."*

"Thanks Uri. You're the best. Talk to you soon."

Cassiel wasted no time returning to the Manor. He hoped that Chance's point of origin teleport would give him what he needed. Finding Clotho in her office he was almost rude in getting to the question. "Lady Clotho, I hope you're well. I have a quick question for you," he blurted.

Clotho looked up startled. "Good to see you too Cassiel. When did you get here?"

"I have only just arrived. I need to ask you something about Chance." he said almost pleading.

"That's fine Cassiel, but you have to do me two favors for the question," she said raising an eyebrow.

Cassiel sighed heavily and agreed, "If that's your price."

Clotho laughed and said, "They are very simple my friend. Stop calling me Lady, and take a bath. You look like shit."

Cassiel laughed as well. He rubbed his jaw, realizing that he had not even shaved in five days. "Can you show me where Chance first arrived at the Manor? I doubt he realized etiquette is to teleport outside the grounds and announce your presence before entering."

"As it happens, you're correct. He teleported onto the road, right where the apple orchard starts. Will this help with your search?"

"Yes it will Clotho. Thanks. And I'll take that bath as soon as I check out this location." He smiled and ported out.

So much for etiquette Clotho thought with a laugh. *He just teleported into my office.*

Cassiel was able to find the location fairly quickly. He realized that this point of entry was the opposite side of the teleport in the warehouse that had started his quest. For once luck was on his side. He had all he needed to get a full picture of Chance's soul signature. Relieved, he teleported back to the rooms he used when staying at the Manor and turned on the shower. He made quick work of getting cleaned up as requested by Clotho, and even shaved. He dressed in clean clothes and went to the arena. He sat in the same seat Chance had been in and brought the young man's soul signature to the forefront of his mind. Holding that picture he traced the teleport out of the arena. He was surprised at how much effort it took to pinpoint an exact location. It was as if Chance was trying to mask his teleports. It was tricky work but not impossible for someone of Cassiel's skill. He ported and found himself in an abandoned camp in the woods.

He knew the camp had only been abandoned a few days ago. He felt Athena's energy here, and knew she had used it for some reason. Chance's energy was all over the place. The kid made a beacon of himself without knowing it. He looked for the echo of a teleport having both their traces. In essence it would look like overlaid tracks with both his and her signatures, the lead energy on top of the following. Athena must have given him some tips. There were at least twenty traces here. Cassiel focused and immediately discarded the first four. The echoes were too old to be their destination. He took a seat and started concentrating on the others. He felt some other people's blurred energy but left those alone to focus on Chance. Slowly as the hours passed, the sun trailed lazily across the sky from east to west, and still Cassiel sat and focused. Pushing his ability to the outmost limits, he unwove the strands of energy and echoes around him to find the one that was strongest. Time was getting short and he didn't have time to trace the destination of each one. Finally, he felt a tug in his mind. One of the four traces left also had four other indistinct energies going off in that direction. He knew he had it and that the Hunters had found them too.

Cassiel spent the next thirty minutes tracking the location. He was standing now, weapons at the ready. He was not sure what he was going to run into but he wanted to be prepared. Once Cassiel had the destination locked he teleported, and fell down on his knees crying at the scene before him. A circle fifty feet in diameter was completely destroyed by an intense fire. The energy used to create this was far beyond what he thought the two were capable of and the trace had a sickly feeling to it. Cassiel's fears had been realized. He was too late and he had failed. The teens were dead.

● ●

Sitting in her room at the Seraphs building, Uriel felt her friend's grief, it was so intense. Immediately she tried to contact him and found a wall of anguish and guilt blocking her. Not understanding what had happened she contacted Clotho and told her what she was feeling. Cyrus was brought in on the conversation next, they met at Manor to discuss it. The three friends were afraid of what it could mean and did not want to contact Horatius until they knew for sure. As they were discussing what could have happened, Cassiel walked into to the room. His pants and arms were covered in ash. He had smudges on his face and in his hair. Tears left streaks in the ash on his face. Uriel ran over and put her arms around him for support. "I failed," he said in an anguished voice. "The camp was completely destroyed."

"What?" Cyrus cried out. "Tell us what you found Caz."

Collecting himself, he spoke in a solemn voice. "I managed to find their last two camps. Athena had been teaching him to mask location with multiple jumps. It was not enough. When I arrived at their second camp..." Unable to describe what he had seen, he sent a mental picture of the devastation to his three friends. Their connection was deep enough to share memories this way.

"My god," whispered Clotho, her hand covering her mouth. Cyrus stood in stunned silence. Uriel continued to support Cassiel, wiping soot and ash off his face. They had all lost friends, lovers, and in some cases spouses, to battles and raids. The teens being killed in such a way still crippled them with pain. They didn't know Chance, but Athena was like a beloved niece to all of them. She was feisty and smart, kind to her friends and clever in training. As they stood there sharing in their grief, Cyrus started laughing.

"What the hell is so damned funny Cyrus?" Cassiel spit out in anger.

"Think about it for a moment," Cyrus said calmly. "I was just as upset as you but I have had more rest and can think more clearly."

"What do you mean Cyrus?" Clotho asked, for some reason feeling hopeful.

"These Hunters had orders to capture Chance at all costs. Capture not kill," he explained. "I think the kids escaped again and that the camp was destroyed out of anger. Chance has been evading them for how long now?"

Cassiel let out a sigh of relief body shaking, realizing that Cyrus must be correct. "From what I found, it may have been years." He briefly described all the places he had been.

"We saw from how quickly he got out of the arena that he is resourceful," Cyrus continued his train of thought. "Your findings only confirm in my mind that they escaped again. You have done well Cassiel. Take a mental and physical break. Then find them, we all know you can."

Uriel and Clotho both sighed in relief and nodded agreement with Cyrus. Cassiel took another deep breath then walked back to his quarters to once again get cleaned up. This time he intended to grab a full meal. Time may be getting short but he realized he could not afford to make such a mistake again. If Cyrus had not been thinking with a clear head they would have abandoned the search.

An hour later, Cassiel, Uriel, Cyrus, Clotho, Horatius, and Shifter were sitting around a table enjoying a nice meal. Talk around the table was about the teens. Cyrus explained that Cassiel would continue the search after the meal with a clear head and was confident that the tracker would locate them soon. Shifter was brought into the discussion because originally he was going to assume Verock's identity to try to infiltrate the Hunter group. That plan was no longer viable, although the master spy's talents could still come in handy.

"How long does it take you to assume an identity?" Cyrus asked Shifter.

"Well if the person is similar in size and shape to me, a few hours. The energy required to change my bone structure and musculature is pretty extreme and painful so I need to eat like crazy and replenish as I change." Shifter explained.

"If only it were as easy as they show in movies…" Cyrus remarked wistfully. Looking back at Shifter, he said, "When we find the teens, we may still want you to take the shape of a Hunter."

"I really can't make it any faster. Changing bones is not like changing a light bulb," he murmured.

"I know Shifter. I just didn't know if it gets any easier over time. For as long as I have lived I have never tried to alter my form. I know many do, to be more attractive or physically more imposing. I never needed to do that given my size." He smiled winked at Clotho.

"No, it never gets easier or less painful. I spoke to the healers once about it. They said that's why they knock out their patients when healing injuries." Shifter replied.

"Just keep it in mind, we might need you soon." Cyrus said.

"I need to get going," Cassiel said suddenly. "I am still afraid to leave those two out there much longer. When I find them I'll contact Horatius first."

"Good luck," they said in unison as Cassiel vanished.

"He didn't finish his pie," Uriel said picking up the plate. "He'll find them first H. No one tracks as well he does."

"I have faith in him," Horatius said, "Otherwise I would demand to go with him."

Slowly the friends at the table separated to their duties and various functions, leaving Cyrus to ponder the young man Chance. *Who are you young one? And why on earth are you so hunted?*

• •

Cassiel arrived at the burned out prairie camp with a clear head and a renewed sense of vigor. Hovering above the dust he walked around sending out his senses. *Athena you clever girl, you learned to teleport* he thought sensing her echo in the area. He continued to reach out but didn't find a dual port sign in the area. He knew it had to be there. There was only one echo of a teleport out that had the same taint as the fire energy. *So, the kids gave you a hell of a fight, if only one of you made it out. I wonder if it was Chance or Athena who did the damage.* He widened his search.

He walked nearly a quarter mile circle around the camp and still could not find the echo. *Think. They needed to port out to escape, and Chance ironically enough doesn't seem to take Chances.* Looking up, it hit him. *The kid can fly! Or at least levitate. That must be it."* He expanded his search to include the sky. After another hour, he found it and another piece of the puzzle made sense. *That's why I have such a hard time tracing you. You're a kinetic porter. By its very nature your energy is scattered.*

Having a clear path to track he closed his eyes and leapt. Looking around, Cassiel was genuinely surprised to find he was near a large shopping area. Shaking his head and putting two and two together he laughed when we realized where he was. Walking the boardwalk, he could not sense them anywhere. *Clever kid, but not clever enough. I know the places where I will most likely find you"*

Cassiel began porting to the various parks. Thinking it might be the kind of irony that would appeal to an e-worlder to go to Harry Potter land, he started with Universal Studios.

• •

He contacted Horatius when he found them at Disney World. They were following the Parade of Lights Down Main Street. Both were dressed well, and smiling. Horatius met him and they watched the youngsters from an angle slightly in front of them. Athena's father just stared at his daughter, his face a mix of emotions. When she put her head on Chance's shoulder and smiled wide at the spectacle around her Horatius came to a decision.

"Cassiel, can you follow them for me?" he asked.

"What? You don't want to take her home after the fireworks?" Cassiel responded, surprised.

"Look at her face Caz. I have not seen her look that happy since her mother died." He smiled. "Just keep an eye on them for now. Call in some of the Protection Force if you have to, but let her enjoy being happy. I think she will make the decision to come home on her own soon."

Still greatly relieved that he had found the duo, Cassiel also smiled at how happy the girl he thought of as a niece looked. "Alright Horatius, inform the others of your decision will you? I don't want to be distracted and lose them." Nodding Horatius stepped into the shadows and vanished.

Recovery II

Chance woke up from his nightmare shaking. It was hard to get the faces out of his head. He knew in his heart that the men deserved to die; however, his mind still refused to let up. Trying to lessen the shakes, he thought about the day at the park and a small smile returned to his face. As bad as the prairie had been, he could not remember ever having as much fun as he had yesterday. Athena he discovered was just great to be around. She was smart, witty, strong and beautiful if he let himself think it. She was bringing out sides of him he didn't realize he had, like wanting to open doors for her and be a gentleman, also that protective nature that caused him to kill without hesitation. He didn't have a whole lot of experience with girls. He was a little young when he fled the Crèche and being on the run is not conducive to dating. "I'm thinking too much about this," he quipped. "Time to make breakfast."

To his surprise when he walked into the kitchen, Athena was there already cooking. She was wearing the grey shorts he bought her and a blue tank top. She had her hair pulled back into a ponytail. He stopped in his tracks looking at the young woman who was unware he was in the room, she grabbed things out of the fridge that they had purchased the night before on their way back. She was singing a pretty song he had not heard before.

Transfixed listening to her voice, she sang, "All the

birds in the forest they bitterly weep, saying, 'Where will we shelter or where will we sleep?' For the Oak and the Ash, they are all cut down, and the walls of bonny Portmore are all down to the ground." She turned around to see him staring, and blushed to her ears. "I didn't know you were up yet. I thought I would make you breakfast for a change."

"That was beautiful. What was that?" he asked.

"Oh, that. Myriam, Gerrod's wife, always sings that song."

"I didn't know you could sing. And I didn't know you knew Gerrod either."

"Well, I don't really know him," she protested. "He knows my dad." She realized she had said a little too much and was trying to recover.

"His wife, Myriam, is she the woman that guy Talon liked?" Chance asked.

"It's complicated," she said evasively. "But more importantly, how do you like your pancakes?"

Chance knew there was more to this then she was letting on but let it go. "Are there many ways to have them? I always assumed they were, you know, round," he joked.

"You sir, do not appreciate the fine art of pancakes!" she exclaimed happy to have changed the subject.

"Sir even!" He laughed. "Ok madam, please enlighten me," he bent forward in a mock little bow.

Athena made pancakes of various sizes from dime sized to dinner plate, then played with the thinness of them and tried to make ovals. She thoroughly enjoyed herself. She tried to fry up some eggs, and wound up breaking all the yolks so she scrambled them in the pan. Chance watched the spectacle before him and gave her encouraging words. It was quite obvious Athena had not cooked often. When the meal was served, with coffee of course, they sat down at the eat-in kitchen counter and dug in.

"Hmmm..." Chance offered after taking the first bite of a half cooked, sort of chunky pancake. "Maybe while we are together I should do the cooking."

Athena made a face and stuck her tongue out, then took a bite. She chewed slowly, then suddenly laughed. "Did I just poison us?" Chance laughed with her and they continued to eat their slightly inedible but fun breakfast.

"Tell me more about you," Chance said suddenly.

Startled Athena answered, "Isn't that a rather forward question for someone who is planning to ditch me soon?" she regretted it as soon as she said it.

At little hurt by the answer Chance protested, "What do you mean? If I was going to ditch you I could have done it any time I wanted."

"Our deal is complete Chance," she asserted. "You can read soul signatures and I can teleport. Not very far yet but I can do it. You said we were not compatible. How did you put it? 'This partnership is not going to work out.'"

"That was before..." He paused and then snapped, "Fine, I'll pack my things and go if that is what you want. You can stay here for a few more days I'll teleport from the Marketplace and draw them off." Chance stood to leave and Athena grabbed his arm.

"No that's not what I want!" she yelled. "I don't really know what I want yet but I don't want it hanging over my head the whole time that you are going to leave!"

"Athena," he said calmly. "You have a home, and a family, and apparently you are important in some way even though you won't admit it. I am just some runaway. Why would you want me around?"

"Why would I care if you are a runaway?" she challenged.

"I don't know. That's why I wanted to know more about you!"

"So, you're not looking to bail out as soon as I am feeling stronger again?" she asked.

"As long as I get to do the cooking, no I am not," he said, trying to lighten the mood. "I should. It's not safe for you to be with me." He walked over to the window and stared out wringing his hangs together. "But if not for you I would have been caught. I am somehow better when I am with you."

Athena blushed and looked down. "I feel the same. Better."

"So," Chance sat down again. "Tell me about yourself then."

"That still sounds like the kind of personal question you ask on a date Chance," she joked.

Now it was Chance's turn to blush. "I've never been on a date before Athena.".

"What was yesterday?" she asked, smiling.

"Ah...well...was that a date?" he stammered.

"Well if it was a date it was a good one."

"Have you been on dates before? Wait. Don't answer that. Of course you have, with that Caval guy you keep mentioning."

"Caval?" laughed Athena. "God no. He is like a brother to me and way too sure of himself." She held her sides as she laughed at the thought.

"Oh, I just thought...would you want to go on a date with me?" he said not really asking a question.

"There is only one way to find out Chance." She smiled.

"How's that?" he said.

"Ask me," she said still smiling.

• •

They decided to hold off on the whole official date thing. However, they did want to eat at some restaurants while they were recovering. Athena knew the events on the prairie still weighed in the back of Chance's mind. She also realized she was more and more drawn to the young man. She was not kidding when she agreed she was better with him. She was somehow sharper; they learned mental communication in a day! Even her father had trouble talking to her mentally. She tried not to think about her father but knew that he was probably going out of his mind by now. She knew she should be going back soon; but she just did not want to leave Chance alone.

They took the bus back to the Market place. Chance was not worried because it was so public there was no chance of getting snatched, although he did advise switching buses at least three times at random, to get back several blocks from their Timeshare.

Always so cautious, always so careful, he told her that she saved him from getting captured. Athena knew the truth though. He would not have been in that position if not for her. He would have left that camp before they found him. "Don't stay in a private camp too long," he said once. "It's too isolated and easier to capture you."

But while training her, they had stayed in an isolated camp too long. She may have saved him, but she created the need. She also made him a killer. For all those reasons and more she wanted to stay with him. Her father may or may not approve of him but she had fallen for Chance as well. She knew she would have to convince him to come back with her. She could show him the location mentally and he could take them. Athena was not strong enough to port that far yet.

They ate lunch at a dinosaur themed restaurant with some really cool animatronics. Chance had seen the place half dozen times and always wanted to have a meal there. Sitting in a room that looked like a glacial cave that kept turning from red to blue she contemplated how to bring up the subject.

"This place is pretty cool," Chance commented, bringing her back to where they were.

"Yeah, the light effect is eerie."

"How's your food? You've barely touched it."

Athena looked at her grilled chicken salad and said, "Oh, it's actually really good. I was just lost in thought." She was surprised that Chance ate the asparagus that came with his steak and potatoes, first. When she questioned him about it he told her he didn't always get variety and the vitamins were good for him. Thinking of their time camping, she realized he was right. Meat he could get easily, but veggies and sides he only had when he stole them or when he had a brief stay at a Safe House. It made Athena wonder briefly if the lack of proper nutrition had stunted his growth. She looked at him critically while he ate. He was a handsome young man. She smiled at his new short haircut. Athena had forced him to get it cut at a proper barber shop before they went out for lunch. It took away from the wild look he had and showed more of the guy he should be she thought.

"Are you ok?" he asked. "You keep getting spaced out. If you're tired, we can go back."

"No," she laughed. "I am fine really. I just thinking I like your new haircut." She smiled.

"Oh, thanks," he stammered, going a little red. "You look nice today too."

After lunch they rented a paddle boat and went out on the small lake. She was holding an oversized Mickey Mouse doll that Chance won for her on a ring toss game, swearing (and lying) that he didn't use his telekinetic energy to make the ring land on the correct bottle.

"Where do we go from here?" Athena asked.

"I don't know yet," he replied. "Sometimes I pick at random when I port out. Other times I have a destination in mind. If you want to learn to port better and if there is any other training we can teach one another, it should be another open camp. This time we stay only two days though."

"Always running," she murmured.

"What was that?".

"Chance," she said delicately. "There is another option."

"I don't see one. We need to keep moving and I don't trust the Safe Houses anymore. I wonder if they found Sabre's book," he mused.

"You could come back with me." There, she said it, it was out there now. He really could come back with her. He would be safe, and properly trained which someone with his obvious ability needed. Chance looked at her with hard, cold eyes. She could see just a hint of energy built up behind them. She knew she had caught him off guard but she had to talk to him about it.

"That's your home Athena, not mine. I don't trust groups. Even your friend Clotho was not able to stop them from trying to get me at the Manor," he argued.

"Clotho is my father's friend," she corrected. "She didn't know you needed protection, or else those men would never have gotten in. Besides, that was just a Safe House, a rest stop, not a full-fledged group."

"I just don't trust it Athena," he repeated.

"Do you trust me?" Athena asked.

"Of course I do," he exclaimed, "You know I do!"

"Then trust me when I tell you that it's safe," she pleaded. She locked eyes with him refusing to leave his gaze. She could see the struggle in him. He was tired of running, but the fear planted in him was so deep seated that it was hard to overcome.

"I'll think about it," he said.

Smiling, Athena said, "That's all I ask, and I won't bring it up anymore today."

"Ok, let's get this boat to shore and pick up supplies. We have clothes and food at the timeshare, but we need camping gear packs and outdoors equipment." he explained.

"Alright, let's go," she answered.

They changed buses twice before finding a sporting goods store. They found a couple of decent sized tents, a cooking kit with various pans, light but thermal sleeping bags, and other small amenities they would need for another outdoor adventure. Chance was in the archery section looking at broad head tips for his arrows and was surprised when Athena picked out a bow of her own. They also each picked out a couple of hunting knives and Athena selected a pack of throwing knives.

"Not all of us can shoot rocks like bullets," she said when he raised an eyebrow at her selection.

He frowned at the thought, then decided to pick out some large steel balls for sling shots. When Athena looked over at him he shrugged as if to say "you never know." When they were outfitted they took several buses before getting off and walking back to their rooms. They passed a few people on the way out, seeing smiling kids with light sunburns who had obviously enjoyed their day at one of the various theme parks in the area.

"I chose where to eat lunch, you choose dinner," Chance suggested.

"Do you like Italian?" Athena asked.

"I'll try whatever you want."

"Ok, Italian it is. Keep the jeans but put on a nicer shirt," she admonished. "I'll be ready in a few." Athena went to her room and grabbed the only dress she had purchased. She didn't know why she bought the blue summer dress when she did, only that she thought it was cute and she had been in dirty clothes for over a week. She brushed out her hair reminding herself that this was not a date, and met him in the common area. Chance had put on a nice button up black shirt. He smiled at her and the two left the room for a nice evening out.

"What are these called?" Chance asked, taking another bite.

"Tuscan pork chops," Athena laughed. She was currently eating his stuffed chicken masala. They had each ordered and then switched food halfway through the meal.

The pair talked, but avoided the elephant in the room. Were they on a date or just two good friends sharing a meal? Athena asked Chance how he was feeling about the events at their last camp. He let her know that it was hard, but more and more he realized it was necessary. Maybe all the training he had growing up and all the near misses prepared his mind for the inevitable. Athena avoided all talk of returning to the Argonauts. That conversation could wait until Chance felt ready.

"Not trying to jinx our nice meal or anything," Chance whispered, "but do you feel like you are being watched or is it just me?"

"Damn," Athena whispered back, "I thought I was just being paranoid."

Chance smiled at her like nothing was wrong and took another bite of food. *"It's time to go back,"* he thought to her.

"Alright," she acknowledged. *"Let's head out."* She took her cues from him and kept smiling and talking as if nothing were wrong. They paid quickly, left a healthy tip and took six buses to get back to the timeshare. They both changed into traveling gear and packed their camp gear. They agreed that maybe one more day here was all they could swing. In the common room, they were looking over their gear one last time before heading to bed, when a man walked in the door. Looking at each other, Athena grabbed Chance's hand. They each grabbed a gear bundle and they were gone as he ported out with a 'pop'.

Mistakes were made

Caval was bored. That was never a good thing. Being able to use energy on an adult level, he didn't have many friends. The kids his age had a hard time relating to him. Athena understood. She was pretty much his only real friend, but she was still off on her adventure which left him alone. He had been given an assignment by his teacher who was away on a business matter, but Caval had mastered that in two days.

He sat in a room, manipulating energy the way a master composer can manipulate music. Fire danced down his arm as he levitated in the center of the room. He was freezing water in ice trays while causing a paper airplane to fly around the room on an eddy of wind. The T.V. was on and he was playing a game consul but neither was plugged in; a trickle of electric energy from Caval gave them the power they needed. He was not allowed to have anything plugged in. All power had to come from him per his teacher. It was same with cooking. Caval was not allowed to use gas and had to use his own heat to cook his meals. The water in the trays could be drawn from the pipe or created by separating hydrogen and oxygen molecules in the air.

According to his teacher, the necessary resources were always around if one just looked. Drill, drill, drill. He was bored. He counted the energies he was manipulating currently; fire, ice, wind, electric, kinetic, and molecular. Six was not enough. He needed to be able to control at least eight variations at once by his fifteenth birthday. If he could, he would be allowed to finally have a challenge match in the arena.

It isn't fair, he thought. *No one else my age can even control three at once. Teacher was a jerk. Athena's already had a few fights, until her dad got all over protective.* That thought brought Caval back to the reason he was alone and bored. *Athena! Where are you? Is that guy Chance still with you?"* he thought as he made a stream of sunlight in the room split into a rainbow. *There we go, seven.* Then he realized he was back on the floor. Still six.

Caval could drill for hours before he needed rest. It was almost second nature to him now. His teacher told him he was unique. He did not have a singular or main affinity, but was adept using energy in its purest form, the raw stuff that the universe was made out of. Only a few hundred energy users like him had existed as far back as anyone could remember. They were able to do things no one else could including create new variations of energy use that no pattern existed for yet. The trouble was that they usually died very young. Other energy users feared them or wanted to use them. So Caval's talent was kept a secret. Most people didn't know what he was capable of.

That left him bored without his one friend. He needed to fix that.

• •

Cassiel had assigned four people to protection detail over Athena. They were to have at least two of them watching at all times. The Protection Force was made up of individuals who had various skill sets from trackers to all out brute force attackers. They all shared one common goal, protect high priority assets. Usually they were assigned when a member living in the normal world was under threat of assassination. Sometimes they stood as guards for e-world leaders, like the secret service does for presidents and diplomats. Most of the time, their job was guarding against assassins.

It was still legal in the energy world to assassinate a target. Teens were taught about this in school around age fifteen, or if they are targeted. Assassination was considered a less respected, underhanded way to take out a rival than a head-on challenge, but it was still used. Anyone who managed to assassinate a target would get nothing from it, unlike a sanctioned challenge. However, evil energy users like those in the Overlords didn't mind using assassins to take out an enemy they would rather not risk losing a challenge against.

Unknown to Athena and Chance, the Pro-Force were looking out for them and keeping an eye out for the Hunters that seemed hell bent on capturing Chance. When Cassiel left the teens to go home and get some much needed rest, they had just left the park and were taking multiple buses to wherever they were staying. To prevent any chance of losing them, he made sure one member of the team assigned to watch over them was an astral expert. Wisp was able to astral project and follow the kids that way wherever they went. There is no way to lose an astral tail unless you know how to banish a soul back to its host body. The other bonus of having Wisp on the team is that she could see anyone else attempting to follow that way. Her partner, Nexus, would watch over her body to make sure nothing happened to her. Cassiel was certain that, between the two teams, the teens would be ok. He informed Horatius and Cyrus of the status of the kids then teleported home.

Caval was waiting for him in his living room. All the plugs in his quarters were out of the wall sockets but coffee was brewing and Caval appeared to be playing some video game that Cassiel was not aware he owned.

"I started the coffee pot when I heard you pop in," Caval yelled from the other room. "Should be done in a minute."

"Hey Caval," Cassiel said cautiously. "How did you get in?"

"The door was open," he claimed.

"Ok we both know that's a lie," Cassiel sighed. "So how do you get in?"

"Does it really matter how I got in?" Caval questioned lightly, "The fact that I am here and we are together is enough." He smiled.

"The door is still locked; you don't have a key; and I shielded this place from teleports. How did you get in?" Cassiel asked in a steady voice. "Not that I mind you are here kid, call it my need to know."

"Fine, but you're no fun when you're surprised Uncle," Caval quipped. "I teleported onto the roof then jumped down to your balcony. That door *was* open. So I didn't lie when I said your door was open. I just didn't say which one."

Cassiel sighed again, "So, are you going to tell me what you're doing here?"

"Waiting for you," he said without missing a beat.

Cassiel walked into the kitchen and poured a cup of coffee. He did not need this right now. "You're beginning to be as annoying as your teacher," he growled.

"I knew you would be back soon, because I saw Uncle Horatius back at the Argos table smiling last night. I assumed you found Athena and she is well or else that would not have happened. I miss her and I want to know where she is," Caval explained.

"You could have asked Horatius," Cassiel replied.

"He's still mad at me for covering for Athena, so he wouldn't tell me anything if I asked. So I came here," He beamed a big smile.

"Well you came a long way and broke in for nothing. Horatius knows she is safe and does not want her bothered till she decides to return. And I," Cassiel asserted, "will respect his wishes."

"Come on Uncle! I am so bored, and Athena is my only real friend. You have to tell me where she is," he complained.

"Caval, did you ever think if you were not such a pain in the ass, you might attract more friends?"

"Most people are boring anyway," Caval dismissed the remark. "I just want to hang with Athena and show her some of the things I have learned."

Cassiel felt Caval's energy reaching out to his entry point. "Caval, you're good kid, but you won't be able to track my teleport yet."

Realizing he was caught, Caval retracted his energy. Stalling for time he changed tactics. "What did you learn about Chance? You were tracking a long time for you."

Not seeing any harm in telling Caval he explained, "Cyrus told me you were able to pick up on him being on the run. That was very true. From what I could find he has been running for well over a year." Cassiel took a sip of his coffee. "I don't know how trained he is, but I did realize he is a strong kinetic. It makes him hard to track."

"Ouch! That's a harsh way to port," Caval interjected. "My teacher said it is one of the most painful."

"It is. I imagine Athena was having a rough few days when they started out together." Cassiel said.

"So he's a tough kid, but can he protect Athena?"

"You and I both know she does not need protecting. More likely they are sharing some knowledge and just enjoying being young." Cassiel laughed. Wisp contacted him then to let him know the kids were in a timeshare, doing well and probably headed to bed.

Caval had been watching him and recognized the signs of a quick mental chat. "Who was that?" he asked suddenly.

"Wisp," Cassiel said before he could stop himself. *Damnit. He got me,* Cassiel thought to himself. "She is working on a project for Uri, and needed to know if the prisoner was available," he said trying to recover.

"Oh. Ok. Guess I'll be going, I'll let you get some rest. Sorry for barging in on you Uncle Caz."

Before Cassiel could stop him the young man was out the door to the deck and vanished. "I think I just screwed up there," Cassiel said under his breath.

• •

Alright thought Caval. *Wisp always partners with Nexus and Illyria will tell me where he was sent on assignment. That will tell me where they are!* Proud of himself for working it out, he teleported to the Forum and went right to Illyria and Nexus' quarters. Knocking on the door he waited for her to answer. A pretty woman in her late twenties opened the door. Her hair was so black it looked bluish. She had green eyes like an ocean storm. Currently the lady in question was holding a little boy named Dexter.

"Hello Caval," she said with a smile. "How can I help you today? I am afraid Nexus is on assignment."

Nexus was a good sparring partner for Caval because he could reverse an opponent's powers and send them back. Named for the nexus of energy where energies meet, he could use energy in various ways, but he used his reversing specialty to devastating effectiveness.

"I was going to ask him to spar. Do you know when he'll be back?" Caval questioned innocently.

"Afraid not," Illyria explained. "When he left for Florida this morning he did not have a return time."

"No big deal. I'll look for Typhoonus. I need to work on water energy anyway." Caval said, "He's lucky to be in Florida this time of year. I heard it is going to snow at the Manor soon. He getting a tan?" Caval laughed.

"God no," Illyria said about her very pale husband. "But I made him promise to get Dexter some Mouse ears while he is in the area."

"Thanks, Illyria. Tell him I want to spar with him when he gets back!" Caval called out as he walked down the hall. *So, they are near Disney World* he thought." as he walked down the hall. Having never teleported there, he needed coordinates.

••

Illyria sat playing with little Dexter, so pale like his father but with her dark hair. Not long after Caval left she felt the familiar tingle of someone trying to contact her mentally.

"Illyria, have you seen Caval?" Cyrus's mind asked her.

"He was here about five minutes ago why do you ask? Is he in trouble with Sabastian again?" she responded.

"No nothing like that. He's searching for Athena," Cyrus explained, *"Nexus is on her guard duty."*

"Oh dear," Illyria thought. *"I told him Nexus is near Disney World."* She heard Cyrus sigh in her mind.

"He is keeping one step ahead." Cyrus informed her, *"Cassiel had to contact me to ask you as you two are not familiar with each other's minds. Thanks for the information. He's probably in Florida by now knowing him."*

"Good luck finding him. That boy is so rambunctious," she exclaimed.

"Talk to you soon. Clotho and I will have to have you and Nexus over for dinner soon." Cyrus closed the connection.

Illyria had the feeling she just made a rather large goof without knowing it.

• •

Orlando was bright! Caval had to purchase some sunglasses from a street vender. *So this is where they are. I'll bet she went to Disney World without me."*

He looked around to figure out where they would be hold up. With no fake ID hotels would not work. Neither would a youth hostel or camp. He knew that Athena had taken a money belt for fuel and food on the road. He had only grabbed a few hundred dollars as he was not planning on an extended trip. Right about now his father was probably looking for him. He had to act fast if he was going to make Athena come home. He began searching for Nexus' and Athena's energy signatures by walking casually and stretching his search capability to its limits.

When he felt several other e-worlders he didn't know in the area, he quickly pulled back. His teacher had taught him how to conceal his presence, and made him practice so much it was almost always on. He took some of the local free buses that went from parks to hotels and continued to look for signs. After several hours he was just about to give up when he saw the telltale sign of a Pro-Force car. They were always silver SUVs with temp tags, brush bars and a rear bumper guard. They never knew if they would have to ram something. Caval knew he was in the right area.

The SUV was parked on a street that had several large luxury hotels and vacation spots. They would not park too close but not too far away either. He jumped off the bus at the next stop and began looking for Athena's signature in earnest. They were so in tune he could find her half mile away if he had to. He was walking back in the direction of the Pro-Force SUV but on the other side of the road. If she was anywhere in the area he would find her. Another hour passed, it was getting dark. Suddenly a bus passed by and he felt her on it. Looking up he saw her and Chance inside, looking a bit agitated and talking on the bus. She looked nice in a blue dress with her hair done. They got off the bus at the next stop and entered what looked like a hotel that was still under construction.

Caval made a note to ask her how they could be staying there. Being careful not to be seen, he found their room by walking almost directly under it the first time. Taking the elevator, he double checked the signature. *Yup. That's her. This is going to be fun* he thought. He opened the door to yell surprise, and had just enough time to see Athena and Chance vanish. *Damnit that was a mistake!* Half a second later he teleported as well.

Forces of Nature

When they arrived at their first destination Chance immediately felt they were followed. Not knowing how they were tracked so fast, he ported again. Their second destination was near a safe house. Chance was trying to move fast so the destinations were not as important as losing their tail. Once again he felt the presence appear behind them and off they went again. *Something is not right* he thought. Athena was more used to teleports but quick ports like this will have her on her knees in no time. Gathering two destinations in his head he made two quick jumps, the last to an open field in Nebraska. He stopped and pulled moisture out of the air for his attack. When the Hunter appeared Chance blasted him with the full force of water.

Caval was right behind Chance and Athena when they ported out. He kept trying to yell stop but there was not time. No sooner would they arrive they were gone. The last port was so quick he almost lost them. It took a full seven seconds to find the path then jump. The blast of water that hit him knocked him off his feet like a fire hose. *Ambush* he thought, quickly turning the water to ice shards and throwing them back at the attacker. The shards hit an energy barrier and shattered. He felt energy to his left and fired a bolt of lightning.

Chance felt more then saw the water being changed into an attack, *Ok don't use water* he thought and put up a kinetic shield. Then he teleported thirty feet to the right pushing Athena down to keep her safe. He tossed the bag of steel shot into the air as soon as they arrived. He registered the electricity flying at them and erected a wall of earth to intercept it. Chance's mind had never been so clear. He had to stop this Hunter and keep Athena safe. He then sent out an underground attack that caused the roots and plants to grow up and wrap around the Hunters legs and lower body. He had just finished this when the wall of earth in front of him exploded.

The wall of earth that blocked Caval's lightening was a surprise, whoever ambushed him was good. He could not see the person clearly but knew they were still behind the dirt wall. He used an air attack that destroyed the wall from the inside when the vines grabbed his legs. Looking down he was about to use a molecular blade just as something shattered his right leg.

Chance watched as the wall exploded. He could not make out his attacker but he could see him. He sent the steel shot from the bag he had tossed in the air at his target. His intention was to use the twenty steel balls to turn the man into swish cheese. He saw the first steel ball pass through the man's right thigh.

Caval barely managed to get up the temporal field. Anything entering the field would look as if it were almost stopped. He had the opportunity to see another nineteen steel balls coming for his body. When he finally saw his opponent, he was shocked to realize he was fighting Chance. He was also losing from the looks of his leg. He had never been hit before. He brushed all the projectiles aside with his hand so they would pass harmlessly to the left and then burned the vines off his body. He had to move quickly because he could only keep the temporal field up for a short time. He knew on the outside of the temporal field everything would look like a quick blur.

Chance did not understand how all the steel shot seemed to stop moving then shift aside. The man, no boy by the looks of it, that he was fighting must have used hyper acceleration, but that should not have stopped the ballistic attack. Chance started using his kinetic energy to try to set the boy on fire like he saw Lord Gerrod do. Then he wrapped energy around himself and flew at the boy.

Caval felt the attack; he knew what it was. Chance was speeding up his cells to make him spontaneously combust. He was countering the power when Chance soared at him and his fist caught Caval in a vicious punch. *Christ the guy can fly too* he thought as he fell back. Years of combat training kicked in and he quickly grabbed Chance's arm. Using his own momentum he threw the older boy to the ground. As he continued his spin he knew what he was about to do would hurt. Caval then used levitation to shoot himself sideways trying to take pressure off his injured and badly bleeding leg. More roots were shooting out of the ground trying to take hold of him. Chance was already up and facing him getting ready to attack again. He put his shield up as best he could hoping it would hold while he tried to figure a way out of this mess.

Chance connected with the young man's cheek, hurting his fist. He felt hands grab him and toss him at the ground at break neck speed. He sent out a kinetic pulse into the earth the instant before he stuck it making it as soft as a bunch of foam pillows. The impact still hurt a little but he turned in time to see the boy shooting sideways as if he was on wheels. *Who the hell is this guy?* Chance thought. He fed the ground attack more energy and charged up a blast of fire like he had seen Athena do, determined to end this fight quickly.

Son of a bitch! That's Athena's best attack. How the hell did he learn it in a week? As the blast hit him in a reddish blue inferno, he switched his shield to absorb the energy. Knowing the exact nature of the attack he had the perfect counter. *Is it getting darker?* he thought as he screamed, "Chance, I am not your enemy!" The shockwave that hit him was not only a surprise, but knocked him to the ground where the vines wrapped him like a spider wraps its meal. For a moment he thought he was dead till his saw out of the corner of his eye that Chance was picked up and tossed liked a rag doll a good forty feet. When landed he did not get up. Only ninety seconds had passed from the time he arrived in the field.

• •

When Chance first turned to attack whoever was following them Athena could hardly keep her feet from the quick ports. She had been getting used to them but the rapid nature of the last few played hell with her equilibrium. Just as she thought she had it, Chance ported them again across the field they were in. She rolled over as he pushed her down and continued his assault on their attacker. Athena shook her head to clear her eyes. She had to get up and help but needed to shake of the effects of the ports and get ahold of herself. She heard the sounds of the battle raging and registered that Chance was fighting Caval and was Caval was bleeding.

The two boys met in a crash as Chance flew into her lifelong friend and then was tossed into what looked like a fluffy sandbox that appeared out of nowhere. Chance then turned to once again attack Caval who had glided to the right when she tried to scream "STOP" but it came out as a whisper. Athena's voice was too soft to be heard over the wild crashing of energy. "Chance, Caval, stop fighting each other," she tried again to scream, hurting her throat in the process.

The two young men were so wrapped up in their fight neither boy heard her.

The sky had darkened blocking out the moon and the stars, and she knew Chance had done it. He had said he was able to control the weather. Putting her hands in front of her, Athena unleashed a wave of pure power out of desperation that knocked the two apart. She saw Caval get saved from any real harm by the roots that pulled him to the earth. Her heart sank when she saw Chance picked up and thrown, arms flailing and hit the ground in a solid crunch. Athena was worried about her bleeding friend; however, she was more worried about the boy who had captured her heart. She ran over to him yelling his name. She could hear Caval hysterically laughing from his cocoon-like prison.

She dropped to her knees by Chance and took his head in her lap. "Chance, Chance," she said with tears in her eyes, lightly tapping his face. He was not moving. He had taken the brunt of her blast and she knew he was not shielded. He had only just begun to use a proper shield and could not yet sustain it. Athena was terrified that in her desperation to stop the two from fighting she had accidentally killed the boy she now knew she loved.

As Caval lay there he had time to register that the vines had stopped squeezing and the sky was clearing again. *Wow, I just got my ass kicked* he thought still laughing about the situation. He hoped Chance was ok and knew the whole thing was his fault. *I am going to be in so much trouble* he thought, as he snapped the vines. Caval sat up and looked around the battle field. It didn't look good and was bound to get someone's attention. He used a piece of his shirt to tie off his leg, trying to stop the bleeding with the few healing techniques he had actually paid attention to.

"My teacher was right. I am too sure of myself," he muttered as he hobbled over to Athena and Chance. She was holding Chance's head in her lap and crying telling him to wake up over and over. It took him a moment to realize that the blast that had ended the fight came from her. *She's stronger than I remember* he thought. He had already pieced together why Chance was so sought after. If the boy was alive he would have to tell him and Athena. They also would need to get the hell out of there and soon.

"He's too tough to die from that attack," he assured his friend.

"What the hell do you know?" she spat. "This is all your fault. What were you thinking walking in on us like that?"

"I know this will sound lame in spite of everything that just occurred, but I missed you and wanted to surprise you."

"Just how on earth did you follow us through five teleports?" she demanded, wiping the tears from her face.

"I attached an astral thread to you when I saw you in the room. It's the same type of thread that anchors you to your body when you're astral projecting."

Athena laughed bitterly. "I hope you're happy with yourself," she said with venom in her voice. Chance had still not woken up.

"At the moment, I am just surprised to still be breathing if you really want to know," he replied softly.

Athena looked at Caval for the first time. He was pale and could hardly stand. The look in his near purple eyes was one of concern. He had none of the bravado she usually saw. "You look like shit."

Caval kneeled down wincing in pain and put his hand lightly on Chance's chest. "May I?" Athena nodded and watched Caval close his eyes to concentrate. He made a small bluish silver pulse of energy glow in his cupped hands. The energy shot out and hit Chance who gasped for breath as if it were his first. He was still unconscious.

Startled, Athena pulled Chance into a tight hug. Still crying she whispered, "You're alright, you came back to me."

Caval knew time was running short. He was tired like he had never been before.

"We don't have much time. That fight is sure to get several people's attention and not all of them from our world. I know you're mad and I don't blame you. I just wanted to surprise my friend. I should have thought about it more when I found you. But all of that can wait for another time. Right now, I need to tell you a couple of things and you need to get out of here."

Caval wasn't usually so serious. Worried, Athena shifted position so her arm was behind Chance and she faced Caval. "What it is Caval?"

"Well for starters I know why those people want Chance so badly. Also, that fight we just had has probably generated a huge heat signature that can be spotted by satellite. It's one of the main reasons most official battles are all underground in sealed rooms now or officials are bribed to redirect satellite imagery."

"I never knew that!" Athena exclaimed.

"My teacher told me. You would have been told soon. Your dad was planning to tell you about it."

"Why do you think they are after him?"

"Because Chance is like me," Caval explained. "People like us are unique. We don't have a main and we can control many things at once. Here I thought I was the best in a generation, and I find I am not even the best in my age group,"

"Is Chance really that strong?"

"Well, if you hadn't intervened he would have killed me for sure. I am running on empty here." Caval replied. "On top of that he is only half trained and I have had the best teachers in the world. The earth and roots helped him here, outdoors. He would not have had them in an arena, and I probably could have taken him. However, all things being equal as they were out here, he beat me fair and square." Caval looked a little bitter about the acknowledgement.

"Why are we talking about this here? We need to get you both to a healer. Just port us home."

"Two reasons. One, I am too tired to port. I have been training for weeks straight and that battle took everything I had." Caval confessed. "Second, what would happen if Chance woke up at the Argos? Or even the Forum?"

"Oh my God, you're right," Athena said, realization dawning on her. "He would never trust me again if I took him there without his consent while he was unconscious."

Caval defended her, "Your judgment is clouded by emotion, or else you would have realized he needs to make the decision on his own. I'll contact Dad soon and have him pick me up. You two will be gone by then. The second thing you need to know before you go is to never fight like this outside again if you can help it." Caval cautioned. "My teacher told me there are government agencies who know about us, not who we are but what we can do. He was captured once as a teen. By now the activity here has been picked up via satellite and there are probably choppers on the way."

"Great," Athena said. "Chance is out, you're weakened and people are probably coming to get us."

"Grab your gear. I'll wait." Caval said. Athena laid Chance down and left to grab the packs. She scooped up a handful of steel bearings on her way back to a still unconscious Chance and a very tired looking Caval.

When she returned Caval asked, "Did Chance teach you to teleport? Knowing you that would be something you would want to learn."

"Yes he did," she replied.

"Good, then port out of here. Take at least three jumps to where you want to go. His Hunters know his trace not yours, which will stop them from being able to track you for a long while," Caval assured her. "I'll tell dad that Chance flew off with you to avoid detection. I'll also take my thread off you. I don't want to know where you are going."

"Why don't you want to know?"

"Because, Uncle Cassiel found you two, and there were guards. If Chance found out, he would suspect the worse about groups. I don't know him as well as you do, but that fight told me a lot about him. He is desperate, and he was pushing himself to the limits to protect you." Caval pointed out.

"Damn," she swore. "I knew we were being watched."

"Chance needs to be with us, he needs proper training, but until he makes that choice you two need to be free to move." Caval insisted, "So I don't want to know where you are. The adults won't understand and I'll be in some trouble but that's ok. Now get out of here. Remember -- at least three ports."

"Are you going to be alright?"

"Yeah. My pride took the biggest hit, but next time he and I face each other when we spar I'll be ready for him," Caval laughed. "Now go, get out of here before we're found."

Athena nodded her head, closed her eyes and disappeared.

Caval waited a full fifteen minutes before contacting his father. He told him he was hurt but nothing more. His warning to Athena about outdoor battles was accurate but he highly doubted they were picked up, the fight was too quick and it's not like governments were looking for activity all the time in all places. He just wanted to give Athena the motivation she needed to teleport the distances she would need. He sincerely hoped it worked. Looking at the night sky he said his version of a prayer.

"So," a voice behind him said. "You look like holy hell."

"Hey Dad," Caval said looking up into the face of Cyrus before losing consciousness. Cyrus scooped his son up in his arms and took him straight to the healers. Questions would come later...

The Cabin

Three extremely draining teleports later, Athena arrived at her final destination. She was standing before a cabin in the Pennsylvania woods. The place was moderate sized and in the middle of nowhere. It belonged to Athena's mother Andromeda. When she was young, they would take an annual trip there. Her mother wanted her to get the full experience and made them back pack for six days through the woods. Of course her mother could have just teleported them but she told Athena, "Anything worth having is worth the wait getting." Athena wished she remembered that before all the craziness had started. Then again if she had, she would not have met Chance. She would wait until he was ready to come with her because she knew he was worth the wait.

Tired and low on energy, she had a hard time getting Chance inside and had to drag him. Once inside she went back out for their gear. This place was the reason she knew how to use a bow. Her mother had taught her to hunt. Bows were not useful in the arena but it was nice to be able to catch your food. Since both she and Chance could hunt they could stay here as long as they wanted. Athena didn't think her dad even knew the location of the cabin. It was her mom's special retreat. She went to the bedroom and took some blankets off the bed. They were a little dusty. The place would need a good cleaning. Not able to drag Chance to a bed she unrolled one of the sleeping bags on the floor, rolled him on to it, covered him in a blanket then collapsed on the couch and fell asleep.

When Athena woke she was freezing and it was dark. It took her a minute to remember where she was. The familiar smells of the old place brought her back to her senses and she began looking for the tinderbox to light a fire because her energy level was *still* so low. The fireplace was always stacked with kindling in case it was needed. She recalled there was a stack of firewood on the side of the cabin. Striking the flame and getting the fire going she went out to get some logs for the fire before the kindling burned out. When she opened the door she was surprised by the snow. Athena paused for a moment listening to the silence. The snow muted the landscape like a dampening field muted power. Shaking her head, she walked around the cabin and gathered some wood. She placed the logs in the fire and made sure it was roaring before she grabbed an old rocking chair nearby and sat by the hearth. She wondered if they had any coffee in their stores then remembered her mother used to drink it too. She would check the pantry later to see what dried and canned goods remained. The cabin had not been used in years so she was certain some of it had gone bad.

Athena looked over at Chance who was still out on the floor. She was not certain if was the high amount of energy he had expended or her blast that did it. Whatever it was, he would need rest. It seemed funny to her that they wanted to rest and recover and needed it even more at the next place they wound up. Even if Caval had not shown up, they had planned to leave the timeshare that day. Feeling like they were being watched was too uncomfortable for either of them. For Athena, knowing it was guard detail set by her uncle made it easier to accept, but she wondered if Chance would have reacted badly if he had spotted them. He probably would see it as invasion rather than protection.

The cabin was starting to warm up. She knew she should sleep more but she just sat by the fire watching Chance in his sleep, or coma. Athena hoped he woke up soon. She wanted to talk to him about what happened and about how she felt. Mostly, she just wanted to see him open his eyes.

When she woke again, she was slumped in the chair with a stiff neck. The cabin was getting cool again but not cold. Her mother had built this place well with modern windows and insulation. There was no power here; her mother had liked it that way. There were kerosene lamps and candles everywhere though. She stoked up the fire that had died down to embers and pulled Chance closer to it. She probably should have done that last night but she was so tired. He stirred in his sleep and she took that as a good sign.

Athena walked around the cabin remembering good times here. *We will be safe here* she thought. The cabin had a good sized living room. The kitchen had an old wood-burning stove and a small table for eating. The pantry was larger than the kitchen itself and went down into the cool earth where meat could keep fresh longer. She looked at the shelves and saw they were still fairly well stocked. Athena did not remember if her mother had restocked after their last trip here but apparently she did. None of the cans were swollen which was a good sign. The dry goods were in airtight Tupperware so there was no chance of bugs or vermin getting into them. Speaking of vermin, she knew she should check the place for mice.

There were two bedrooms. Her mom's old room was twice the size of the guest bedroom with a nice Queen sized bed. The guest room she slept in had a twin sized bed too small for Chance. She would think about the sleeping arrangements later.

Both had small fireplaces in them. Her mother loved having a fire. She once told Athena that it was in her marriage contract with her father that anyplace they lived had to have a fireplace. The small bathroom had a working gravity shower. Rain water ran through a sand and charcoal purifier then collected in a small cistern on the roof. Reinforced beams and another small wood burning stove meant she could have hot water. The chimney was just a simple pipe exiting the roof. There was a stream nearby where she could wash the dust from the sheets and prepare the beds for the two of them. Athena did not want to leave Chance alone in here but she knew he would be ok. When he awoke she did not want him to have to worry about anything other than recovering. She went to the small closet in the living room and found the two winter coats were still in there. Hers and her mothers, they were the same size. She was supposed to grow into hers and she supposed she had.

Athena grabbed her coat, stoked up the fire a bit then took the short trek through the mounting snow to the river. The water was cold so she warmed it with heat energy, glad her strength was returning, and quickly cleaned the linens. Once back in the cabin she placed her shoes on the drying rack by the door and again used heat, this time to dry the linens. Her mother preferred not to use energy in the cabin but desperate times and all. Athena then practiced some levitation, bringing in a stack of firewood for each fireplace and for the stoves. Once she was confident that her weariness was not affecting her control she used it to levitate Chance to the large bed.

He was still wearing his shoes. She thought that odd for some reason and removed them. He was still out, breathing steady but still unconscious. She stripped his shirt and looked at his injuries. Chance had bruises all over a rather strong looking body. Using the first aid kit, she wrapped his body and injured hand in gauze and tape for support. It was the best she could do for now and she hoped nothing was broken. Had she been a healer she could have diagnosed it better but as she explained she was weak to water. Perion the head of the healing ward had once explained that healers were almost always strong water users because of how the human body was comprised mostly of water. Although healing occurs naturally on a cellular level the water in a person's body makes it possible. Chance had been out at least twelve hours. Athena lit a small fire in the hearth in the master room and closed the door to a crack.

She found her mother's old boots and was surprised when they fit her. Donning her jacket once again and taking the bow she purchased with Chance, Athena went out to hunt. She returned an hour later tired and cold with a rabbit and a squirrel. Not her best hunting trip but at least it was meat. She considered teleporting to buy some but did not want to risk it. They were here, they were safe, and here they would stay till they were ready to leave together. She would wait. Skinning her catch was more difficult than Athena remembered. She usually just watched while her mother did the work. She remembered her mom telling her she might need this skill someday and thinking at the time that her mother was nuts. Well someday was here and she was doing her best regretting not paying closer attention.

She took a page from Chances book and made a stew on the wood burning stove. She used the canned vegetables and potatoes from the pantry. Athena wondered how Caval was doing. Chance had hurt him pretty bad. That fact alone made her believe what Caval said was true. Chance was special. She knew it from their first lesson but to see the example of his potential greatness was frightening. She was strong, and a very good sword fighter. Athena knew she could hold her own in a fight against most people; however, she knew she was greatly outclassed against those two boys. She peaked in on Chance then took a short nap on the couch.

Athena woke to the smell of rabbit, squirrel stew permeating the cabin. She checked on it and gave it a quick taste. *Not bad considering I cooked it* she thought to herself. She plucked a book off the bookshelf, one of the many romance novels her mother liked to read, and sat down to kill some time waiting for Chance to wake up. Several times she got up to walk around the cabin, dusting or cleaning. The cabin was looking decent and clean when she looked in on Chance again. She tried to reach out with her mind and touch Chance's but his lack of consciousness prevented contact. She wondered if Aunt Uriel would be able to break through and wake him up. It had been eighteen hours and he was still not awake. Athena was sure of Caval's assessment. She knew her friend for too long to think he was wrong. He was confident and arrogant, but he was usually right. She ate another quick meal, keeping a low flame in the stove to warm the stew. She pulled the rocking chair into to the room and sat beside the bed. As the sun began to set on their first full day in the cabin she fell asleep.

• •

When Chance woke, the first thing he noticed was that he was in a bed and covered up. He looked around and found himself in a strange room. It was dark but warm, with faint light coming from the remains of a fire in a small fireplace. Athena was asleep in a chair with a blanket pulled up around her.

He hurt all over, and was incredibly thirsty. *Where am I, and how long have I been out?* It was painful to sit up but he managed. His hand was throbbing but he could move all his fingers so he knew it was not broken. Trying to reach out with energy to get a better understanding of his surroundings Chance was both surprised and frightened that he could not. Even the effort made him more tired. Looking at Athena sleeping in the chair he trusted that they must be safe. She must have been keeping watch over him. When she woke he would have to ask her about their present situation. Even though he had just woken up from being out for he knew not how long, he was already drifting back to sleep. It was more comfortable on what he assumed were bruised ribs to keep upright, so he fell asleep that way looking at the girl sleeping in the chair.

The next time Chance woke there was sunlight streaming through the window. The fire was roaring nicely in the fireplace and Athena was gone. He tried to get out of bed but lacked the strength to do so. Calling out for Athena she quickly ran into the room and jumped on him hugging him.

"Ouch..." He winced from the pressure on his ribs.

"Sorry," she replied sheepishly. "I'm just so happy you're awake!" She let him go. She kissed him lightly on the cheek and stood up. "Welcome back." She smiled and left the room again.

"What was that?" he whispered more confused than ever. Chance watched her leave and thought he could hear her banging around pots and pans. When she returned she had a bowl of stew broth, a glass of water, three Advil, and a cup of coffee.

"Don't worry," she joked. "This time it's edible." She handed him the bowl of broth and his stomach did flips as he realized how hungry he must be. Taking the glass of water, he sipped then gulped as his body demanded more. Athena grabbed the glass. "Only a little at time," she explained. "We don't know how your body is going to react to food."

"Thank you," he said taking a spoonful of surprisingly tasty broth. "How long--"

"Food first, then I'll tell you everything," she cut him off. "You need your strength."

"Alright," he responded spooning more broth in his mouth. He swallowed the Advil with the coffee which was wonderful. He wondered how she brewed it but he didn't ask and continued to eat. Athena watched him cautiously. He could not figure out why she was paying so much scrutiny to his pain. He briefly wondered if he killed that kid he was fighting or if he just escaped. Handing Athena the now empty bowl he looked at her expectantly.

"I guess I should start with where we are at," Athena began. She set the bowl on the floor, smiled at and took his hand. "We're safe. This was my mother's cabin. We're somewhere in Pennsylvania. She and I used to come here once a year for a retreat."

"How did we get here?" Chance asked, surprised she was holding his hand.

"When the fight was over I teleported us here," she stated. "It took me three ports but we made it."

"I didn't think you had that kind of control." Chance said surprised.

"Well I didn't really have a choice. You were out and people were coming." Athena explained. "It motivated me to do what you always said I could."

"What happened to the kid? Is he dead?"

"Yeah, about that," Athena said. "That was actually Caval. The whole thing was a big misunderstanding. You didn't kill him by the way."

"That was the guy you are always going on about?" Chance exclaimed. "The one who is supposed to be so strong? Holy shit! I'm lucky I'm not dead. I take it he got tired of playing with me and that's why I was knocked out?"

"That was kind of my fault," she confessed. "When I saw you two fighting, I sort of blasted you both to separate you when it looked like you were about to kill him." She sighed, "I'm really sorry. I didn't mean to hurt you so bad."

Chance laughed, "Ok, how long was I out for?" trying to comprehend what she had told him so far.

"Best guess without clocks, thirty hours give or take, I lost my watch somewhere."

"Do me a favor. Just start from the moment I was knocked out and finish up with the food you brought me, please? I need to get my head around everything going on," Chance pleaded.

Athena spent the next three hours talking to Chance about the events in the prairie and the cabin. During this time she went and filled up another bowl of broth this time with some vegetables in it, and of course more coffee. By the time she was done she was tired of talking and Chance looked like he had more questions than answers. "And that brings us to where we are. Safe for the time being, and it's a good thing because you are in no shape to move for a couple days."

"About that, I tried to reach out with my energy earlier and could not. Do you know why that is?" Chance questioned.

"Well, I don't think you have ever expended that much energy before," she explained. "It's like using a muscle or cardio training. If you push yourself too far without building up to it you can hurt or exhaust yourself."

"So you think I just pushed too far?" he asked.

"Chance, you are used to teleporting and practicing, but have you ever really pushed yourself to that level before? I mean you nearly killed Caval who has been trained by some of the best in the world, since he was like, four."

"I was just trying to protect you," he disclosed. "I guess I didn't realize how much I was pushing. Besides, that guy was probably holding back."

"Chance," Athena laughed and kissed his hand. "Have you not been listening to me? Caval thought he was ambushed. He went after you with all he had and you won. You're special! We don't know your limits. That's why the Hunters want you."

"I'm just me Athena," Chance said. "Nothing special about me, I probably just got lucky." Shaking his head he felt even luckier to be alive. He also was a little embarrassed at how affectionate Athena seemed to be, not that he minded it was just unexpected.

Athena smiled at him. She took his bowl and said, "We will try to get you out of bed a little later. Maybe have dinner in the dining room. For now, just rest up a little more." she walked out the door looking back for a second before heading into the kitchen.

So, that was Caval Chance thought to himself sipping his coffee. *I wonder how much he was holding back.* His mind was reeling from all that Athena told him. He agreed that the cabin was probably a safe place; however, he quickly assumed her father knew of its location. From the way Athena had described her father's reaction to losing his wife, they were very close. Chance imagined that they had their own retreats here. He began to think more about the girl he was traveling with. She seemed different. More than just being affectionate, Athena was more confident. She took charge and found them a safe place to rest. She took care of him pretty well considering she admitted early on she was not a healer. He wondered if the young woman was homesick being here. It must make her think about her father more.

He was touched by the streak of loyalty. She could have taken him back to her group but she respected his wishes enough to put herself through the hardship of getting him there. It must have been hell on her the first night, trying to get the place warm and worrying about him. Chance decided he would not worry whether her father knew of the cabin. He would deal with that if the man showed up. Right now he had to concentrate on getting out of bed. He felt weak, not just physically but at his core. He could not remember a time when he could not reach out and touch energy. Athena was probably right; he was just not used to using energy like that. He would need to fix that in the future. Start pushing his limits when he trained so he would never feel this drained and helpless again. Although he had to admit to himself, a part of him did like Athena taking care of him. He must have trusted her more than he knew, because without realizing what was happening he closed his eyes and fell asleep.

• •

Athena walked into the kitchen with tears in her eyes after talking with Chance. She realized how little he thought of himself. Part of her was dying inside wondering at all he must have been through that he was still hiding. So much pain, so much suffering, and yet, with all that time alone he was such a good person. He had goodness and honor to his core. He could not even accept the fact that he is exceptional. Where did he learn to be like that, she wondered, abandoned by his parents, raised like a weapon at best or lamb to the slaughter at worst. Looking at her own life made her feel ashamed. How spoiled and naive she thought she must seem to him. Looked after and cared for by loving parents and friends of the family who she thought of as Aunts and Uncles. Money just for the taking if she wanted and she shamed him for stealing to live. *"Forgive me if I can't empathize with your situation,"* he had said to her and she realized he was right. Even after that he still took her with him, protected her, and helped her. Athena the spoiled run away no real clue about life, no real clue about true pain. She had lost her mother, but she was still sheltered and nurtured. Athena never went hungry, never went without a place to sleep, and was never made to feel like she was worthless.

She loved him, she knew that. She was probably in love with him, and she never felt more unworthy of being loved by anyone. She had to do better, to be better, to become a person worthy of his love. Athena could not imagine her life without Chance now. It had been less than two weeks and he captured her so completely without even trying. He would laugh at her if he knew how hard she had fallen. She recalled that her mother met her father around the same age.

Energy world relationships were complicated. People who could die young tended to follow their hearts more quickly. E-worlders were considered adults at sixteen. Most of the laws and rules in the world were set down over two thousand years ago.

She knew that her father would approve of Chance if they met. Now she just had to make Chance approve of her. Athena went to check on him and saw he was asleep again.

The amount of energy he displayed and the control he has is staggering. She told herself. Again she was struck by how different their lives were. He was an out-caste child; she was loved by leaders and powerful people. He was selfless and giving, and she had to admit she had been selfish. *That's behind me now* she reminded herself. *Chance has brought out the best in me and I intend to stay this way. When I convince him to come back with me the first thing I am going to do is apologize to my father.* When she thought about it she realized she owed quite a few apologies. *How do I convince him to come back with me? How do I show him I am not a spoiled brat? This sucks.*

Checking the pantry, she realized there were ingredients and pans for baking bread. Athena did not know how to bake bread but she was certain she and Chance could figure it out. Walking to the small bathroom lighting a fire to heat the water she felt confident that things would work out. After everything that they had been through it had to. The shower was on the smaller side but it had a seat. *Well at least if I have to help him in here he can sit down to wash up* she thought while she waited for the water to heat up. Checking on Chance again and building up his fire she realized they would need more wood soon. Luckily there was plenty outside.

After showering and filling the filter with snow to replenish the water supply she started on dinner. Making oatmeal was easy and it was filling. She reasoned that Chance would need something filling when he woke up again and it was the best thing she could think of. She took the two-steaming bowls into the room she was already thinking of as Chance's room and gently woke him up. On the tray were a couple more cups of coffee and a little sugar that had been in a sealed container. Handing him the bowl she asked how he was.

"Still tired," he replied, "but feeling better. My stomach is fine by the way."

Smiling at him she replied, "That's good. The small amount of food was only a precaution."

"Good to be cautious," he agreed. "Are you sure Caval took that link off you?" he asked suddenly.

"He wouldn't have lied to me about it, and he wants to train more before sparing with you again," Athena replied. "Remember, you hurt him far worse than he hurt you, and your vine attack actually protected him."

"I must be the only combatant in history to save my opponent with my attacks," he joked.

"Well," she laughed, "that not usually how it works but I am certain it has happened before." They sat in silence for a short time just eating their oatmeal it was a little chunky.

"I thought we were going to try to get me to the kitchen," Chance said suddenly.

"Well, you were asleep again so I assumed you didn't have the strength."

"Tell me more about who you really are," Chance asked.

"I am not much more than I already told you really. At least not personally," she admitted. "Although, my father, Horatius, is a leader of the Argonauts."

"Well I knew you were not just anybody based on who you seemed to know. Clotho told me she was in charge of the Manor and not just anybody gets a responsibility like that."

"Well, that's one of the reasons they had Uncle Cassiel trying to track me." Athena had still not told Chance that they were being guarded by people. At this point she was not sure how he would take it. It made her feel guilty again.

"How long did Caval have that tracking thread on you?" Chance asked.

"Well, probably from the beginning. I don't know a lot about it but I think he could keep it up while he slept," she ventured.

"I wonder if he told your dad about it." Chance uttered.

"I don't think he would have; he was the one covering for me when I ran." This was not going in a direction she wanted to go. *How can I become a better person lying to him?*

"Well I think Caval's advice to you was good. The Hunters shouldn't be able to track us here. So even if your people discover us at least it won't be them," he concluded.

"We can decide on how long to stay once you are up and about. First thing in the morning I'll help you to the shower."

"Well actually, if there is a bathroom in this place, I kind of need to go now," Chance said, his face turning red. "I have been drinking a lot of liquids today."

"Oh!" Athena turned red herself, "I'm sorry. I didn't think. I can levitate you. It's how I got you on the bed." Laughing together she helped him into the small bathroom and closed the door.

"Thank you," he called through the door, laughing. Athena made herself scarce for a few minutes. Chance pulled himself into the small shower, hurt hand an all. It wasn't too long before he contacted her mentally asking for her to toss in a towel. She threw a robe in that she had taken from the timeshare. If he was able to talk mentally she knew he must be getting some energy control back. Athena helped him back to bed where she left him a pair of sweats and a t-shirt. He apologized about the mess of clothes and bandages in the bathroom. Athena simply left him some privacy and went in to throw the clothes and bandages away; they were ruined anyway. When she arrived back at his room he was settling down under the blankets.

She kissed his cheek, wished him pleasant dreams and went to bed herself. When morning came he was already feeling stronger. The rest from the day before and the food helped greatly. Athena was already up and he called to her. She helped him to his feet and Chance was glad to see that his legs held his weight. With his arm around her shoulders and hers around his waist knowing he was on the mend he said "Well, let's go cook some breakfast."

Promises

Caval woke up in a Tank. He knew he was far more hurt than he originally thought if they had tanked him. Tanks were used for healing fighters who were really hurt. The patient would be submerged in super oxygenated liquid keyed to their own DNA. It was particularly effective for burns. The Forum had some of the best scientists in the world working for them. A genius in biology, robotics and computers name Gyro ran the division. When you can offer unlimited funds and one hundred percent free reign you tend to get the best and the brightest. No FDA or other agencies telling a scientist what they can or can't do, willing human subjects who volunteer for procedures that could fix what energy could not. The main thing that came out of Gyro's research though was the Tank. It had saved many lives.

Currently Caval found himself suspended in the liquid. He had been unconscious when lowered in so he was "breathing" the liquid as well. Really he was not doing much of anything other than letting his body naturally pass oxygen from the liquid in the tank to the liquid in his veins via his lungs. He looked over through the murky whitish liquid and saw Clotho asleep on a small couch that had been brought in. He reached out and touched her mind waking her. *"Hi Mom,"* he thought to her. *"How much trouble am I in?"*

"That depends on how much you tell us about what went on and why your father found you in a field half dead."

"How long have I been out for?"

"Eighteen hours. That wound in your leg nearly killed you. It shattered your femur and severed several arteries," she explained.

"Yeah, I thought it was pretty bad. I used the technique my teacher taught me to stop the bleeding as much as possible. Didn't heal it though," he responded.

"So are you going to tell me what happened?"

"As much as I can, but I think I should probably tell everyone. Uncle Cassiel and Uncle Horatius should be there. When can I get out of here."

"Well we had Perion and Hippocrates working on you so you are pretty much healed. Sabastian had them keep a scar on your leg as a reminder."

If he could have seen her Caval would have realized how angry his adopted mom really was. *"Can we meet in a dining room? I am starved."*

Half an hour later, washed, dressed and feeling more like himself, Caval entered the living quarters of his father. Cyrus, the main leader of the largest and most powerful e-world group The Forum, had very spacious penthouse quarters. He knew that his father preferred to live in their private villa but his duties required him to be here more often than not. Looking at the table where there was food provided for him, he saw Clotho, Cassiel, Horatius and of course Cyrus waiting for him. None of the adults looked pleased. He took his seat and waited for the questions to start.

Cyrus began. "So, why don't you start with what happened at the field. We have already pieced together how you found Chance and Athena at their hideout."

"They are safe aren't they?" Horatius asked quickly.

"Yes Uncle, they're safe," he revealed, looking at the worried man. "Also, Athena is in really good hands with Chance. Between the two of them it would take a small invasion force to capture them." He smiled. Horatius did not smile back.

"At least we know they were not captured," Clotho said putting a reassuring hand on Horatius.

"As far as what went on in the field, well that was my fault." Caval frowned. "When I found them at that hotel, I just wanted to surprise Athena and take her home. I attached an astral thread to keep a trace on Athena and it was a good thing because Chance ported out, in like, a second."

"When did you learn to use that?" Cyrus asked. "That is a very advanced...never mind. Go on." He sighed.

"Well after like the fifth jump Chance turned to attack me," Caval explained. "He thought I was a Hunter," he added quickly before anyone at the table thought Chance was an enemy.

"Ok, so who hurt you so badly?" Cassiel asked, still angry that all his work in finding the pair was wasted.

"Chance," Caval stated. The adults around the table all looked a little disturbed. Caval went on to describe the fight. He spoke of the ease in which Chance was manipulating the different type of energies. He spoke about the wall being used as a diversion so the steel shot could be used to kill him. Then he told them Athena interrupted the fight and briefly introduced the two.

"Are you sure this was Chance?" Clotho asked amazed.

"Yeah, it was him. When the fight was over and I was lying on the ground, he flew off with Athena. I lost sight of them going south I must have passed out or something. Then I contacted dad. I was too trashed to even teleport home," Caval finished.

"I looked all over that field for his teleport trace and could not find it. If he flew it would explain why I was unable to," Cassiel mused.

"That's it?" Cyrus asked. "You don't have anything else to tell us?" Looking at his adopted son, he knew the boy was holding something back.

"Well, I got so messed up because Chance is like me," Caval explained. "He certainly didn't have a main, and his level was frightening high considering his lack of formal training." He frowned. "My teacher is going to be pissed."

Still concerned, Horatius asked, "Your certain Chance was not trying to take her?"

"Yeah. Like I explained, when Athena introduced us and we realized what a mistake had been made, he apologized for hurting me. Said something about only wanting to keep her safe," Caval lied. "Then when Athena asked if I would be ok and I said I was going to contact dad, they left." He looked around the table with innocent eyes and started eating some of the food put on the table for him.

"You should stick to the truth," Clotho said darkly, "because you're a horrible liar."

"What?" he asked startled.

"Ok so after the fight what really happened?" Cyrus asked. "We know the fight was accurate. You're not that self-debasing."

"They flew away!" he exclaimed.

This cycle of questions repeated for roughly two hours with only slight variations the whole time Caval protesting he was too weak for mentally sharing the events.

"Son," Clotho finally said trying to keep her temper. "Please don't make us use your Aunt Uriel on you. Tell us the truth." For the first time Caval looked a little frightened.

"Fine!" he yelled suddenly. "She took him away. He was out cold and hurt. I advised Athena to port because the Hunters don't know her trace. That way they could get away and rest somewhere. I don't know where they went and I didn't ask." Clenching his jaw tight and looking away.

"I should have guessed," Cassiel said. "I did pick up a port trace from her but assumed it was a battle jump, like the others on the field."

"Just let them be!" Caval pleaded. "Chance will be back on his feet in no time and Athena will convince him to come back to the Argos. If you pressure them, he will bolt. Then those Hunters will catch him." He said trying to make them understand the way Chance thinks.

"Cassiel, see if you can find a location," Horatius ordered. "Just to make sure they are safe. Caval gave my daughter some decent escape advice. We'll consider guards when you know where they are. If Chance is like Caval, the Hunters will not give up until they find him.”

“I’ll find them; I know her trace very well.” Without saying goodbye, Cassiel teleported back to the battle field.

The young woman called Wisp entered the room a moment after he left. “Have you found them?” she asked, worried. “It was my detail that lost them. I have been sick about it. Nexus wants to resign from the Protection Force over this.”

Caval looked sick. He thought very highly of Nexus and did not want the man to leave his job over his mistake. “Excuse me,” Caval said quietly and stood up. “I need to speak to Nexus and Illyria. I can’t let him quit because I was stupid.” As he left he heard Cyrus tell Wisp she was welcome to join Cassiel on the search.

• •

Cassiel found himself standing in another field. He was angry to say the least. All his hard work tracking down Chance and Athena was wasted. He only hoped because Athena did the teleports he could track them quickly. Knowing that Chance was unconscious was actually a relief. If he was awake, they could have teleported to a city, taken a bus a hundred miles away, and teleported again to confuse their trail. Then it would take months even for Cassiel to track them down. It has only been twenty hours. The trail was fresh and if Caval was correct Chance might still be out.

Looking around the battlefield. it was hard to believe that two teens had fought here. Cassiel had seen fights with well-trained adults that did not cause this much damage. They were definitely on a different level. He found Athena’s port location easily and began tracing its destination. Soon, he felt the telltale pop of air of a teleport. Wisp walked over and immediately began sharing her energy with him.

"I want to help you find them," she explained. "It was my duty to keep an eye on them and I failed."

"Alright," Cassiel replied, "but you can cut off the energy link. I am fine." He felt the flow of energy from her stop just as he located the destination. "Grab my shoulder," he said, and they vanished. The next two traces were just as easy to follow. Athena had no method of diffusing her trail and her type of teleporting was not like Chance's. Just as he was about to make the final port, Wisp made a suggestion.

"Pick a spot a mile or so away if you can," she asked. "If they are keeping watch it will be far enough out of their range. One of us can then astral around to see if they are safe."

"Makes sense," Cassiel said, "but I can't exactly see the area, I can feel the rough layout of the land and elevation. There are a lot of trees. I'll shield us from popping into an object but we may wind up off the ground to protect us."

"Would not be the first time," Wisp sighed. "It amazes me that you are able to track as well as you do and not get hurt."

"I spent close to a decade just perfecting this skill Wisp," he explained. "I wish I was half as strong at my combat skills but we needed a good tracker when I was given the name Cassiel. Unlike many other angels, Cassiel is known for simply watching the events of the cosmos unfold, as a tracker it is usually my job to find and watch."

"Alright, let's go." She smiled.

They arrived in a freezing river. Shocked by the cold water, they were happy that at least they were not falling to the ground. Even as they made their way to the shore, Cassiel was already probing for energy. "I feel something to the southeast," he reported. Once on land, they were afraid to use heat to dry themselves, for fear of alerting the kids to their presence if they were close.

"Hold onto me please," Wisp requested. "It's freezing and I need to be a little more stable before I can astral over there." Taking the young woman in his arms they sat with their backs to a tree. Cassiel tried to warm her with his body heat as he felt her go limp. He knew she was astral and looking for the missing teens. Twenty minutes later she returned, and they were both freezing.

"They're here," she said with chattering teeth. "In a cabin. It looks like Athena has fires going and the boy is asleep in the master bedroom. No sign of anyone else. There are a couple of pictures of Athena and what must be her mom on the walls. It looks like the pair is safe enough for now."

"Ok," Cassiel said. "Let's report the location, good work"

"Thanks" she smiled.

After quickly warming himself, Cassiel went back to Cyrus's quarters where the group was sitting discussing possible plans. Still cold, he took his seat and asked the server for a cup of coffee. All eyes turned to him.

"Please tell me you found them," Horatius began.

"We did," Cassiel explained. "They are holed up in a cabin in Pennsylvania. There are pictures of you guys there. Do you know where that is?" he asked.

"Oh thanks gods," Horatius laughed. "That's Andromeda's cabin. No one knows where it is; it was her family retreat spot when she wanted to get away. I have not even thought about it since she passed."

"So they're isolated and safe?" Clotho asked.

"Yes. It's safe to assume that. Andromeda used to keep it stocked with canned and dry goods. Plenty of game in the area, they won't even need to teleport for anything. My daughter chose the perfect camp," he said proudly.

"That's the best news I have heard since she went missing," Cyrus said. "We can only hope she is able to take care of Chance."

"Wisp said he was sleeping," Cassiel reported. "Do you think he might still be knocked out?"

"While you were gone I had Caval show me the fight from his perspective," Cyrus explained. "Chance was positively blasted. He was lucky he did not die. Caval restarted his heart. It may be days before he can even walk depending on his overall constitution and if he can heal himself with energy."

"Well count Athena out on that part," Horatius cut in. "She has a hard time with water energy which is the basis of healing."

"Yes but if he is sleeping he is alive," Clotho supplied, "and Athena would not risk his life if she felt he was in danger of death. She is too smart for that. So, what do we do about them?"

"We leave them be," Horatius announced. "We send Cassiel to check on them every four or five days. She will either convince him to come to us as Caval suggested or she will leave him."

"You're ok leaving your teenage daughter alone with him for as long as it takes?" Clotho asked cautiously.

"Clotho, I don't like it but if I tried to force her to come home she would be even more rebellious and run off again." Horatius laughed.

"Yes, I know that," she acknowledged, "but this is your little girl we are talking about. You are usually so protective, and well, Chance is a young man…" She squinted in thought. "We don't know how old he is, now that I think about it."

Horatius shrugged. "I am more concerned that she will miss Thanksgiving. I was hoping to spend it with just her and me this year. I know now that I pushed her to this by being too protective."

"I am not worried about how old or young he is," Cyrus added. "We have never seen or heard of him till now so he is not an adult in our world. Also Caval might have been an idiot, but he loves Athena like a sister. If he thought there was a problem with Chance, he would not have advised her to run with him."

"Well I can check on them every few days," Cassiel offered. "I'll need to be careful though. There's snow in the area and I can't leave any tracks."

"Using energy to levitate is also out of the question," Cyrus added. "Just astral. Wisp had a good idea. You are not as strong as her at it but you can use it for the short distance you need."

"Will do. I'll check one more time tomorrow to see if Chance is up. If he is, then I'll check the day after Thanksgiving. That will give them five days," Cassiel decided.

"Ok, we have our plan. The teens are safe, and we will continue to look for these Overlords in the meantime." Cyrus declared, "Meeting adjured."

Early the next morning Cassiel was bundled up and trying to keep his distance from the cabin. He sat down near the same tree he and Wisp were at the day before. Going astral was always frightening for Cassiel. He found the detachment from his physical being very disorienting.

The thin thread of energy that attached someone's soul to their physical body was close to impossible to cut; however, there were several people who had learned the method. If the thread tying your soul to your physical body was cut, it caused your body to go into shock and your soul could not return without a soul the body cannot live, it was not a pleasant way to die.

Shaking off thoughts of this, Cassiel went to the cabin. Athena and Chance were in the large bedroom. Chance was eating a bowl of something and they were talking about the fight. He still looked tired and weak but he was up and alive. Athena looked good. She was watching Chance intently. Cassiel smiled to himself knowing he was seeing what Horatius had seen at the fireworks show. Athena was falling in love with the young man. He could not help but be happy for the young woman he thought of as a niece. Going back to his body he felt good about the situation for the first time. Finding the pair out here would be close to impossible for a tracker with less than his abilities. Teleporting home he reported his findings to Cyrus then returned to the Seraph house for breakfast. He would check on the teens Friday.

Overlords

Inferno stalked down the hall, energy crackling off him like sparks off a live wire. To say he was angry would be an understatement. He was furious and looking to take it out on someone. His prey had escaped again even after the spy had told them the location. *Disney World?! Are you kidding me?* he thought to himself.

When the trace first showed up outside of the shopping center and then just disappeared, Inferno assumed they had hopped a bus north. When the spy confirmed that Chance and his little fireball had actually stayed in the area he simply could not believe it. Then some punk friend of the little fireball shows up at their room and Chance bailed! By the time the team was able to locate and track the ports the entire area was a battle zone. His people nearly ran into Lord Cyrus who was just standing in the field looking around. He knew the little fireball was the daughter of an Argonaut leader, but how did Lord Cyrus fit in the picture? Inferno needed to talk to Harbinger now!

Years I have been chasing this kid, we could have brought back twenty or more kids by now. Chance is a challenge, and an escapee so that makes it personal but who cares! If I had my way I would just kill the kid the next time I saw him and be done with it. Inferno thought. He was tempted to hire an assassin to do just that. The only thing that stopped him was wanting the pleasure of killing Chance himself. He knocked on the door to the office, then just barged in. He was shocked to see a young woman seated on Harbinger's lap.

"Inferno," Harbinger said. "So nice to see you again. I take it you recognize my guest?" He looked at the woman who was climbing out of his embrace.

"She's the spy?" Inferno asked, stunned, all anger drained out of him.

"Yes, and I would like to keep her a secret. Your barging in here uninvited leaves me with a problem to say the least." Harbingers voice was icy. "What am I to do with you failing to follow protocol?"

Inferno felt pressure forcing him to the floor. Trying to fight against it proved useless, Harbinger just stared at him as he was forced to his knees. He could feel his joints popping as he was pushed harder with almost crushing force to the ground.

"That's enough my love," said the woman sweetly. "I think he has learned his lesson don't you?" She put a hand on Harbingers shoulder. "I must return before they notice I am missing."

Inferno grabbed her hand and kissed it briefly. He eased off the pressure as Inferno watched the woman fade away.

"Consider yourself lucky. She is much more forgiving then I," Harbinger announced.

"I did not realize you were on intimate terms with anyone. What will your wife say?" Inferno challenged as he stood up, his body aching from the pressure that almost killed him. His mind already on what he could do with this new piece of information, he thought he could turn this meeting back in his favor after all.

"She's a toy. Nothing more," said a tall woman walking in the office from the same door Inferno entered. "My husband is allowed his playthings when they are useful to us." The raven haired woman with dark, almost black eyes, leaned in and kissed her husband. Standing slightly behind him she faced a once again stunned Inferno.

"As Melaniya pointed out, the woman is a toy. As long as she is useful we will keep her around." Harbinger looked pointedly at Inferno. "You had hoped seeing me with her gave you some leverage over me, didn't you?"

"Yes," he answered knowing that a lie could get him killed. "I did not know you and your wife played such games. Melaniya always seemed a jealous type." Behind Harbinger Melaniya smiled.

"Now that we have that out of the way, why are you here?" Harbinger asked in the same cold voice, not bothering to answer the implied question.

"I..." with his anger gone and cold fear in his body, Inferno forgot what his initial purpose was. Recovering, he stated, "We lost the trail on Chance. He disappeared from the hotel he and the little fireball were staying at. When we were able to track his location Lord Cyrus was surveying the area. Also I am tired of chasing him. It's a waste of time in my opinion."

"Old news," Harbinger stated, "and your opinion does not matter. So again I ask, why are you here?"

"Um..." Inferno was now totally thrown off and once again in fear of his life. Until the crushing weight was placed on him he always considered himself stronger than the man before him. Harbinger was a politician in his eyes, not a warrior like himself. Now all these assumptions were gone. He just wanted to get out of the room alive.

"Let me tell you why you are here," Harbinger began. "You lost your intended target yet again and do not know how to proceed. So you come in here acting tough when what you really need is for me to tell you what to do again." He smiled. "You are a tool, a weapon, that is all. Don't try to rise above your station and pretend you can think. We will let you know where the boy and his lady friend are soon enough."

"Yes my Lord," Inferno replied, feeling humiliated and angry again.

"Your anger serves you, but never try to use it against me," Harbinger stated simply. "When we locate the boy, and we will, you are not to harm the girl, she is to be left out of this. We do not want a war with her father and his allies. We are not ready for that. Do you understand?"

"Yes my lord."

"Good, then leave us, you're no longer needed."

Realizing he was dismissed Inferno hurried out of the room. Once again he felt angry, but didn't know what to do with that anger. Walking down the hall he recognized that there was much more going on than he had been told.

• •

"Would you really have killed him?" Melaniya questioned taking a seat on the desk.

"No, he's an idiot but useful," Harbinger explained. "His control of wind and fire makes him a powerful warrior when we need him."

"And what of our little toy? Does she know as much as you pretend she does?" she asked.

"She is not a member of the inner circle, but can squeeze information out with her looks. She is charming when she wants to be and can play up vulnerability." He smiled, "All those things she thinks she does with me."

"And me," his wife laughed. "How much longer do you think we will have to play with her?"

"Once we capture Chance, her usefulness will drop tenfold. She is also getting a little too daring trying to please me." He mused, "She will get caught soon if she keeps this up."

"If that happens can she lead them here?"

"No. She doesn't know this location and I was porting her. The only thing she could tell them was she would meet with me and you and report her findings as well as more embarrassing times spent with us." He smiled thinking of those times.

"Well then, maybe the Argonauts will take care of her for us. Although I would enjoy letting her know she was a plaything before she died. So devoted to you over nothing." Melaniya laughed as she left the room.

"And people think of me as evil," he responded to his laughing wife's back. Harbinger knew it would be several hours possibly a day before his spy contacted him with the information he needed. *Where did little Athena take you Chance?*

He faded out and arrived at a small camp. There were children of various ages running around using the meager skills they possessed. He went to the two small cells to check on his prisoners. The two teens looked at him in disgust and fear. Both of them were tired, malnourished and beat-up looking. Harbinger used the two as an example to the other children of what happens when they fall out of his favor.

"I have good news for the two of you. You may be getting out of here soon. A proper meal and bath would be nice wouldn't it?" The teens nodded but did not say anything. They had long since learned that to speak to Harbinger meant more pain for them.

Leaving the two in their cells, he sought out Warden who ironically enough was given the name because he was "the Warden" of the camp to see how things were progressing. He found the man punishing a student with an energy whip. She was cuffed to a pole by hands and feet. A chain ran between them that hooked to a power cable. A guard stood by, manning the switch. Harbinger watched as the whip slashed the girls back open another three times before making his presence known.

"Ah, Lord Harbinger. What brings you to camp today?" Warden asked.

"Checking to see how the future troops are progressing." With a head nod to the girl on the post, he asked, "What did this one do to deserve your personal attention?"

"She is hard to break," Warden explained, "I have seen grown men take less punishment and submit." He looked at the girl who glared back with cobalt colored eyes.

"She strong?" asked Harbinger looking at the frail looking girl who met his eyes.

"Too strong for her own good," Warden grimaced. "She challenged, then took down a teacher who disciplined a younger student." He nodded to the two guards who took the young woman to the healing wing to tend to her back. Her eyes never left Harbinger until she was out of sight.

"Strong will that one," he mused. "Is she usually so defiant?"

"No. Her will is mostly broken like the rest," Warden commented. "It was just when Zarra slapped a little girl that she reacted so strongly. When she tried to put her back in her place Mouse attacked and landed Zarra in a healing wing half-dead."

"Mouse? You call the girl Mouse?" Harbinger laughed.

"Wasn't me, my Lord. The other kids call her that, probably because of her mousy brown hair."

"Interesting. How goes the rest of the camp?"

"Very well. The kids are all coming along nicely. Fully half of them are little more than cannon fodder as you know. But they should be able to take out one or two people who are not expecting such savage attacks."

"Good, very good," Harbinger smiled. "Have your guards learned the teleport lock power yet?"

"Yes my Lord," Warden replied. "They keep it up at all times now. I have them doing it in shifts. Not that any of the kids here know how."

"That's what we thought about Chance when we lost him," Harbinger reminded the man. "I would not put it past that girl Mouse to learn it on her own like he did. She has more fight left in her than you think. Keep up the good work;

we may have another guest for you soon." Not waiting for a response Harbinger walked to the edge of camp. When he was beyond the range of the lock he faded out and returned home. Everything was looking good. In a few more years they would be able to launch a war in the e-world the likes of which had not been seen since the dark ages. Harbinger could hardly wait.

••

After his humiliation at the hands of Harbinger, Inferno went to the training center. Taking out his anger on some of the weaker members of the Overlords did not satiate his rage. He had no idea that the politician was so damned strong. What was that power that had been used on him? Why did his shields not work against it? More importantly, what was Harbinger hiding? There had to be more to Chance then he was being told. Why was this boy such an important target? He had seen several children brought in who were stronger. Yet, this boy remained at the top of their list. Inferno has chased him around the country and back. He even had a brief stop in Europe which caused problems with the anti-energy users in Scotland. The battlefield was impressive but no better than Spark could have done. Now the trail was cold, there was no trace to follow. Harbinger's spy supposedly could ferret out the information leaving Inferno with nothing to do but wait and brood.

He considered his options. *Maybe I can accidentally kill Chance when capturing him. After all, the boy is bound to put up a fight. I could always blame it on another member of the team. It's a pity we have to leave the little fireball alone. I'd like to play with that one myself.* As he walked to the mess hall, he began to formulate a plan.

Holidays

Chance got stronger every day. After the initial shock had worn off, he was able to tap into energy again at will. Athena went hunting and bagged a deer. They were once again eating venison steaks and stews. He missed eggs but there was no way to get them without teleporting out and they both agreed not to do that. So far they had not sensed any energy around them other than their own. Chance felt safe and comfortable for the first time in a long time. The Hunters could not track Athena; they were in the middle of nowhere; they had food, a nice place to sleep; and he was beginning to be happy. Athena and he were getting closer and closer as well. Late night kisses by the fire in the main room were getting heated. He really liked having a girlfriend. Chance thought back to that first morning making breakfast when he could still barely stand.

"Are you going to teach me to cook us a proper meal or do I continue to feed my boyfriend inedible food?" Athena asked suddenly her face turning a little red.

"Is that what I am?" Chance asked, startled.

"If you want to be." she responded shyly.

"Well, yeah, I mean I have never had a girlfriend before, I may be a bad boyfriend." He stammered.

"Does that mean you are?".

"Isn't the guy supposed to ask the girl to go steady or something?" Chance laughed.

"Well then, ask me." Athena stated with a coy smile still blushing a burning shade of red.

Chance took a moment and looked at the young woman. She took his breath away sometimes and made his heart skip a beat. He didn't know when it happened, only that it did. Realizing the depth of his feelings for her was a pleasant surprise. With a smile he asked, "Would you like to be my girlfriend?"

Athena leaned forward and kissed him full on the lips. "I thought you would never ask."

After that they made breakfast. Chance taught her how to properly make waffles substituting apple sauce for eggs. They came out pretty good and the two laughed and fed each other as they talked about what to do next. The next few days were a blur of cleaning, light calisthenics and stolen kisses. They baked bread to dip in their stew and make venison sandwiches. Chance knew Athena wanted to go home, he could tell. However, she respected his wishes and never brought it up. He was enjoying his life and recovery so much he began to wonder if this was what people always talked about.

Was this the kind of life he could have with her back at the Argonauts? Would her father approve of him or get between them? He was seriously considering going back with her now; however, life was so good he was afraid of anyone or anything getting in the way of it. Athena was amazing, strong, brave, and resourceful. There was no hint of the naïve and well semi-spoiled girl he had first spoke to just a couple weeks ago. Twice he had tried to bring up the idea of letting her take him to the Argos as she called them but his fears got the better of him.

It was day five in the cabin when, out of the blue, Athena asked him a question. "What are we going to do for Thanksgiving?"

"What?"

"Thanksgiving, the Holiday It's tomorrow."

"Oh, I didn't know that. I don't usually celebrate it."

"Well I do," Athena responded, "and I think this year you have something to be thankful for too. Don't you?" she questioned with a playful smile.

Smiling back, he answered, "Of course I do." He walked to the door pulling on his coat.

"Where are you going?" she laughed.

"I am going to get us a wild turkey or a pheasant," he replied picking up his bow. "It's Thanksgiving and all. We should have one, yes?"

"Be careful," she said smiling ear to ear. "I'll see if we have a pan around here big enough to cook one."

Chance spent the next couple of hours searching for a habitat where wild turkeys would be. He knew that they were in swampy forest areas so he followed the river to a more open location. As luck would have it he came upon a small flock. There were seven to choose from. Chance didn't know turkeys lived in flocks. He had hoping to be able to find one if he was lucky. Drawing back with arms that were a little shakier then normal, he shot a decent sized turkey. The others took off in a flurry of feathers and sound. He took his kill back upriver to the cabin, grinning. So caught up in his new found happiness and security he missed the patch of beaten down snow where Cassiel and Wisp had been.

"You actually got one?" laughed Athena when he walked in the door, freezing.

"Yes. I hope you found a pan," he responded setting down his bow and walking over to the roaring fire.

"Well I don't know if it is big enough but I found one."

"I'll get this guy ready then, after I warm up a bit," he smiled.

"It's cold enough that all the meat is keeping. I guess it's a good thing we came here in the winter."

"Plus the fires are nice," he responded blushing.

Walking into the main room and pulling Chance forward for a quick kiss she said "They are nice aren't they."

Chance smiled at her and took the turkey outside to clean it. His ribs and hand were killing him. He went over the stores in his head. They had plenty of food. Maybe they could stay another couple weeks then go to the Argonauts. He wanted to keep this time alone with her for as long as he could. The practical side of him honed by years on the run knew that she would need to get back to her father.

Two more weeks. That will have given us three weeks at the cabin and a little over a month together. She will be home in time for Christmas. Smiling at the thought he let the turkey hang on a line high enough to keep it safe from any wild animals and went back inside to get some pain medication, regretting that he had gone hunting so soon." Athena was singing a pretty song he did not know. He smiled once again at how much better his life had gotten since meeting her.

• •

Athena was beginning to wonder what was wrong with her. Who was this forward kiss-steeling lap-sitting girl? She was never one to chase boys or get involved in gossip with the other girls at the Argos. Hell, her best friend was a guy and she never even showed interest in him! Yet here she was with Chance, in an almost blissful mood, half the time kissing him by the fire till her lips felt bruised. Something about him just made her lose all control of herself. Her mother would have laughed at her acting like such a girl. Athena was a warrior! She was strong! She was helpless when it came to Chance.

At least he never pressed her to go any further. He was a gentleman at all times. Ok, most of the time. She thought about the previous night when his hands wandered a bit more than normal. She hadn't stopped him and that was part of the problem. Shaking off these thoughts, she waited for Chance to come back in. When he did he looked tired, and she noticed his arm shaking. Athena noticed anything that had to do with Chance. Without realizing it she starting to sing.

"Baby, baby, yeah, are you listening? Wondering where you've been all my life. I just started living. Oh, baby, are you listening? When you say you love me know I love you more. And when you say you need me know I need you more. Boy, I adore you. I adore you..."

"What song is that," Chance asked, "It's pretty."

She blushed as she realized she was singing out loud not just thinking of the song. "Um, it's called *Adore You.*"

"Don't be embarrassed. You have a great voice." He smiled. "I love to hear you sing."

"You look tired. Are you ok?" she asked changing the subject, still blushing furiously.

"Just a little sore," he admitted. "Don't think I was quite ready to hunt yet."

"Sit down Chance!" Athena exclaimed, "I'll get you something for the pain." She ran to the medical kit and grabbed a couple of Advil and some water. Chance was seated in the living room in the rocking chair by the fire. She handed him the medicine and glass of water and asked how bad it was.

"Not real bad," he lied. "I just pushed myself a little too hard is all." Smiling he swallowed the pills.

"You're still a bad liar," Athena quipped. "On a scale of one to ten, how bad is it?"

"About a seven," he laughed and winced. "I'll be fine. But you'll have to do the hunting for a few more days."

"What am I going to do with you?" she asked exasperated.

"I'll be fine. Just let me sit and warm myself by the fire for a little bit."

"Alright. I'll get something for lunch. Would you like venison or venison?"

"I'll have the lobster," he joked.

"I'll get right on that," she replied. She leaned down to kiss him before going to the kitchen. *It's a good thing we can rest. he still needs it* she thought as she put the plate of food together. Grabbing a cup of coffee for good measure she walked back to the room and sat on the stool next to him.

"Thinking about home?" Chance asked suddenly.

"A little," she admitted. "I wonder how Caval is doing. You really messed him up."

"From what you have told me about him, he is probably just mad he could not get you home," he posed.

"Well we have healing tanks at the Argos too. They help a lot." Athena said.

"What are those?"

Athena launched into an explanation and history of tanks. Talking about e-world history led her to another thought that made her smile. "Do you know about the moratorium on fighting, raids and everything else during the holidays?"

"No, what's that?"

"Well because almost all the major religions of the world have their holy days in December, the energy world at large ceases all fighting for the month. Even the winter solstice is celebrated this time of year."

"So, what are you saying?" Chance looked perplexed.

"I am saying that pretty soon we should not have to worry about the Hunters, for like a month."

"The Hunters never stopped chasing me." Chance said a little bitterly.

Now it was Athena's turn to look confused. "Didn't they ever take a break?"

"I guess I don't even get a break when the rest of the world does." His jaw tightened and he looked ready to scream his frustrations.

"Chance," Athena said cautiously. "That group must be really evil. Only the worst kind of people would ignore the traditions of our world."

"The more we talk, the more I think you are right," he admitted. "I was thinking that maybe in a couple weeks..." he took a deep breath and paused. Athena held her breath, hoping for a change of heart. "We could go to your group."

"Really!" Athena exclaimed jumping up. She knocked the plate out of his hand between hugging and kissing him. "Are you serious?!" She caught herself and realized she had once again climbed into his lap. When she realized that he was trying to smile around a grimace of pain, she jumped off his lap and apologized. "I'm sorry, I'm sorry, your ribs."

"It's ok," he laughed. "I take it you like the idea?"

"I love it," she agreed.

Athena was both overjoyed and shocked at the turn of events. She had wondered how to start subtly convincing him. Chance surprised her at every turn. She picked up the plates and caught him staring at her with happiness on his face. *Two more weeks,* she thought. *Then he'll be safe, and we can be happy without the black cloud over us.*

Several hours later after another night spent by the fire Athena was still excited about going home. She had given him the larger room and was currently tossing and turning in bed trying to fall asleep. Her mind went back to his comment about not getting to rest when the rest of the world did. At times like that she was reminded again about how hard his life has been.

Athena woke early in the morning. She was having trouble sleeping anyway. Walking around the cabin she built up the fires in the three rooms and went outside quickly to grab the turkey. There was no stuffing but she was still happy they would be having one. Her uncle Cyrus who was originally Egyptian she thought would always throw a huge party on Thanksgiving. Aunt Clotho and he had a villa that was roughly the size of small village. It was really ridiculous how big it was. In her uncle's defense, she reasoned it did not start out so large and he usually used it for parties. She thought about how her father had wanted to have a private Thanksgiving with just her this year, the last one before she became an adult in the e-world. *Sorry dad* she thought as she got ingredients out for their meal. The cornbread was difficult as they had no eggs, but Chance had taught her that vegetable oil, cornstarch and baking powder could be used. He had confessed that he learned that from a group of homeless people in Boston. It was not the first time she thought that if she had been in his place she would have curled up into a ball and died. Chance reminded her when she mentioned that to him, that necessity bred innovation and she would have been fine. It was way too early to actually start cooking but she was trying to keep busy. Making coffee, she laughed at how addicted to the stuff she had become. Before meeting Chance, she had never even drank it. Now she had it with every meal. Little changes, little differences, she hoped she was making changes in Chance as well. Working in the kitchen she was singing again.

• •

When Chance woke he knew he had pushed himself too hard the previous day. His bruised ribs were sore again.

His hand felt ok which was good but breathing hurt. When he thought about it before he slept he realized he could have used a stone and his ballistic attack to kill the turkey. Too late now. He got up and heard Athena in the kitchen. He heard her singing that same song as yesterday and smiled. Walking to the bathroom he saw the fire had been lit in the small water heating stove already. Stripping off his clothes he let the semi-hot water sooth his bruised ribs. It felt good to just to stand there and wash away the problems. Chance had a nightmare again about the men in the field. He was coming to terms with it more each day but sometimes his conscious got the better of him. Today was not the time to think of that. Today was going to be a good day. His girlfriend, he could not believe he was able to call her that, was in the other room singing a beautiful song and it was Thanksgiving. He was thankful for the first time in his life. Chance was so wrapped up in his thoughts her did not hear Athena.

"Do you want anything for breakfast?"

"Athena," he jumped and covered himself. Looking at her face half-way into the room, his face turned bright red. "What are you doing?"

Laughing she said "Asking if you want food?" he could see the coy smile on her face.

"I am in the shower!" he stammered still feeling hot all over.

"I can see that," she replied playfully. "Now do you want breakfast or not?"

He could tell she was enjoying his discomfort. It reminded him of how she played with him the first day they met. "Yes I'll have some breakfast," he laughed. "Now get out and let me shower."

"Fine fine," she replied "But don't use up all the hot water, I still need one."

He could hear her giggling as she left the room. Shaking his head and smiling in spite of himself he finished his shower to save her some hot water. Of course she could always just use her energy to heat it. He came out for breakfast; her cooking was getting much better. She was still smirking and laughing under her breath.

"That was not as funny as you're making it out to be," Chance said.

"It was pretty funny," she replied. "Bedsides, you've had me stammering and caught off guard for three days. I owed you a good startle."

When they finished eating she announced she was going to get cleaned up and he could do the dishes. When he commented that she better lock the door she just stuck her tongue out and laughed as she went into the small bathroom, which didn't even have a lock. When he heard the water falling he was tempted to peak in on her to give her a start but remembered her comment about him keeping her off guard so he didn't. He heated the water in the sink happy that he was able to call upon energy easily again and quickly finished the dishes.

The rest of the day went pretty much how it started; Athena was playful and flirty all day. Chance was not about to let her win this game and he flirted back. Both of them made comments that made the other blush and laugh. He knew he was going to miss this free feeling they had when at the Argos so he was going to enjoy every second of it. They talked again about each other's lives, spending time by the fire and in the kitchen working on dinner. Athena talked about good times with her mom, and learning to harness fire from her dad. They seemed to be in constant contact most of the day. When at the fire they were holding hands or closer, touching arms or hips in the kitchen when making bread. Dinner was better than they expected although the turkey proved to be much trickier to cook then they realized.

While they did have a big pan, it didn't fit in the space that passed for an oven on the wood burning stove. Chance laughed as they cut the legs and wings off the bird to shoehorn it in. They cooked those separate in a pot stripping the meat off to make a turkey stew. Chance reflected that he ate a lot of stews. They toasted with a bottle of sparkling grape juice Athena's mother kept in the pantry and loved the day.

"You know," Chance said. "Since I have met you, I have had the best days of my life." He smiled at her feeling joy.

"They have been great for me too. Happy Thanksgiving Chance."

"Happy Thanksgiving."

"So, I was thinking about what we have been doing and what else we can do..." Athena said with a sly looking smile.

Chance looked at her with wide eyes. "Um, are you suggesting we take things further?"

"What do you think?" she smiled giving him an expectant look.

"Ah, well...I'm not sure..." he stammered his face going red.

"Well," she sighed, still with a demure look. "We are never going to get any better unless we practice."

"Well yeah, haven't we kind of been doing that?" he questioned feeling hot all over.

"I was talking about getting back to training. What were you thinking?" She held expression of mock outrage as long as she could before laughing, knowing full well what she was making him think.

"You are evil," Chance replied frustrated. "You made me think you meant something else and you know it!"

Still laughing she kissed him lightly. "I think that part of our relationship is just fine as it is for now."

"You're going to kill me, that's all there is too it," he exclaimed.

"Don't be mad," she was still laughing. "So what do you think? Will you be up to training next week?"

"As much as I want to, I don't know if my body will be ready." He sighed. "Let's see how I am feeling by Sunday."

"Sounds like a plan," she agreed. "Now let's go sit by the fire for a while and then get some rest."

Getting up and walking to the blanket he sat by the fire and motioned for her to come over. She went over and tucked under his arm leaning against him. He enjoyed his evening fires with Athena. Each day was a time of peace he never thought he would have.

• •

Athena woke in the late morning. It was almost noon. Chance must really be recovering because he needed so much sleep, he was still out. Unknown to the teens, Cassiel had been to check in on them before either of them woke.

Seeing that they were safe he reported back to Horatius. Athena decided she needed a walk to clear her head a bit. She had been very flirty yesterday. She knew she needed to scale that back a bit and keep herself in check. Chance was a young man and could only take so much teasing. She blamed her mother for this. She had always told her, "When it hits you, bam! Don't hold back."

"In our world we die young. Maybe I am not being too forward or too fast she thought as she walked. *As long as we keep from getting a little too carried away what's the harm in enjoying our time by the fire? Well other than driving Chance insane with desire. Yeah we should scale back a bit.*

Having made that decision and also looking forward to possibly more training next week she continued her walk. It was peaceful here; her mom had good taste. Athena could picture bringing her own kids here someday. A day many years in the future, but a day she could still see clearly. Unbidden the image of a grown Chance standing next to a little girl both in winter jackets came to her mind. It was with this image in her head, and smiling, when she was knocked out.

Captured

Inferno had waited what felt like an eternity for this raid. When the spy reported Chance and the fireball were held up in a cabin in the woods he could scarce believe it. Over the course of the next five days he planned their attack. Seven of them were spaced out evenly. He had taken one of Warden's guards, the one best at the teleport lock, to prevent escape using that method. He made sure the woman, whose name he did not get, knew to use the lock in a large sphere to prevent Chance from flying above and porting out as he did last time. Nothing was preventing Chances capture today.

They kept a safe distance using augmented vision to look at the cabin. His people had been watching for days. Chance was still weak. They just had to wait for the signal from Harbinger's spy. When she reported that Cassiel, a pathetic name to Inferno, had checked on the teens that morning he knew it was the day to strike. He was just about to give the signal when the girl walked outside.

He watched her take a deep breath and walk in the direction of one of his team, smiling and laughing to herself as she walked. Inferno signaled Dunstan mentally and told him to carefully move back. This would go easier than he expected. His orders were still clear, leave the girl alone. Originally he was going to break the door in and try to stun the teens before they knew what happened. With the fireball out of the picture it would be even easier to capture Chance.

"When the girl is far enough away," He thought to Dunstan, the strong earth user who was following her, *"knock her out."* After a couple minutes of silence he heard the telltale signs of a body hitting the ground.

"Done," Dunstan thought back.

"Good, get back in position,"

Inferno took a final look around the area and saw his men were all in place. He changed his plan and sent a fireball the size of a small fridge at the cabin. The impact was devastating, blowing the side of the small structure and the roof completely off. He could see a very startled half-dressed Chance stumbling out of a doorway in a room that was falling apart around him.

His men charged. The six of them kept an even distance and surrounded him. Inferno was surprised when fully half the logs from the cabin that were currently still on fire lifted into the air. Chance looked possessed. He could see the energy swirling around his body. Four of his men in Chance's line of sight had flaming logs sent at them. Two of his men's shields were shattered by the force of impact and killed instantly. Inferno watched as Dunstan blasted the log coming for him out of the sky with a huge stone that came from somewhere. The woman called Shard sent sparking pieces of what looked like diamond dust at the logs causing them to practically disintegrate. The team had been assigned to Inferno because they were supposed to be quick thinkers. From what he saw, at least two of them were morons. The cabin was falling apart and still burning. Chance was untouched by the flames. Inferno could see the boy's legs were not steady and he chose this moment to attack.

• •

Chance woke to the sound of an explosion. Years of instinct kicked in and he tried to port out immediately. Still in bed, his port failed but he was glad for that because he assumed Athena was in the cabin. He cursed himself for trying to port as the roof lifted away. Everything going on around him seemed to be in slow motion. He was up and out of bed before he realized it and out of the door to his room. The walls were collapsing around him, and there was fire and smoke everywhere. He called out for Athena in his mind and could not reach her. With the fire blazing and the front room completely gone he knew she must be dead. Something snapped inside. He looked out to the trees and spotted several people. He did not know how they found him.

His energy reached out and grabbed the wood all around him and he sent it like missiles at the enemies he could see. Tears streaked down his face thinking he caused Athena's death. He would kill every one of these people if it was the last thing he did. Two of the people he could see managed to escape his attack. Chance felt weak and unstable on his feet. Taking hold of the trees he grabbed the woman who was shooting ice shards at him. Before she could scream he had the trees rip her apart. He felt something hit him in the back in several places and turned to face this new enemy. A man stood on the small slope above shooting slivers of energy so compact they were like arrows. He blocked the rest by summoning the stove, combusting the material and then sending the liquid metal to cover the man head to toe. Turning back to find the man with the large rock Chance was smashed with a solid wave of concussion force. He knew it was the man from the field. "I'll kill you," he thought and lost consciousness.

• •

Inferno rushed to a position still in Chance's blind spot and was shocked when he saw Shard torn apart by a hemlock tree. *Merry Christmas* he thought twistedly as he continued his advance. Ivor managed to hurt Chance using his signature power. It looked like he was going for a kill; not capture after everything he had seen. Before Inferno could react to stop the man, Chance had turned him into a living screaming statue. He saw the teen turning to attack Dunstan who was disrupting the ground around him pulling rocks and boulders up for protection. *I have you,* Inferno said to himself and let loose a torrent of air determined to take him down. Chance never saw it coming, he was knocked to the ground already out before landing in a pile of ash.

Looking around the vicinity, Inferno could not immediately grasp that it was over. Two and a half years of chasing the brat and he had finally done it! He had won; the kid was his. The casualties were nothing to him. Although surprised by the brutality that Chance displayed he didn't really care. He had him! Dunstan walked down from his rocky perch and spit on the kid.

"Are we done here?" he asked Inferno.

"Yes, we are done," he replied.

"Good," Dunstan spat. "Then have that woman lift the lock and let's get the hell out of here." The woman in question was currently walking in the direction of the two men and the unconscious boy.

"The lock is lifted; I am going home." She looked at Inferno. "This is your mess; you clean it up." Before she could port away Inferno reached out and grabbed her hair pulling her towards him.

"You will leave when I say," he commanded. "We don't teleport home from here or have you forgotten their tracker?" Looking a little afraid she nodded in agreement. Inferno then picked up the boy and tossed him over his shoulder like a rug. Closing his eyes, they left the remains of the still smoking cabin and Athena knocked out somewhere in the hills.

• •

Walking into Harbinger's office Inferno dropped a heavily sedated Chance on his desk. "I told you I would catch him this time."

"Yes, and it only cost you four people to do it," Harbinger replied.

"You were the one who gave me that team!" Inferno shouted.

"And you in your infinite wisdom decided to start the capture by blowing up half the cabin," he replied icily.

"I thought it would harm him in the process making him unable to retaliate." Inferno insisted

"No, you thought you might accidentally kill him and have an excuse." Harbinger explained like he was talking to a child. "Only you were wrong. He was incensed more than likely thinking you had killed the girl and took out most of your team."

Looking at the boy lying on his desk, half-dressed and singed, he tried to fathom how he had done so much damage to the team that had captured Spark unscathed.

"Why is this kid so important anyway?" Inferno demanded.

"I really don't know," Harbinger admitted.

"Why he is important is none of your concern Inferno," Melaniya informed him as she walked into the room. "That knowledge is above your station.".

"Yes milady," he responded, thinking, *your husband doesn't know either.*

"So our little toy served her purpose after all," Melaniya smiled. "Maybe we will keep her after all."

"It's possible, my love," Harbinger agreed. "However, I grow weary of how clingy she has been of late. Maybe I will give her as a gift to someone loyal," he added.

"Why not the boy?" Melaniya asked. "He will need someone to properly educate him on his place in the world and she might fit that role."

"Excuse me," Inferno interrupted, annoyed that the two seemed to have forgotten he was in the room. "But the boy was in love with the little fireball we left behind. I doubt for a moment your used goods will appeal to him." He threw a look of contempt at a glaring Melaniya.

"For once you make a good point," Harbinger agreed. "Take Chance to the camp. Inform Warden that you will be stationed there as a guard as well. Penance for loosing most of your team." Furious at having been demoted after close to three years of work, Inferno picked up Chance and teleported out without proper dismissal.

"Do you think that was wise my love?" Melaniya asked.

"Everything is playing out as I thought it would. Soon we won't have to consider Inferno at all."

• •

Arriving at camp with Chance on his shoulder Inferno *reported* to Warden. "I was instructed by Lord Harbinger to bring you this boy and inform you that I am to report here as a guard.".

"Damn, what did you do? Sleep with his wife? Warden asked.

"I simply carried out my assignment as instructed," Inferno insisted.

"Spectra told me the story already," Warden explained. "I was just being nice. You screwed up catching the kid and it took you close to three years. Take him to the cells by the west side. There are dampening fields there. He may be surprised by the company he keeps when he wakes."

"Yes sir," Inferno spat. He was tired of the treatment. Something had to change his fortunes and soon. Spectra must be the bitch that controlled the teleport lock. She would get hers as well. No one made fun of Inferno for long and lived to tell the tale. Maybe he would challenge Warden for his position. It would be nice to torture Chance for the duration of his stay at camp. It turned out that there were two emaciated looking teens in this section of the camp. The guards were attentive as they knew any slip up on the dampening fields meant a prisoner had access to their energy and could be deadly.

"New prisoner for you lot," Inferno said as if he had any power in this place. "His name is Chance. Harbinger has wanted him back for years. Don't underestimate him." He dropped Chance on the ground in front of the guards and walked off, trying to imply authority. However, he did not notice the looks the other two prisoners gave the heavily sedated young man, or the looks of contempt by the guards.

Leaving Chance with prison guards, Inferno went to check on the rest of his new assignment. After all the time he spent trying to capture Chance and bring him here he was curious as to what kind of world he was leaving the kid in. The fact that this was now his world for the time being played on Inferno's mind. He walked the camp examining the children and teenagers who inhabited the place. He observed that the camp was and abandoned prison with barracks, a mess hall, a yard, and plenty of guards. Aside from the cell area that he associated with solitary confinement, there was an area for capital punishment. Inferno viewed the punishment location with some interest. At the current time there were a few young children, maybe eleven years of age cleaning the area. It was apparent they were mopping up blood from some sort of punishment. A bored looking guard was overseeing the process.

"Who's blood?" Inferno asked.

"Mouse, again." The guard stated. Inferno vaguely remembered hearing about the girl called Mouse. They say she is very strong.

"Are they always this rebellious?" Inferno questioned.

"The Crèche kids were usually obedient." The guard explained, "The captives always take some time to break."

"Interesting, this Mouse is a capture then?" he asked.

"Yeah, she was a special case. Our Leader took out an entire group to get her." The guard shrugged. "Not sure why, she doesn't seem to be all that special to me, just defiant."

"Since this is my new post, any other kids to watch for?" inquired Inferno.

"Yeah," the guard laughed. "Spark, but you know him. That kid's dangerous. He's also beat, but not broken."

"Thanks. You may want to know that Chance is back," Inferno said and walked away enjoying the stunned look on the guards face. Looking into the yard he tried to see if he could find Spark, by how the kids reacted to him. People were always attracted to power. He then made his way to the infirmary to see who this Mouse was.

• •

Chance woke in pain and in darkness. He reached out for energy and felt nothing. Not even the dulled sense he had after his battle with Caval. He felt empty and digging deeper did not help. The energy was just not there. He was about to call out for Athena when everything came crashing back. Tears ran down his face as he remembered the fight in the woods. Athena gone, dead, her bright light snuffed out because she was with him. A sob escaped his lips. He tried to sit and the injuries protested. The shoulder that he did not feel in the wreckage of the cabin flared up like a hot poker in his back. He cried out again this time in pain. His memory vividly replayed the fight; the man he killed with molten metal had hit him in the back with some kind of attack. Chance could move his arms but slowly. He hoped his eyes would adjust to the lack of light soon as he needed to see where he was. The pain of losing Athena hit him like a tidal wave and he was crushed under the weight. Again sobbing, falling out of bed onto the floor not caring. She was gone, and he was captured, his world was shattered.

Betrayal

When Cassiel left the Friday after Thanksgiving, he was in a great mood. Dinner had been beyond fun. The party at the Villa had been crazy and full of life. Cyrus had invited all the leaders from the Argos, the Seraphs, and the Forum plus their families. The insane man did not stop there. He invited most of the Protection Force and allowed his invited guests to invite anyone they wanted. All in all there must have been two hundred people at the Villa. Music played all night on a stage set up specifically for anyone to jump up and grab an instrument. The result was a crazy eclectic mix of people, some who had never met, playing any songs and music that they all happened to know. It was truly glorious.

Cassiel and Wisp went together; he had spent the last three days with her. Until this craziness he had only really known her as a member of the Pro-Force. He was pleasantly surprised to find out how much they had in common. After getting over her initial guilt over the teens, she asked Cassiel to dinner to thank him for taking her on the recon mission. She felt so much better knowing they were in a safe place. Said woman was currently asleep in his bed at home.

He left early allowing her to sleep so that he could verify the teens were alright before they woke up. All looked good. There was remains of a Thanksgiving dinner in the kitchen. Athena and Chance were asleep, looking peaceful and nothing seemed out of sorts. He did a quick sweep of the area and only saw the trails left by the two as they hunted. After informing Horatius, he returned home to grab a quick shower and maybe get some breakfast in bed for Wisp.

••

Wisp woke and stretched with a smile on her face. The party had been glorious and the after party even better. She looked around the room and frowned a little that she was alone. Pulling on a shirt over her small frame she heard the shower turn on. Cassiel must be back. She wondered where he went so early in the morning. As a member of the Pro-Force she was used to getting up early. It was part of her duties to always be prepared and one step ahead of her assignment. That's why it had stung so badly when she lost Chance and Athena. She had never failed in a mission before. At least she knew where they were now. Wisp still did not know all the details of why they left. She had been taking a short nap at the time. She had heard about the fight, but had not been given those details. She made a mental note to ask Cassiel about it later. Standing by her clothes which were currently on Cassiel's dresser, she heard the bathroom door open.

"Good morning," Cassiel smiled at her, wrapped in a towel.

"It is a good morning isn't it," she smiled back matching his grin. "I borrowed your shirt, hope you don't mind." Currently it was all she was wearing.

"No, not all," he laughed, "It looks better on you anyway."

"Where were you off too so early in the morning?" she asked, "I am usually the first one up."

"I didn't know you were such an early riser," he replied. "I was just checking on the kids. Wanted to get there before they woke so I would not risk being discovered,"

"I trust they were safe?" she asked, interest piqued.

"Perfectly, I already let Horatius know; he was expecting an early report." Cassiel supplied. "He told me to take some time off." He laughed and shook his head.

"That sounds nice," Wisp answered as Cassiel approached her.

"We could go to the Island for a short vacation maybe?" he asked her tentatively putting his hands on her waist. "Just a few days," he added quickly.

"That could be fun," she smiled giving him a quick kiss.

"Yeah? You would like to take a trip with me then?"

Laughing lightly, she told him, "Of course I would. Let your group know and we can leave today if you like. I don't have a current assignment so I'm free." She watched him close his eyes and knew he was talking to someone. She waited patiently, still smiling as her new lover informed the proper people he would be gone for a few days.

"Done," he said opening his eyes. "We just need to pack a few things and we can go. The house on the island has everything we need."

"Great," she whispered pulling him in for another kiss. Cassiel responded wrapping his arms around her. It was at that moment when she pushed the dagger that had been hidden in her pile of clothes between his ribs into his lung. Still holding him in the kiss as his breath exhaled into her mouth, Cassiel fell to the floor. She tried to remove the dagger as he fell but it was stuck in a rib. No matter there were hundreds that looked like that one. Looking down at the man she purred, "Thank you for the great night, and for the information. Harbinger will be thrilled to know he can finally capture Chance." She took off his shirt throwing it on the bed. Standing naked she gathered her clothes in her arms and teleported to her rendezvous point.

• •

In the early morning hours Cyrus was cleaning up the Villa. He had servants and staff to do this but he always liked to lend a hand. He only needed two hours of sleep a night so he liked to keep busy the rest of the time. Clotho was asleep having been a great hostess last night. Caval had attended the party with his teacher who managed to make it Sabastian usually did not attend parties. The night had been a training exercise for the boy because of that. Horatius had contacted him to let him know the two runaways were safe. The poor man had been on pins and needles all night knowing Cassiel was going to check on them the following day. A short time later the man himself contacted Cyrus knowing he would be up, to request a short vacation. Cyrus smiled, happy for his friend's budding romance. He had seen how Wisp and Cassiel danced close all night. He did frown for a second thinking of Uriel who was in love with Caz, but afraid to tell him. Wishing his friend well, he said he would inform the others and to have a good trip. Being primary leader had its advantages. He briefly wondered if Wisp could be used in a new position other than Pro-Force.

Looking around at the mess he laughed and realized it would take him all day to clean up. Maybe he would wake Caval and make him help. It would be good for the teen to learn to act like a leader. Leadership was in his future as far as anyone could tell. While thinking this Cyrus was surprised to see the teen walking towards him. It was still early and unlike Cyrus, Caval actually needed sleep.

"Hey dad, need some help?" he asked.

"Thanks," he nodded, "I could."

"Where do you want me to start?" he questioned looking around at the remains of the party.

Cyrus laughed, "Pretty much anywhere. Your mother is going to have a fit when she sees this place." He watched the teen started picking up dishes that were scattered on the tables. He pulled over a serving cart that had at one point in time held a massive cake and was stacking the dishes on it. Cyrus could not place the odd feeling he had until he realized Caval was picking dishes up by hand, not just using energy as he usually would. "Son?" Cyrus asked, "Why are you picking them up by hand?"

"My teacher," Caval supplied. "He says I need to find a balance. I use energy for *everything* because I can. He wants me to not rely on it for everything."

"Cyrus smiled at the young man. "Sabastian is a wise man. I saw you two talking last night." He continued to clean up while talking and noticed Caval was doing the same. "What did you two talk about? Or is it something I can't learn?" he ventured.

"No, nothing like that," Caval murmured. "Mostly he wanted me to watch people and their interactions."

"Oh, and what did you see?" Cyrus was curious.

"Well, he was really interested if I could read intentions of people, like who was trying to impress someone, things like that." Caval offered. "Like how Marshal only went up to play the violin to try and impress Kirin."

"You saw that too?" Cyrus stated with another round of laugher. They spent hours cleaning and spoke of other meetings of people, what their reactions meant and how he thought they would play out. Cyrus was impressed with how much Caval had picked up. At some point Cyrus noticed Clotho walk out and watch the two with a smile. The day was going by quickly as father and son enjoyed each other's company in this simple activity. Of course he always knew the boy had good instincts. It was the reason Cyrus had shown him the memory of Chance and Athena. Thinking of this he mentioned to Caval that the pair were safe having been checked on by Cassiel that morning.

"That's an interesting paring," Caval said suddenly.

"What do you mean?" Cyrus asked cautiously.

"Well, Uncle Caz is obviously getting really serious about the lady he was with last night." he responded.

"Yes, and...?" Cyrus prodded.

"Well she was noticeably feigning interest." Caval frowned.

"What do you mean by that?"

"She was slightly turning from him all night, her body language suggested she was both trying to seduce him and was not really all that into him at the same time." He supplied, "I felt bad for Uncle Caz but was told it was not my place to step in."

"Are you absolutely sure about this?" Cyrus demanded.

"Yeah dad. I had my teacher confirm everything I was seeing." He stammered. "It was all part of my training last night." Cyrus, feeling scared all of a sudden, tried to contact Cassiel and could not.

"Oh Gods," he said and teleported. When he appeared in Cassiel's room he found his friend on the floor in a pool of his own blood. Quickly he reached out with his energy and took a pulse. The man was at death's door. Placing a hand on him he teleported the two of them to the healers while his mind screamed for Perion or Hippocrates.

"What the hell?" Peroin yelled as she took in the sight before her.

"He is barely holding on!" Cyrus shouted, "Get everyone! We cannot lose him."

The next moments were a flurry of motion. Cassiel's body was levitated gently into the air. Several healers teleported into to the room in various stages of dress as some had obviously been sleeping. Perion had her hand on the dagger in Cassiel's back but was afraid to pull it out until he was more stable. Hippocrates was in another room setting up a Tank. The healers poured energy into the almost lifeless body of Cassiel. Cyrus just fell to the floor with his back against the wall, his friend's blood on his hands.

• •

Horatius was informed that Cassiel was in critical condition in the infirmary. Cyrus related Caval's thoughts and what he found in Cassiel's room which of course was nothing but blood. He put two and two together fairly quickly and teleported to the cabin. He was so shocked by what he found that for a moment he lost the power of speech. He reached out for his daughter's mind. Even if she couldn't talk to him, he should be able to feel her if they were in close proximity. Nothing, he felt nothing. He reached out with energy looking for a sign of a teleport by her. He was not as good as Cassiel; he could not track but he could still see the marker. There was none. Her energy was all over the place, but no teleport.

Concentrating hard he was shocked by the amount of energy that must have been Chance's. He saw a couple bodies and blood splatter in the woods. Turning slowly in circles he was almost sick when he realized the iron stature that looked vaguely like a man was in fact a man! *My gods what went on here?* he thought as he continued to scan. Pushing his energy up to overcome the energy in the area he searched again. When he expanded the circle around him for a good half mile, the felt it, Athena's soul. A father would never miss the soul of his child.

Running in the direction of what he felt, he ran past the body that was torn to pieces and over a large outcropping of rocks that did not look natural. Horatius picked up a trail of footprints after the rocks in the same direction as Athena's soul. He charged himself for combat just in case. When he saw her his heart almost stopped. She was lying face down with a layer of fresh snow on her body. He could see her breath condensing in the cold air and knew she would be ok. Picking her up gently and warming the air around them, the snow began melting off her body. She had a knot on her head that he could feel and he realized she had been knocked out. *They wanted her out of the way,* he thought. He was holding her close thankful that she was alive and safe when she spoke.

"Dad?"

"Yes baby, I'm here."

Athena's eyes open wide, "Chance!" she screamed.

"He's gone, sweetheart," Horatius explained, "but I swear to you baby we will get him back!"

Athena hugged her father and cried. He held her close and took her to the healing ward. She was so caught up in her grief she did not notice the teleport did not hurt.

• •

When the news reached Clotho about Wisp's betrayal she left for the healing ward immediately. Caval had been telling her about his conversation with his father when she was contacted. She had a moment to realize that twice today they had left their son wondering why his parent teleported out. Cassiel was in bad shape she was told. They had found a blood donor for a transfusion and were preparing to place him in a Tank. Perion informed her that if the dagger had been pulled out instead of left in him he would have died hours ago.

"Wait, you mean to tell me you have the weapon that the murderous bitch used on him?" Clotho asked in a voice that demanded answers.

"Yes," a stunned Perion reported. "I have it in the other room. We only took it out a couple minutes ago."

"I need to see it," Clotho insisted.

Perion led her to the adjoining room. Cassiel was floating in a tank surrounded by healers feeding energy into him closing the wounds and repairing internal damage. It would take hours if not days. The Tank was constantly filtering out blood seeping into the oxygenated liquid and replenishing what was drained out. Knowing how expensive the Tanks special liquid was the cost of this operation was staggering. There was an operating table in the room as well and Clotho knew this was where Perion had extracted the dagger.

Pointing to a dagger in a bowel of cleaning fluids Perion stated, "This is it, it was stuck in a rib. I am afraid we did some more damage as we pulled it out."

"It's not your fault Perion," Clotho answered kindly "I am sorry if I snapped at you. This whole situation is just unbelievable." Cyrus entered the room and looked at his wife.

"Love, you don't need to do this," he said knowing what she was thinking. "We can find her another way."

"We don't have time," she sighed. "We both know it. That dagger is the quickest way for us to see where she is hiding."

"Remember what happened last time?" Cyrus warned.

"I remember." She smiled lovingly stroking his cheek. "I became Clotho." With those words she picked up the dagger. Her energy flowed through her and she used psychometry on the weapon. Her natural affinity to all things soul related made her an expert at the ability that slipped the grasp of most energy users. Clotho knew she had to be careful when she used the energy because unlike Uriel who could purge a memory extraction she could not.

Psychometry was dangerous. Unlike books or movies that played it off as a simple object read, the true power made the memories permanent. Because of this side effect it was hard to differentiate absorbed memories from real ones. This had caused her personality to shift in the past depending on the strength of the object. Clotho became Clotho when she read a necklace belonging to Cyrus' late wife. The necklace had been a present for their first anniversary and the woman called Cassandra had worn it until the day she died.

Clotho knew the danger as the memories flooded into her but they had to capture Wisp. She could feel Cyrus holding her empty hand. As Perion had been the last to touch the dagger, Clotho got a few snippets of memories from her. *Interesting. I understand the basics of being a surgeon.*

Wisp's memories were shocking, Clotho tried to compartmentalize as they assaulted her mind. Even after all the years of learning to cope with psychometry she still feared the changes that could come with it. When she reached the end and started seeing the man's memories that placed the dagger in the armory she cut off the power she didn't always know how to do that but Sabastian had helped her learn. She was sweating and breathing hard. Clotho could feel the teleport lock power that had been enacted while she was reading the dagger and knew it was coming from her husband. When she opened her eyes he was looking at her with love and concern in his dark eyes.

"Clotho?" he asked gently.

"It's still me my love," she responded. "I didn't own the dagger that long..." She shook her head. "I mean she did not own it that long. Get Uriel to confirm it. I won't block her probe." She smiled at Cyrus, although she felt a little ugly inside.

Twenty minutes later, Uriel, who had been keeping vigil by Cassiel's tank, announced that Clotho was in fact still Clotho, but she had some "rather unpleasant memories" and went home. No one missed the fact that she did not go back to Cassiel's side. Everyone felt a little guilty about that as well.

"What did she see?" Cyrus asked his wife, knowing she had knowledge Uriel did not want.

"Probably the start of last night's festivities for Wisp and Cassiel," Clotho said a little colder than normal. "She needs to purge out the kisses, gropes and, well, other memories of Wisp and Caz. I don't like having that kind of intimate knowledge of my friend either, but Wisp was wearing the dagger at last night's party."

"Focus love," Cyrus interrupted. "Can you tell us where Wisp might be hiding?"

"Of course my love, I can take us there." She half cried. "After all, I feel like I have been there before."

Taking his wife's hand he updated her on the situation. "Athena is back. She is in a tank being worked on for possible frost bite." Clotho looked shocked. "She is safe, her father is with her, but we need to catch Wisp. It may be our only way of saving Chance, and avenging Cassiel."

"You're right. Get a small team ready, I'll open a gate." Clotho vowed. Gates are portals to places like small wormholes that can be opened. Similar to teleporting but allowing multiple people to pass through, Clotho had studied long enough that she knew how to open one easily.

"I prepared a team when Uriel was examining your memories." Cyrus smiled. "I knew you would be ok by the look in your eyes." The team in question, which included Nexus, filed into the room.

"Well then, let's go get the bitch," Clotho stated.

"That's my girl," Cyrus grinned as the gate opened.

"She should be alone. Harbinger only meets her at midnight." Clotho declared.

• •

Two hours to go, then all this would be over and she would be in a position of power. Consort to the great Harbinger. He loved her more than his wife, he had admitted on several occasions. They included her in their affairs sometimes to placate the woman until she was allowed to challenge her. Just two more hours and Harbinger would come collect her. Part of Wisp felt guilty for what she had done to Cassiel. Really she didn't need to kill him. There was always the 'thanks for a great night' speech and then she could just leave him. However, once she learned that only she and he knew of the cabin's location his death was essential. She gave the location to that manservant Inferno and eliminated the only other tie to the cabin. If the plan was followed correctly Athena would be half frozen when she woke and no rescue operation could be launched until she found her way home which could take days. Cassiel was supposed to be on vacation, so no one would find him in his room until he didn't report for duty in three days. Wisp smiled thinking of the rewards awaiting her.

She was daydreaming of these things when people stormed into the room. Her confusion was quickly dispelled when she saw her old partner Nexus. Wisp did not understand how, but she had been caught. She was just about to attack when bands of energy picked her up and pinned her to the wall. There were bands around her wrists, ankles, waist and neck. Wisp could not move, still she fired off a blast of energy from her outstretched hand only to have it caught and looked at by the man in front of her. Guards lined the room and Clotho walked in behind Cyrus who currently held her energy blast in his hand like an apple. He was looking at her as the band around her neck tightened. Cyrus crushed her ball of energy like a grape, then Clotho spoke.

"Hello Wisp," she said with a deathly quiet voice. "I think we have things to discuss, but first," Clotho charged her fist with energy and punched her in the stomach, causing Wisp to retch and cough.

She thought she may have broken a rib but collected herself and laughed. "How is dear Cassiel?"

Clotho drew a fist back to hit her again but Cyrus touched it lightly, and that was enough to stop her.

"Don't give this evil thing the satisfaction my love. She wants you to kill her rather than capture her." Clotho was frowning.

"Secure the room," Cyrus barked to the men he brought with him. "She was waiting for this Harbinger; let's prepare a surprise for him tonight." He smiled darkly.

"You will never catch him," Wisp laughed. "He is far stronger than any of you!"

Clotho looked at the woman whose life she now had a small part of, with contempt. "If I were you Wisp, or Whisper as he calls you, I would be more worried about Uriel." She turned away from the younger woman and vanished through the gate.

Wisp began building walls around her memories. She did not know how Clotho knew her lover's pet name for her but she would not let Uriel in. She had to defend her mind! The bands around her pulled her forward as Cyrus walked through the gate. She vowed to herself she would resist. She would not betray Harbinger! His Whisper would be too strong to break and he would save her soon.

Consequences

The guards pulled Chance to his feet and threw him on his cot. The man who walked in the cell exuded authority without even trying. He was much more intimidating then the man who called himself Warden. Chance was not going to give this man anymore satisfaction then he gave the last though. He still refused to eat or drink, it had been three days. His lips were parched and his throat dry but he didn't care. Death would take him soon enough and there was nothing they could do about it unless they sedated him and give him fluids intravenously. The man looked at his meal and water, again untouched, and frowned.

"This will simply not do Chance," he said in a reasonable voice. "I can't have our star pupil starving himself to death after all the time we spent trying to bring you home."

"Not my home," Chance barely whispered. His throat was so dry he found it hard to speak. "I don't care."

"Well I have a couple people who might care," the man stated. The guards pulled in two teens that Chance immediately recognized. Jim and Eliza looked beat up and thin. But were gagged and stared at him. "If you let yourself die, I will kill these two as punishment."

He pulled out a long knife, grabbed Eliza by the hair and pulled her head back. Lowering the knife to her throat he said, "Drink the water, only a sip at a time. I will wait until you have consumed the entire glass."

Frozen in shock, Chance did not know what to do. He thought that Jim and Eliza were dead or moved on to whatever came next. Eliza's light brown eyes were pleading with him.

"You have ten seconds to pick up that glass," the man stated in that same calm voice. "Ten...Nine...Eight."

Chance picked up the glass and took a sip. His body reacted to the water in ways he did not even have words for. Still looking at the man who had the knife to Eliza's neck he took another sip. The process took longer than Chance could believe. An hour? Maybe two? When the glass was empty the man with the dark eyes took the knife from Eliza's throat.

"Don't kill them," Chance pleaded.

"That is entirely up to you Chance," the man promised. "We've already treated your back, hand and ribs with our healers. Eat, drink, get well. Then maybe they will live. Defy me, and they will most assuredly die." He motioned for the guards with his head. Jim and Eliza were taken away. "I am Harbinger, Chance. The lives of people around you depend on the choices you make. Remember that." And the man left.

Chance looked at the meal in front of him. His body was rebelling against his decision to starve to death. He looked at the guard standing outside his door. "Can I get some more water," he requested and took a bite of his meal.

When the water arrived, the guard set it down on the ground between the bars and backed away. *He's afraid of me,* Chance thought. *Interesting.* Harbinger was not afraid of him, that was obvious. He did not remember him from the Crèche. *Jim and Eliza are still alive -- barely.*

He chastised himself for his decision to starve to death, although it was the lack of water that had been killing him. How could he avenge Athena if he died? She would have been so angry at him for being weak. What was it she said? If she had his life she would have curled into a ball and died. He told her that would not happen and yet he just tried to do that same thing. Stupid, he had to be better, get stronger, find a way to make these people pay. He was weak again but this time it was lack of fluids which was his own fault. At least they had healed his injuries. He should recover quickly if he rehydrated. The question was what they wanted from him. He had always wondered that when he was on the run. Maybe Harbinger would give him some answers but he doubted it. For now, he would bide his time, use the observation skills he picked up on the run.

Star pupil? Well your star pupil will be gone at the first opportunity. This time I'll take Jim and Eliza with me. I can teleport back to the Manor and ask for Clotho. She would keep them safe, he thought, already planning a way to leave this place. *As for me,* he vowed, *I'll kill them all, starting with the bastard that killed Athena and captured me.*

• •

"You're kidding me, right?" Inferno demanded.

"No, no joke. Chance has never had a debut fight," Warden replied.

"So what are you suggesting?"

"We need to find him one of course," he stated as if it were obvious. "However, he's already slaughtered your men. He is too proficient to fight any of the other teens here, with the exception of maybe Spark or Mouse."

"So use Mouse. She seems like trouble anyway," Inferno suggested.

"She is too important to Harbinger, something about the next generation," Warden grumbled. "And Spark, well he is not ready."

"Let me fight him!" Inferno countered with a sick smile.

"You? Do you really want to kill him that badly?"

"I spent two and a half years chasing the brat around the globe, and my reward was to be stuck here as a babysitter." He spat. "I could have killed him several times but I was ordered to 'bring him in alive.' In a sanctioned fight I can finish him and not get in trouble."

"I'll run it past Harbinger," Warden said. "He wants the kid to have a hard first fight, maybe you would be it."

"Push it hard," Inferno growled. "This kid is mine, and we both want to be rid of him after how he treated you on your first meeting." Turning and leaving the office Inferno knew his challenge would be accepted. Harbinger wanted him out of the way he knew that. However, Harbinger did not know that Inferno had a plan to counter Chance's control of kinetic energy. Walking to the edge of the teleport lock he went to see an old friend.

• •

"Inferno?" a woman asked. "Is that you?"

"Hello Joule. It's been a while. How are you?" he responded with a smile.

She looked at him sternly. "What do you need Inferno? You never just pay a social visit," she claimed.

"Sharp as ever. Yes, I need to call in that favor." His eyes were deadly serious as he spoke.

"I was beginning to think you liked me," she mocked. "What do you need?"

"I need to know how to counter your powers completely, and in return I swear I will never challenge you in the future." He asserted, "More than fair for the favor you actually owe me."

"I'd ask you why, but I'm afraid I would rather not know." Joule, the foremost expert in kinetic energy, picked up a small dagger off the table and sliced open her hand. Holding the dagger out to Inferno, she replied. "You have a deal."

"I knew you would agree, and you're right, you don't want to know." Inferno smirked and sliced open his own hand, and then clasped it with hers. The deal was made, sealed in a blood handshake. Joule would teach him to counter everything Chance could possibly do. Inferno smiled knowing victory in the upcoming challenge would be his.

• •

"Well sir you were right, Inferno jumped at the opportunity to fight Chance." Warden thought to Harbinger.

Laughing while his wife looked at him with a raised eyebrow he answered, *"I knew he could not resist the opportunity."*

"Do you think Chance can win against Inferno?"

"If the boy can't win then we don't need him. Set the fight for Christmas eve." Harbinger ordered, and cut off communication.

"What was that about?" his wife asked, knowing he was taking mentally.

"Just setting up Chance's fight against Inferno," he smiled.

"Do we have authorization to put Chance in harm's way for his premier fight?" Melaniya questioned.

"I am tired of listening to directives I don't understand or have a say in." Harbinger snarled. "If Chance dies, then he is not worth all the effort to catch him, is he?"

"We have already lost our spy..." she cautioned.

"I was never going to meet her anyway. The guards they left at the rendezvous point were for nothing." He scoffed. "We had everything we needed at that point. She was a fun toy but there are always others."

"Yes my love," she soothed, "but the loss of our spy was considered a failure. I don't want to add another one by losing Chance. We need a backup plan, or at least an escape route."

"It is all planed out heart of my heart," he promised. "Cyrus has seen to that even though he does not know it." Harbinger laughed and smiled at his plans. If the boy died he didn't care, there were always other children. As far as Whisper went, she could not tell them anything useful. Her few rendezvous spots were double blinds and she did not know the existence of the camp. "We are quite well my dear, quite well."

Melaniya looked at her husband, not as certain as he was. For their safety, Chance had to win against a man who had fought in the arena forty-three times.

· ·

The next time Chance spoke to Harbinger things did not go as he had planned. Two days had passed; he was feeling better. Rehydrated and fairly well fed he was more bored than anything. He took to doing some exercises in the cell when the man arrived with Warden. Chance looked up but continued to do pushups. He did not acknowledge either man until he saw guards bringing Jim and Eliza with them. He understood that this was a planned meeting and decided to play along. "How can I help you gentlemen? As you can see I am eating, drinking and staying in shape." He stated.

"Excellent," Harbinger responded. "I see you have taken our little talk to heart."

"I understand that I am captive and that I must do as you say," He responded automatically. Mentally he added, *also that I will kill you the first chance I get.*

"There is still the matter of your punishment for leaving us without permission." Harbinger frowned. "You see, when that happened we had to make some changes. I will let Warden tell you about those later."

"My punishment?" Chance asked fearing for what came next.

"Yes, your punishment," Warden said smiling. He brought Jim and Eliza forward. Their bonds were cut.

"If I need to be punished, then do it to me and leave them out of it!" Chance fumed.

"You don't understand," Harbinger spoke. "We realize your life and well-being mean nothing to you. However, the lives of others, that's another story."

"Don't hurt them. I agreed to live. What else do you want?" Chance yelled.

Warden stepped forward and threw a long thin knife known as a misericord at Chances feet. "Choose," he stated.

"What?" Chance asked startled looking at the weapon.

"Your punishment for leaving us is to choose which one dies." Warden declared.

"I can't...they are both innocent," Chance stammered.

"Let me clarify," Harbinger spoke. "You choose one, or both die"

Chance stared at the two teens who were his friends when he was in the Crèche. Athena had mentioned how he had chosen to abandon people, leave them behind. Harbinger told him his choices would decide people's fate. Chance realized in that moment how much his actions and decisions had weighed on other people's lives.

"I can't..." he sobbed, "I can't choose."

"Either you pick one now, or they both die now," Warden told him.

Harbinger nodded in consent letting Chance know this was his only choice. He looked at his two friends; the two who had grown up with him. Chance had tried not to think of them while he was on the run, but they were his only real friends before Athena. Suddenly Jim dived forward taking the misericord and drove it into his own heart. Chance lunged forward trying to stop him but it was too late. His hands were over his friends, blood pouring over them. Eliza screamed and they dragged her out of the cell screaming Jim's name. Jim locked eyes with Chance and mouthed the words "Protect her" before his head fell forward on Chance's shoulder.

"I will find a way to kill you both," Chance declared looking at the two men tears drying on his cheeks. Warden pulled Jim off Chance and extracted the misericord.

"Perhaps someday you will get that opportunity," Harbinger mused. "However, understand this Chance, if you escape, she will die and so will three random kids. All of them under eleven years old, all of them on your hands." Harbinger smiled at Chance locking eyes with the boy who wanted nothing more than his death. "Warden, give our star pupil the rest of the good news. I have business elsewhere."

"Well Chance," Warden began, "do you understand your station?"

"Yes sir," he replied viscously. A guard brought in a pan of warm water and a couple towels. Chance started to wash the blood off his hands but he felt them forever stained.

"Good, then you need to know a few things before I let you into the compound." Warden informed him. "First off, we are willing to kill Eliza and three others just like this sack of meat on the floor." He kicked Jim's lifeless body for effect; Chance flinched.

"I understand," Chance intoned.

"Second, we have learned to teleport lock; however, I don't think we need to worry about that anymore. Do we?"

"No sir," Chance affirmed gritting his teeth and standing up.

"Lastly, we have set your debut battle in the arena for Christmas Eve. Today is December the second. You have twenty-two days to prepare for the fight." Warden smiled. Chance shook his head, not at all surprised; he knew they would pull this on him. All of this was calculated to break his spirit. He would have to play along for now but they would not control him.

"Who is my opponent and what are the terms?" Chance requested trying to keep his head.

"Inferno, the man who brought you to us, unlimited combat, no real bonus for you other than you get to live," Warden remarked. "If you will follow me, I will show you to your new barracks." Chance fell into step behind Warden actually smiling at the opportunity to pay the man Inferno back. He unwillingly left the corpse of his friend behind. Walking with Warden he felt his energy return once they crossed the cellblock threshold. He did not try to attack. What was the point? Eliza was being held in another cell and other innocent people would die if he tried. "You might be interested to know that the Crèche concept has been abandoned since your escape," Warden told him suddenly.

"What do you mean?" Chance replied.

"When you escaped, the leaders decided that the Crèche environment was too soft," Warden explained. "All children regardless of age are here now. No more coddling them till they reach twelve." The man had a sinister smile on his face. "Also all but two of the teachers and care givers were executed for allowing you to learn teleportation. So many changes based on your decision to leave us."

"So many people...the kids...you mean they are all raised without any concept of caring?" Chance stammered. Walking through the camp and seeing children and teens, it was all falling into place for him.

"One little choice," Warden chided.

Chance was stunned into silence. Warden showed him around the rest of the camp, mess hall, training area, yard, infirmary, punishment section, practice battle area and finally the barracks. There were kids of all ages here. Some teachers were instructing 'students.' Chance knew the horror of this place was somehow made worse because he had left almost three years ago. Athena was right; he didn't realize what he did when he left or the consequences it would have for other people.

Decisions

Caval was currently sleeping in a cot next to Athena's Tank. He wanted to be there when she woke up. She was close to frostbitten when Horatius found her and had suffered damage to her hands and feet. Perion assured him that she would be ok; she just needed a day of recovery. Horatius had her sedated as soon as they arrived because she had been hysterical with grief over Chance.

Athena was hurt, Uncle Cassiel was in a coma, Chance was captured and Caval felt it was his fault. They had been safe; they had four guards although one of those guards did turn out to be a spy. Things would have been so different if he had just left her alone. Maybe the Hunters would have come; maybe Wisp would have tried to help them. Certainly Cassiel would not be close to death. Maybe they would have saved Chance. As it stood, Nexus refused to talk to Caval. The spy had been his partner and he felt guilty. Had the attack happened in Florida, Nexus felt he might have been able to stop her before anyone was seriously hurt. Speaking of the spy, she was captured and would soon face the wrath of Uriel. Caval did not envy her. Uriel would not be kind ripping the information they needed out of her head. For now, the teen sleeping by the Tank was worried about his best friend as consequences for his choice clouded his dreams.

Caval woke up startled. He looked at the Tank and his best friend was still floating in it. He thought about what is must have been like for her while she was on the run with Chance. He was both glad and sad that the two had become so close. Glad for his friend who was always so standoffish to boys in general and sad because of how much it was hurting her now. He had no romantic feelings for her; even now looking at her nude form in the tank seemed like a natural thing for him.

Caval briefly wondered if Athena had explained Tanks to Chance. His teacher told him that he did not know how lucky he was to have a Tank. When he was a young fighter it was just healers. You were left with more scars and sometimes they did not have time to heal you back to one hundred percent before you were fighting again. They were lucky. Almost two days, it seemed that people he loved were always recovering but that was just a part of his world.

He knew that when she woke she would be full of fire, ready for action. The sedation and healing was a good thing for her. Athena was strong. He promised himself to fill her in on everything that had transpired while she was out. She was not sedated anymore and could wake up at any time.

Caval had not been to the battle site yet. Horatius had told him about it but he already knew what we would find. Chance was devastating in his energy level. It was uncanny how quickly he could react and fight back. Caval had described his battle to his teacher (once he was forgiven) and offered to show the memory.

"Why was Chance better than me?" he had questioned.

"Chance was probably not even aware of half the things he was doing," he had said.

"What do you mean?" Caval questioned.

"In a true fight you would more than likely do the same thing. You sort of transcend yourself and allow who you were always meant to be to take over. In the case of someone like Chance and yourself, that is an energy warrior of the highest caliber"

"Why did I not do the same thing during this fight then?" he wondered

"Because you saw Chance and went back to your head instead of instinct," Sabastian replied. "You didn't want to kill him so your instinct didn't guide you to do whatever it took to win."

Caval had thought about that for days and realized his teacher was only giving him a half truth. All that did not matter right now though. What did matter was the current situation. How would they find Chance? He owed it to the young man to try to find him at all costs. How would they deal with Wisp?

The leaders refused to call her Whisper; they did not want to give her the satisfaction. She was with Uriel at the moment. They had her under a teleport lock but did not bind her energy. So far, she just sat in her cell smiling. Caval thought that some of the leaders were hoping she would try to escape to give them a reason to act. When the time came she would be tried and found guilty, and then imprisoned or executed. In a world where combat to the death was commonplace and assassination attempts were rampant, betrayal of friends was a terrible transgression and considered the worst crime someone could commit.

Caval looked at the Tank again. Horatius had been down to check on his daughter three times for a status report. Caval thought the leaders must be so used to this that it did not affect them as much. He wondered if one day he would be the same. He needed more information but would not leave the room. Perion was kind enough to have food sent to him. Even restroom breaks were as quick as possible, *"Wake up Athena,"* he thought at her hoping she could hear him.

• •

The day after Chance's capture Illyria and Joule were having tea discussing current events. Joule had been a leader of the Forum but had stepped down a decade ago. The women met several years later when Illyria was looking for advice on a matter of court. Once a week, one of the leaders or their alternate in this case would hold a public open forum court to go over grievances in their groups. Anything could be brought to court from stolen goods to teenage vandalism. The presiding leader would make the decision and that was final, no appeals. Illyria hated court; she could not stand passing judgments on people's lives. There were times when very serious grievances were brought forth. Joule had loved court when she was a leader, so much that she did a week of duty for other leaders occasionally. No one ever questioned Joule's judgments. So Illyria had sought her out and asked her advice on holding court. The two women had been good friends ever since.

"I don't think Nexus should be ashamed of himself," Joule told her friend. "We all get fooled by people."

"I know that, but he doesn't seem to be able to get past it," she sighed.

"It's still too new. He will be fine in a few weeks."

"We have a leaders' meeting to discuss options tomorrow," Illyria explained.

"I am so glad that I am not involved that any more. I like just teaching." Joule smiled.

"You know you miss it," Illyria laughed.

There was a knock on the door; Joule went to answer it. Standing outside was a warrior Illyria recognized from the arena. *What is Inferno doing here?* she thought. The man left after a brief exchange.

Joule came back with an apology on her face. "I'm sorry to cut this short, but I have a training session."

"You do know who that is, don't you?".

"Yes, unfortunately I do," she responded. "I owe him."

"How on earth do you owe someone like that? He's as evil as they come!" Illyria scolded.

"Do you remember Alexander?" Joule posed.

"Yes, the young man who was more talk than ability."

"Well, several years ago after I left leadership Alex and I were in a relationship. Inferno challenged him after an insult." She shook her head. "I met with Inferno in secret and he agreed to spare Alex in the fight in return for a favor later. This is it."

"Joule, you know he can use this against one of us someday," she admonished.

"I know, but you know I can't refuse. Besides, he only wants to know how to counter kinetic energy and swore to never challenge me," Joule explained. "Any other type of energy like what you use for instance would still be able to beat him easy."

"I see," she conceded. "What ever happened to Alexander anyway?"

"Well, he died, two years later." She sighed, "He just kept pissing off the wrong people."

"Ah Joule, one day you will pick a man who is worthy of you," Illyria laughed. "Go train the evil man. We all have favors owed to someone."

• •

Uriel did not know if she was ready to see everything inside of Wisp's head. The information she received when scanning Clotho was already more than she wanted. She knew she had to get everything though; the boy's life was at stake. Looking at the woman in front of her who was smirking, she began her assault. Wisp was well trained in mental defense. As a member of the Protection Force it was mandatory. However, no one so far had been able to withstand Uriel's attacks.

Uriel always found mental defenses like a wall holding back a damn. She could probe around and, without fail, find that one small crack. Once that was complete she would open the crack and out would pour the memories. Nothing was safe. she could see all the way back to childhood memoires. Had she been an expert at torture she could then cause illusions around you to paralyze you with fear and dread. Uriel chose to not go that route; she used her abilities for extraction only. It was true she had the strength to assault a mind so powerfully, it could leave the recipient a vegetable when she was done. Uriel had never done that, but this time she seriously considered it.

The memories she got of how Wisp seduced and hurt Cassiel were almost too much. It was the second time she saw some of them, the first being glimpses in Clotho's head. That was probably the reason she was strong enough to resist the urge to lobotomize Wisp as she read her memories. The energy pattern was simple enough. Brainwaves have a pattern, visible on an EEG. E-worlders and even Non's were able to use the technology to control cars and other electric things, even toy stores carried 'control this with your mind' items. Uriel understood how these patterns worked and used energy to exploit it. It was simple, except for the emotional pain of seeing Cassiel get stabbed again. She continued her mental assault for the better part of two hours. Wisp had long since stopped screaming and trying to fight back. It was always easier when they realized there was nothing they can do.

Michael, the main leader of the Seraphs, walked into the room. He had been briefed on the situation and come to check on his friend. "Uri, how are you?"

"I'm fine Michael, just dealing with all this," she said pointing at Wisp. "I really don't like this woman."

"Uri, you know we all understand how hard this is, but you need to let us know what you found out. Skip the parts about Cass, we know what happened there."

"When is the meeting? I only want to discuss this once."

"Nexus is set to guard her when you are ready," he soothed.

"Well then call him. The sooner I get this witch out of my sight and head the better." Uriel swore.

• •

Athena woke with a bang. The Tank exploded from the force she projected. She stood in the middle of the room with healing fluid dripping off her. Caval who had shielded himself from the blast ran over and covered her in a robe.

"Athena! Are you ok?"

She looked at him with semi glowing eyes. "We need to get Chance," she stated.

"About that, you need to know a few things first." Caval interjected.

She looked around and then at herself and realized she was only wearing the robe Caval had hastily thrown around her shoulders. She thought about how embarrassed Chance would be in this situation. He didn't understand that nudity was not a big deal when you were healed while naked, or in a Tank for an extended period of time naked. She did not think of it the same way he did. That was one of the reasons when she teased him in the shower it was no big deal to her. Athena had meant to explain all of this to him in the two weeks they were supposed to have together before coming home. Now she was home, and healed, alone and furious.

"What am I missing?" She reached out with her mind and saw Caval was shocked she was able to do so, she had forgotten that this was a skill she could not do before training with Chance. He connected to her and shared his memories of events that occurred while she was out. Perion and several healers entered the room but stayed back when Caval put out a hand.

After getting all the recent information from her best friend she took his arm and teleported to her room leaving behind shocked healers. She dropped the robe and went into the shower to wash off the healing fluid, think about what she had learned and process it all. After the shower she gathered clothes from the closet and undergarments from the dresser. Caval waited patiently, undisturbed by her nudity.

"So Wisp betrayed us and that is how they found the cabin?" she asked.

"Pretty much. Right now the leaders are meeting to decide when we can try to get Chance back." Caval replied.

"Simple. We just get him back," she said.

"Well there is a little more too it then that, but I am with you whatever you decide," Caval avowed.

• •

The leader's meeting took place in the Forum's meeting hall. The room had a large oval table with a stone top. Each chair was carved to reflect the house or the name of the leader that sat in it. The Forum was the oldest and most influential energy group in the world. Each of its five leaders could command anyone from the subsidiary groups who were connected to it. Cyrus, Gerrod, Meteo, Typhoonus and Marsal were the current leaders. Illyria is an oddity in the chain of command as she was considered an alternate Leader if any of the five Forum leaders were incapacitated. The second-tier groups were the Seraph's and the Argonauts they also had command of any newer groups that were forming alliances. The Dual Hearts, Wave Runners and few others were in this category. Although each group ran itself, once allied all followed the Forum's rules and precepts. The Forum, Seraphs and Argonauts formed the central core of what was called The Kinship. This alliance considered each other more family than members. Each of the Seraph leader's chairs depicted angels in flight and something akin to their given name. Gabriel's chair for example had the horn of God depicted on it as he was the messenger of God. Similarly, Michaels had the flaming sword, Raphael's a staff, Uriel's a book and Amitiel an angel with broken wings signifying the fall. Some found it interesting that the Seraphs could have any angel name not just the names of Seraphim. There were angel names from all religions in their group. That being said, the current leader's names were what people considered archangels and one fallen angel. The Argonauts tended to keep to Greek and Roman names. Originally the group had been founded using only names on the Argos. As the years passed by however it was changed a bit and any hero or god from mythology would do. The current Leaders were Ares, Horatius, Hera, Demeter and Menelaus. Athena whose birth name was Pamela was the fifth energy user to inherent the fighting name Athena. So long as a person with a given name lived it could not be bestowed upon another unless combat for the name occurred.

The room Cyrus created was open and large vents were placed in the center for the fire that raged in the open space of the table. Currently sitting around the table were the leaders of the three most allied groups in the Kinship. The Forum, the Argonauts and the Seraphs. They had met per Cyrus' request to hear Uriel's findings and discuss how to recover Chance. Each group had a stake in this and none wanted to be left out. Fourteen leaders around the table listened to Uriel the fifteenth as she described what she found out from Wisp's memories.

She looked around the table and began, "The information about Harbinger and his wife is not really important. He is a leader of some sort and his wife is just as dark and manipulative."

"Although it is important to note that Wisp is infatuated with them both," Clotho added.

"What is important," Uriel added darkly, "is that Harbinger commands these Hunters to find young impressionable energy users. They go to various locations all over the word looking for kids to recruit which actually means kidnapping."

"Why are they kidnapping or recruiting these children?" Ares asked.

"They are building an army for some purpose that Wisp was not aware of. It's important to note that Harbinger is not aware of all that Wisp knows. She was trained as a reconnaissance person. Therefore, even while she was enthralled by Harbinger and Melaniya she was still doing what she was taught to do." Uriel explained.

"What else did she find?" Gerrod asked.

"They search both our world for runaways and the non-energy world in places likes children's homes and orphanages. From time to time they will take a child from a home where the child's parents are unaware their child is an energy user." Uriel continued. "The kids are brought to a camp where they are both trained and broken. Some of this we knew from Verock's memories."

"How does this help us find Chance?" Horatius asked.

"Unfortunately, it doesn't. I can see no way to use this information to find the camp. She simply does not know where the camp is."

"Actually," Cyrus smiled. "We know how they choose their kids. How can we use this to our advantage?"

Athena barged into the leadership meeting. All eyes turned to her, surprised to see her not only up and about, but there in the room.

"Athena? What can we do for you?" Cyrus asked.

"For starters you can tell me what the plans are to rescue Chance and how I can help," she stated simply.

"Honey, we are still trying to figure out where Chance is," Horatius explained. "Then we can mount a rescue operation."

"However, we need to find the location soon. If we don't find it before the first of December we will have to wait until the moratorium on combat lifts." Cyrus reminded everyone.

"You would leave him there for a month!" Athena contested hotly. "You can't do that. He could die in a month in their hands!"

"We can't break the rules we helped set," Ares proclaimed. "There is no fighting for this one month a year."

"Cowards," Athena spat. "Aunt Uri, did you get everything you needed from that woman?" she asked suddenly.

"Yes, but I don't see--" Uriel stopped abruptly when Athena teleported out.

"Lock them!" Athena thought to Caval before she disappeared. Arriving at the interrogation wing she started looking in the cells. She spotted Nexus seated outside one of them; the door was open. Athena realized that this was the only cell currently occupied in the Forum prison. Nexus looked up surprised to see her.

"Athena? What are you doing here?" he asked as she walked into the open cell.

"Athena!" Wisp exclaimed. "So sorry to hear you lost your boyfriend. Rest assured my love will find him a suitable mate."

Athena stood before the woman who had caused her so much pain. Wisp was seated on a cot, looking for all the world like a guest not a prisoner. She was not even bound, just teleport locked.

"You think you're so smart and so protected don't you?" Athena scolded.

"I expect to be rescued any time." She smiled.

"Do you?" Athena whispered and slashed the woman's throat.

She looked up to see Nexus jump out of his chair as the door slammed in his face. He could only watch through the bars, a grim smile on his face as the woman died. Athena turned her back on the corpse and pointed at the door. "You do have keys don't you?"

Just then Cyrus, Ares and Horatius arrived. The cell was unlocked and Ares gave her a dark look as she walked out of the door.

"What have you done?" Ares demanded.

"I performed my Right of Assassination." Athena said coldly.

Cyrus looked at Nexus. "Why did you allow her into the cell?" he questioned.

"Well to be honest I didn't know what she was going to do. But I had been thinking about killing her myself," he admitted.

"Take Athena into custody," Ares said quietly.

"On what charges?" Athena exclaimed.

"As your leader, I did not give you permission to assassinate Wisp," he proclaimed.

"Dad!" Athena pleaded.

"I'm sorry Athena," Horatius lectured angrily. "You wanted to be treated like an adult. You must face adult consequences."

Athena was taken to a cell in another building. She noticed bitterly this area had a dampening field. She paced her cell for several hours in silence. Finally, after brooding on the situation she decided to take a nap. When she awoke, sitting in a cot in the cell next door was Caval.

"Hello Neighbor!" he laughed.

"Caval! What are you doing here?"

"Well," he was still laughing. "When you teleported out and I put up the lock I didn't realize how hard it would be to keep it up with that many leaders in the room." He almost fell off his cot laughing.

"What did they do?".

"Nothing bad. Amitiel was close to me and she shocked me into submission. Then a few people teleported out. I had to be taken to the healing wing for a few hours, and then Marshal had me sent to these cells to decide my punishment for interfering with fifteen leaders." Caval sighed. "So did you do it?"

"Do what? Kill Wisp?" she snapped.

"Well yeah. I felt your intentions when you told to me to lock them," he retorted.

"Yes, I killed the witch. I claimed Right of Assassination and Ares sent me here," she conceded.

"Well you didn't exactly clear it with leadership," he said thoughtfully. "I am still glad you did it though. She deserved to die for what she did to Chance and Uncle Caz."

"Well that makes two people who agree. Nexus was there; he could have stopped me but he just kind of let it happen."

"So are you going to tell me what happened while you were away with Chance?" he asked suddenly.

"Do you really think now is the best time?" she snapped back.

"Well, we have nothing but time on our hands now do we?" Caval laughed.

"He's right," a strong male voice spoke. "Why don't you tell us what happened?" Horatius demanded. He took a seat outside their cells. "After all, you do have nothing but time."

Looking at her father, then back at Caval Athena realized she didn't have a choice. "Well it began when he took me to an abandoned forest camp..."

Training

The camp was not turning out to be anything like Chance expected. For starters, Eliza, who had been let out of her cell, had started telling everyone that Chance was the enemy. Most of the kids in camp knew about Jim and Eliza in their cells. Most knew they were special case prisoners but did not know why. Now with Eliza out of her cell and almost a VIP in their eyes, she was turning everyone against him as fast as she could. He was the enemy. He was the cause of everyone's pain. He was why there was no more Crèche. Eliza had pretty much painted him as the antichrist, and he had promised Jim to protect her as he died on his shoulder.

The first few days in the general population were hell. Kids were encouraged to attack one another; Chance was attacked twelve times. He quietly and compassionately put down his opponents with as little damage as possible. Eliza had a following of several strong energy users and the young and impressionable. She was like a demented den mother. The teachers avoided Chance at first too. Each time he defended an attack it seemed as if he was one step further from getting any guidance. He did not want to be seen this way. He felt guilty about how things were and wanted to make things right for the kids here, but he did not know how to start.

He tried to approach teens who were struggling with something to see if he could help only to be rebuked because of Eliza. The only two who really seamed completely immune to her ravings were the boy called Spark and the girl Mouse. They were almost as isolated as he was, but they seemed to have a following of people they would push away. Chance wondered why they did that. He also noticed they would talk to each other in short bursts then separate. Mouse was not treated well by the guards but she also used her mouth and her power often.

On the third day of his isolation, Mouse was being lead out of the punishment area and almost fell. Chance grabbed her and held her up. She looked at him like she could kill him for helping her. That was when Spark preformed a feat Chance had never seen before. Lightening or electricity surrounded his entire body and he was across the yard and between him and Mouse almost before Chance could register what happened.

"Is this guy bothering you Mouse?" he challenged.

"No, Spark," she responded, "just playing hero again."

"Hero?" Chance asked, offended. He looked at the two teens in front of him not understanding what Spark said. "She was about to fall. I was just trying to keep her on her feet so Warden would not get the satisfaction of seeing her weak." With that said, he stormed off in the direction of the mess hall.

Each of them was RFID chipped for rations. Radio-frequency identification or RFID uses electromagnetic fields to automatically identify and track tags attached to objects. In the case of the camp kids they passed their RFID chips under a scanner to obtain food. If they had eaten already that day, the RFID chip knows. It kept the kids fed well but did not allow for over eating. Chance thought it was probably a GPS chip as well but kept that thought to himself. He could easily short out the chip, but then he would not get the food he needed to survive. He sat down to eat and was surprised when Mouse and Spark joined him.

"You know; we don't believe the bullshit Eliza says about you?" Spark started setting down his own tray of food.

"Whatever she is saying it is partially true," Chance confessed.

"Oh, so you're in league with Warden and the guards to try to keep us all in line?" Mouse mused in a surprisingly high voice. Chance stared at her with is jaw hanging open.

"Well, we knew that was a lie," Spark filled in.

"Is that what people think of me?"

"Most people don't know what to think of you," Mouse answered honestly. "They do know the teachers are afraid of you and that lends some validity to Eliza's ravings."

"She wasn't always like that," Chance whispered. "She was sweet and kind. It's my fault she wound up that way."

"So you are him then." Spark stated.

"Him who?" Chance requested.

"The kid who escaped, the one who that new guard Inferno chased forever and a day," Mouse smirked.

"Yes I'm him, but how do you two know all this?" Chance demanded.

"You think we like getting punished?" Spark laughed. "The guards tend to talk in that area. We tune out and just listen. So much knowledge just blabbed because they think we're in too much pain to pay attention."

"They talk more around me," Mouse added. "After all I am just a girl." She had a 'don't underestimate me' look in her eyes that reminded him of Athena. His eyes tearing up and Spark grabbed his wrist.

"Whatever you are thinking, block it out," he snapped. "You cannot be seen crying. You were right to hold Mouse up; we cannot let them see our weakness."

"You're right," Chance grimaced, fighting back the emotion. "They can't see me cry for her again."

"Even if they are afraid of you, they have to teach you." Mouse explained. "They're afraid of me too for different reasons then you."

"Keep doing what you are doing," Spark added. "Win without really hurting people, and you will have them on your side soon enough." Then they left. Spark went to the restrooms and Mouse went to the yard. Chance finished his meal and theirs, then he watched Mouse freeze training dummies solid then hit them with an energy ball and shatter them. Several kids were watching her including some of Eliza's followers.

The next few days went a little better for Chance. He approached a teacher who used heat energy and requested training. The teacher was surprised and agreed. Although he was competent, it was obvious he had already learned more from Athena. Chance mastered the lessons in half a day. Other teens watched in surprise. He spent the second day with an earth teacher Trand again learned the lessons in a day. Moving on from teacher to teacher the guards were constantly watching him and he knew they were reporting back to Warden and possibly Inferno. He was already down to eighteen days until his fight. One of the teens that had attacked Chance when he first arrived, attended a healing training with him. About halfway through the day he asked Chance why he had spared him.

"I didn't want to kill you or even hurt you. I don't think of anyone in camp as my enemy."

Chance didn't know that those words would be repeated throughout the camp for the next week. When the lesson was over he wondered if Mouse or Spark knew mental communication. Having friends he could talk to at all times would be a great help to him here. He learned that Mouse had mental training and was able to connect with her quickly. They both suggested Spark learn as it was a good skill to have.

When he moved from the earth teacher to the electric teacher who Spark usually studied with, Chance noticed more and more students were attending the same teaching he was. During the course of instruction, they would accept the tips and ideas he suggested. Chance was not mastering everything from every teacher but picking up the skills he could to study more on his own time. One teacher Chance really enjoyed working with was a woman who commanded air and ice. They called her Whiteout which ironically she hated. Mouse worked with her from time to time, but not every day. Teachers were not as afraid of Chance's approach anymore and welcomed him to their sessions as other students would invariably show. He spent a day and a half with a shield master then stopped formal training. There were eleven days left till his fight with Inferno.

"Why did you stop going to the teaching sessions?" Mouse questioned.

"I have to prepare for my fight, and constantly working on new things will not help me, only hurt me." He replied.

"You have almost split the camp already you realize," Spark informed him.

"What do you mean?" Chance replied.

"Eliza had them convinced you were some kind of monster." Mouse laughed.

"Yeah, and now over half the camp sees you as some kind of prodigy to be looked up to," Spark filled in.

"I am no one to look up to," Chance snapped.

"Did you pick fire for your first teacher on purpose?" Mouse asked.

"I had some training from Athena in fire..." Chance responded losing focus, looking off in the distance.

"That's the girl," Spark whispered.

"Yes, that was her name." Chance responded bitterly. "Inferno was the one that captured me and is responsible for her death. I will kill him."

"Don't speak of killing so casually," Spark quipped. "Everyone over thirteen here thinks they are a killer because they fought some scared kid."

"Shut it Spark," Mouse cautioned. "Chance is the only teen in camp that has killed as much as me. I can tell just by looking at him." Chance started at her.

"Is everything they said about you true?" Spark asked.

"I don't know what has been said about me," Chance answered still looking at Mouse. "But yes, I have killed. Four of them died when Inferno brought me in. If I had been stronger they all would have." Chance broke eye contact with

Mouse. He did not know what she had done, but he knew it was harsh.

"So answer the question," she demanded. "Did you pick fire on purpose?"

"Yes. I didn't know I would be done that quickly but I did know it would be quick." He explained. "The stronger I appear the more people will leave me alone."

"And now what is your plan?" Spark asked interested. Chance looked at the two deciding if he should confide in them what he was up to. It was obvious they were hated, and they had already shared info with him. "I started doing something new after electric training," Chance confided.

"What was that?" Mouse asked, her curiosity piqued.

"When I fought a friend of Athena's by mistake I used a ton of energy." Chance announced, "I was off my feet for days."

"Yeah, I had something similar happen to me when I froze a lake trying to escape capture." Mouse added.

"Athena told me to strengthen my energy use, like a muscle." He spoke, "In order to do that, I am using energy even now while sitting here."

"At all times?" Spark retorted.

"I started with a small current of energy all over my body," he described. "I switched it to shielding energy yesterday."

"That's impossible," Mouse admonished.

"Just hard," Chance retorted, "I feel a bit tired but I plan to turn it off four days before the fight and just rest."

"You're crazy!" Spark bawled.

"Quite down Spark!" Mouse hissed.

"I am going to practice in a corner of the yard where I saw Mouse destroying targets," he continued. "I need to increase how much energy I can use overall. I will not be defeated by Inferno, and I will get us all out of here somehow," he vowed.

"If your insane plan works," Mouse quipped, "survive your fight first. Figure out how to get us all out second." She got up from the table and walked to the barracks.

• •

Melaniya spent more time at the training camp than normal. She wanted to see what the young man Chance was capable of before he faced Inferno. She was dedicated to her husband, almost fanatically so. However, she knew that his decision to allow Inferno to fight Chance could be disastrous for them both. She was impressed with how quickly he was picking up his lessons. However, Harbinger was playing a dangerous game with the kid's life. She didn't know why he was so important but felt that their future was riding on Chance staying alive. Inferno had something up his sleeve that he was not talking about. He had been chasing Chance too long to take the teen lightly and still he seemed confident in his victory.

It was her job to analyze the data about a given situation or the kids they "recruited" to camp. The job had evolved over the last few years as Crèche kids were now included in this number as well. Once she had done this, working with Harbinger, they would plan out and execute the next steps. That could be the capture of a child, or the direction training should take. She had left the planning of the cabin raid to

Inferno hoping he would fail again. She did not like the man and his arrogance. He was a caste climber. Little did he know that he would never climb to the rank of General like her and Harbinger.

Few people were viewed by the leaders as anything other than warriors. Their vast power was able to squash even Harbinger's substantial energy control easily. It was said that the main leader and his wife studied under the Queen herself and possibly with Phantom. Everyone spoke of it in hushed whispers as it was known they did not like Phantom, wanted to kill him in fact. Looking over the data for kids like Mouse and Spark had occupied a few days of her time. Melaniya was so good at it that she could tell you a person's main energy, how strong their potential was and if they were worth training quickly. She knew that Mouse was stronger than she let on and was hiding it and that Spark preferred boys to girls. All these details she could ferret out with a few cursory inspections and reading the reports the teachers gave on their recruits. She enjoyed her job and the perks of being a general. With Harbinger the two enjoyed unparalleled freedom and fortune, the best of everything. And yet, here she was paying special attention to this one boy.

Melaniya wondered again why their leader wanted Chance so badly. He was a Crèche kid from what she knew, just one of many. He certainly had strong ability, but not anything overwhelming. Looking at teens like Mouse and Bevan, they were much stronger with energy. Bevan was also vastly better at physical combat which was also very important in the arena. So why was Chance pursued for close to three years and allowed to live after killing so many? The leader's wife Raeya herself had shown up to check on the sedated teen when he was first captured.

After watching for several days she entered the training area like any other teacher and watched him work. The kinetic energy he was using made short work of four battle targets. Chance's choices were interesting. He froze, fried and simply exploded targets. It was not enough though and she knew it. Whatever Inferno was planning he knew Chance could do these things. Shaking her head, she realized he was looking at her with a questioning look. For some reason the kid unnerved her.

"You don't approve of my methods?" he asked her.

"Your technique is very good," Melaniya responded before she could stop herself. "However, I think it would be wise of you to concentrate on other strengths and abilities if you have them. Certainly your future opponent is expecting you to use your main power."

"And who are you?" Chance quipped.

"No one of consequence," she informed him, "Good luck in your fight." Melaniya walked away then realizing she had said too much. Then again maybe she had not warned him enough.

Amends

The days and events since Wisp's death had been surprising for Caval. For two days, he and Athena had been in the null-energy cells while she described the time she spent with Chance to him and her father. The trial that followed was short and Athena's first adult case. She wound up being sentenced to house arrest until Christmas. No energy use whatsoever and her father would be watching. Ares had been lenient. He had considered the events that led to her killing Wisp and Athena's age. These factors that kept her from being incarcerated for three to six months in a suppression ward. Caval was allowed to see her the Sunday before Christmas which he was looking forward to. It felt like months since he had spent any quality time with her.

He was still astonished about the time she had spent with Chance. The more she had revealed the more he realized he was correct about the young man. He discussed this with his teacher who suggested Caval give the leaders some advice based on what he knew. So far though, none of the leaders would see him. Despite being impressed that he was able to contain all of them for a short period of time, they were still angry with him. They deemed his action to be a cursory part of Wisp's assassination, even though he hadn't really known what Athena intended. After two days in the cell he was freed. When he returned home, he was shocked that his mother was much angrier about the events then his father. Clotho had always been more forgiving then

Cyrus. Illyria and Nexus had kindly forgiven him for his manipulations after a heartfelt apology and told him the information that had been taken from Wisp's mind.

At his teacher's suggestion, Caval sent a formal request to meet with the leaders to apologize as well as suggest his idea. He knew he had to make amends with them if there was anything he could do to help Chance and Athena. Caval had discussed his reasons and thought process with his teacher at length, and his teacher agreed it was a solid plan. He knew that the leaders would be missing the obvious choice he had seen. They would be so concerned with protecting everyone and keeping them safe that his plan would not occur to them. For now, he would have to wait and hope they agreed to meet with him to accept his apology and proposal.

With the suspension on fighting the leaders could not launch a raid or an assault of any kind to free Chance. If they went with Caval's idea things could be set in motion to free Chance as soon as possible. As the days passed, the waiting was difficult so to pass the time, he trained in earnest. There was no lesson he did not listen to after his fight with Chance. He spent most of his life learning how to be a calculating fighter and had lost what he considered his first real battle. Caval could no longer rest on the fact that he was supposed to be special. Chance had beaten him as easily as he could have defeated anyone else his age including Athena. Cyrus and his teacher were both kind about the fact, but Caval could not forget the point that he had lost. He was supposed to be the best of his age and he was not. He also realized that had circumstances been different, had Cyrus and Clotho not adopted him, he could be in the same situation as Chance. Now more than ever he owed it to the teen to help rescue him and bring him to a place where he could train. For the first time in his life he had what he felt was an equal, someone who could push him to achieve more.

••

"We really should meet with him and see what he wants." Gerrod suggested.

"He is too arrogant. He probably wants to throw it in our faces that he was able to tele-lock us all," Marshal snarled.

"I doubt it's that," Gerrod countered.

"He is a secondary issue right now," Ares stated. "Our primary concern is how to retrieve Chance."

"We can't even find him," Raphael sighed.

"Even if we knew his location which we don't," Horatius reminded everyone, "we can't attack until after the new year."

"You're right, we can't." Cyrus spoke up. "We set the rules and cannot be the ones to break them. However, I agree with Gerrod. We should allow my wayward son to speak."

"How many kids do you think are being held at this camp?" Amitiel asked the group. "We have no idea what we will be facing when we do manage to find it."

"Given the nature of our world, and taking into account non-energy world kidnappings," Cyrus mused, "we could be looking at hundreds. Plus, we do not know how long they have been capturing kids."

"My daughter almost died in the snow because of these people," Horatius said. "Although we all agree her actions against the traitor were rash, we also know what these people are capable of.”

“They have no problems killing anyone in their way to achieve their goals.” Uriel said. “They took out that group in Kazakhstan to capture kids according to Wisp’s memories.”

“I had a friend in that group,” Cyrus remarked. “We all wondered who had done it as none of the aggressive revolutionary groups took credit.”

“We also know these Overlords do not have a member on the council.” Ares said. “Very few groups stay away from the council. Most groups want to have a say in our laws. What do they have to gain from staying out of the council?

“I don’t like it. It smells too much like how the Queen operated,” Cyrus spat.

“She held you prisoner a long time my friend,” Gerrod acknowledged. “You know her methods better than anyone. If you feel these people use them, then I believe more than ever they need to be stopped and quickly.”

“How certain are you?” Michael questioned.

“Certain enough to bring it up here,” Cyrus quipped. “Let’s talk to Caval and keep options opened. We may need to involve other groups if this is as bad as I fear.”

“Agreed,” Ares spoke. “Let him know we will meet with him.” He looked at Marshal and added, “If Marshal is correct and he just wants to brag, he will find himself in a cell for the rest of the year.”

Unknown to any of them, someone was watching the entire meeting from the astral plane, he didn’t know if he should get directly involved yet. Time would tell and he could afford to wait for now.

• •

Caval was surprised and nervous about meeting with the leaders. He knew at least fourteen of the fifteen would be angry he was there. He reminded himself not to make jokes about the incident and to just apologize, ask forgiveness and then move on to other business. When he walked in all eyes were on him. Marshal's look spoke volumes of contempt and Caval realized he had made an enemy. He took the seat he was directed to and addressed the group.

"Thank you all for agreeing to see me today," he began. "I know what I did was wrong, I should never have used my abilities to confine you all to this room while Athena confronted Wisp. It was foolish and arrogant of me. I offer my deepest apologies and ask your forgiveness for my transgression." He paused and looked at his father before continuing. "I can be manipulative and my energy control gets to my head. I am sorry dad for putting you in this position."

"I don't know if we should," Marshal said speaking up first. "However, I am impressed at how deeply you seem to feel about the situation." His statement surprised everyone. "That being said, you admit that you are manipulative. How do we know you are not trying to do that now?"

"Lord Marshal, I realize you are not as strong at mind reading as Lady Uriel." Caval began delicately. "However, everyone in this room including me can read minds. If you feel I am being manipulative I invite you to read mine now." When Marshal first began to speak Caval had hoped he was wrong about the depth of the man's grudge. The longer he spoke the more Caval realized he had really hurt Marshals pride.

"That won't be necessary," Meteo interjected. "To some degree we all understand that you are sincere and hope to cur our favor."

Marshal looked at his senior leader with some resentment but let it go with a nod.

"Lord Meteo, you are not wrong. I do wish to both make amends and hope to suggest a plan that could get Chance back," Caval confirmed.

"Leave the planning to us Caval," Marshal snapped. "With the experience around this table I think the fifteen of us can come up with a plan that will work."

"I agree you could," Caval responded pleasantly, "My father alone has more experience than all of you put together with the exception of Lord Typhoonus." He watched Cyrus close his eyes and shake his head.

"Ahh, there is the arrogant boy I knew would come out." Marshal asserted

"Lord Marshal, I was simply stating a fact. You know what I said to be truth not arrogance. I am young; I don't know what you know." Caval spoke. "However, I don't dismiss someone out of hand because I'm angry with them."

"ENOUGH!" Ares yelled. "Marshal I know you're pissed, we all were. However, we agreed to listen to what Caval had to say."

"Very well," Marshal agreed, "I will listen."

"Thank you Lord Ares." Caval stated.

"Enough with the lord and lady crap though Caval. You've never spoken formally before; doing it now only makes you look like you're trying too hard." Uriel commanded.

"Ok, you're right," Caval smiled. "Given the degree of loyalty that Athena has for Chance, have any of you considered what she will do come Christmas day?"

"What are you getting at?" Michael asked.

"Athena is smart, powerful and very well liked in all the groups," Caval pointed out. "She is going to have three weeks of nothing to do but brood and think about what is happening to Chance."

Amitiel nodded. "Go on."

"If you don't have a solid workable plan by that time she is capable of rallying the teens and many of the younger adults behind her to go after Chance in any way possible." Caval warned. Horatius visibly paled when realized the truth of these words.

"Then we lock her up in a containment field," Marshal proposed.

"That could work," Caval agreed. "Or it could make her a martyr to Chance's cause and backfire. Word is already out about what she and Chance went through."

"What do you suggest then?" Cyrus asked his son.

"We know they capture teens and kids. We also know from Wisp's and Verock's memories that they have capture teams out everywhere."

"Ok, so how do you think that helps us?" Ares questioned.

"I propose you make me some false credentials and put me in a boy's home in the non-energy world." Caval said. "I will 'leak' energy that is sure to be detected by these Hunters."

"Absolutely not!' Cyrus interrupted. "I know where you are going with this. When they find you we wouldn't be able to do anything. Laying a trap for them to come get you so we could intercede would be a violation of the rules."

"Dad, you wouldn't be laying a trap," Caval responded. "You would let them take me." The room erupted in argument. People spoke over each other expressing how foolish and dangerous the plan was

"LISTEN!" Caval screamed amplifying his voice. When the room settled down, he continued. "It's the only way. I am connected to my dad mentally and that can't be broken. We don't know how they transport to their camp. For all we know they don't use energy at all. It could be double or triple blinds followed by a plane to Europe."

"Caval, you can't be serious," Horatius said. "Why do you think we would allow such a crazy and risky idea?"

"Two reasons," Caval persisted. "The first is that I owe it to Chance If not for me he would not have been captured. And the second is that once I'm at this camp I could feed you the information you need to set up a strike and extraction as soon as possible."

The room was quiet as the leaders considered Caval's plan. Marshal was the first to break the silence actually smiling. "I hate to admit it, but that is not a bad plan."

"Are you crazy?" Cyrus exploded. "Do you think for one moment I would put my son in that kind of danger?"

The arguments started again until a man sitting in the corner of the room spoke, cutting off all conversation. "His plan is the only one that has a possibility to succeed," Sabastian said softly.

"You agree to this?" Cyrus scoffed, "You don't even want him to have a debut fight but you want him in a camp full of killers."

"Dad, don't you see," Caval pleaded. "I'm an unknown. That's why I am perfect. I'm also stronger than most adults."

"Son, this is the worst idea I have ever heard!"

"He is the only one who can do it," Sabastian said. "Think about it with your head not your heart. And while you're at it, find Cinder. When Chance is freed he will need a good teacher. I have my hands full with this one." He motioned to Caval then disappeared from the room.

"Does anybody else hate how he does that?" Uriel asked lightly.

"Everyone, you know we're right. This is the best option." Caval appealed. "If you place me tomorrow I have a little over three weeks to get caught. That brings us to the end of the year when the pause on fighting and raids is lifted. You can bust us out once I give you the lay of the land."

"I still don't like it," Cyrus said. "But I agree we will think about it."

"Don't think too long. The longer it takes to place me the more time we leave Chance in that camp where they can turn or kill him." Caval took a cue from his teacher and walked out of the room. He knew they would agree.

"Find Cinder?" he heard someone question as the door closed.

• •

Locating a boy's home for Caval was easy. They knew from interrogating Wisp the type of homes most frequented by the Hunters. Cyrus avoided the specific ones she had mentioned but found one that was similar. He chose a boy's home in New York figuring that with the population density of the area and runaways, the odds were high that Caval would get spotted by the Hunters. Once located, he instructed Raph to pose as Father Raphael and ask if they had any open beds for a young man in need of a place to stay. It had only taken a day to make the forgeries; Caval was now Cal Adams. His parents died in a house fire, possibly set by him, three years ago. He had been staying at with relatives who could no longer afford to keep him.

Cyrus was still not happy about the situation and neither was Clotho. After several hours of discussion, fights and arguments they agreed however that Caval's teacher was correct and this was the best plan. They spent time together as a family after that and went to work on things like Caval's appearance. He changed his hair color making it darker and Clotho cut it shorter in case he had been spotted in the field, but no one thought he had. They knew Caval could find out everything needed to plan their attack as long as he kept a low profile and did not do anything stupid. That was Cyrus's biggest concern; his son was not known for being discreet.

"Dad, I'll be fine. I promise I will not show what I can do." Caval vowed.

"What about Chance? When he sees you will he recognize you and give you away?"

"He's a smart man. I'll give him a little head shake when he first sees me. He'll figure it out."

"These people are vicious Caval," Clotho told him giving him a hug. "Don't be arrogant! They will hurt you."

"I may have to be a little arrogant..." Caval confessed with a small smile.

"We love you. Be careful and contact me as often as you can." Cyrus said.

"I love you both too. Take care of Mom for me." He turned and walked over to Raph. Waving goodbye they teleported out. Raphael had a car waiting in Maryland and they would drive the rest of the way to New York. They wanted no ties or energy trails leading back to home base.

"Did we do the right thing?" Cyrus asked his wife.

"I don't know my love, but Caval seems to think so. We have to trust him." She was crying. Cyrus took her into his arms and they both hoped this insane plan would work and they would see their son again soon.

Preparations

He was exhausted. After a week and a half solid of pushing his limits Chance could hardly stand at the end of the day. Determined, he dragged himself to bed and forced himself to stand in the morning. Sometimes it required wrapping energy around his limbs to get them to move. He had less than a week till his fight with Inferno. He knew he would have to stop soon and take it a bit easy or he would be too tired to take on his opponent. His mind was in turmoil. He was much stronger than he had ever been before; however, part of him still did not want to fight.

He mimicked the way Spark and Mouse used energy and was able to master it. When he tried to teach them what he did they were only able to pick up the basics, although they kept working on it. Mouse was quicker than Spark. It seemed in a month or so she would be able to use kinetic energy very well. This training was done as secretive as possible. The three wanted an ace up their sleeve if they needed it. They kept in constant mental communication making sure to keep their faces neutral so the guards were not aware of it. Twice Mouse had been taken to the whipping post. Spark would close down mental communication when this happened but Chance refused; he wanted to help her deal by keeping her focused.

The turning point in the camp came when a young man named Bevan, one of Eliza's circle, approached him, and asked for advice on levitation. Mouse and Spark had been correct;

he had won over more than half the kids. When he trained he always had a group around him watching and asking questions. The guards took notice of course and Warden came to pay him a visit. The others scattered when the man approached. Chance ignored him and continued to use only kinetic energy in his presence.

"It seems you have become quite popular in a short period of time." Warden announced smiling at the energy he saw Chance using.

"I just try to help people when I can. If they like me because of that, so be it," Chance replied.

"My men are worried you are trying to recruit your own private army," Warden quipped. "With Mouse and Spark's help of course."

"No sir. Just trying to prepare for my battle." Chance responded still focusing on the dummies and not looking at Warden.

"That's very good Dale, because if you were, remember I would have to eliminate each and every one of them." Warden's voice was like ice.

Chance looked up sharply, not because of the threat, but because of the name the man had called him. "What did you call me?"

"Dale?" Warden smiled. "Oh that's right, you don't know your birth name do you?"

Chance was visibly shaken. "My name is Dale?"

"Yes, it is." Warden still had an evil smile on his face. "I know more about you then you know about yourself."

"Do you know my parents?" Chance demanded. Mouse and Spark were both talking in his head trying to calm him down. The practice dummies were melting from his emotional outburst of pure fire energy.

Warden saw he had finally gotten under the boy's skin and grinned again. "Remember what I said Dale," the man chided, "and continue with your training."

When he left Chance was an emotional wreck.

Was Warden telling the truth or just trying to mess with me? Is Dale really my name? Are my parents still alive?"

Mouse scolded him. *"None of that really matters right now Chance! Warden is just trying to distract and hurt you. Don't let him!"*

Thank you," he thought back to her. *"If he does know something I can find out later."*

"*That's right!"* Spark chimed in. *"First defeat Inferno. We can work on escape and finding out other information later."*

"*You're both right, I...I need to concentrate."* Chance admitted. He went back to training; however, the confusion lingered. He knew he had to defeat Inferno, but what about Warden? Did he really know more about his past than even he knew? Chance had to know for certain. For too long he did not understand why he was left alone in the Crèche.

• •

"And you did exactly as I told you to do?" Harbinger demanded.

"Yes my Lord. I spoke to the boy and called him Dale as you requested." Warden confirmed.

"How did he take it?"

"Well, he was shocked and confused. I acted as if I knew all along whom his parents were of course. He had no idea that a record of his drop-off existed." Warden replied.

"Good, good. Perhaps it will be enough to throw him off. I have been disturbed by the reports I have heard from the camp," Harbinger confessed.

"It is quite remarkable how quickly the others have responded to him. The boy has a natural charisma. It's a shame the record doesn't actually say who dropped him off," Warden mused.

"Well come Christmas eve that should be snuffed out. I expect Inferno has been planning for quite some time to kill the boy." Harbinger smiled. "When that is done, I will challenge and kill Inferno."

"Sir, do you think that's wise considering all the effort expended to capture him?" Warden questioned.

"It's an official challenge. No one can refute it. When the boy dies he dies. It has nothing to do with us and I will be the one to avenge him." Harbinger smiled at the thought. The teen was becoming too much of a problem already. The camp mentality was shifting. In just a couple of weeks, there was less infighting and far more cooperation. It was harder to keep control when they were not at odds with one another. When he died in his initial fight, then it would just prove that all the resources spent capturing him were wasted. This could even mean finally achieving a leadership position in the Overlords. After all, the fifth seat was still empty.

••

The kinetic energy barrier Inferno learned to erect was almost complete. It required a lot of attention but once he learned how to keep it up like a shield he was able to use other energy normally. During the course of a normal energy battle between trained fighters you both shielded and attacked at the same time. He would lose his normal shield and be vulnerable to attacks but the kinetic energy Chance excelled at would be useless. A wicked smile was on the man's face as he thought about finally killing the boy. Perhaps it was petty of him but he did not care. The boy had cost him too much and his death was the only thing that could satisfy Inferno now.

Joule was not happy about having to teach him, but she was good to her word. She never asked who his opponent was and he did not offer it up. He found a twisted joy in anticipating killing the boy on Christmas Eve. The rest of the energy world had that silly no combat rule for the month. The Overlords didn't care. They fought and training and planed and schemed. It's why they were as strong as they were. No down time, no slacking, and no mercy for the weak.

• •

When Athena learned Caval was being used as bait she was furious. Furious with her father, with the leaders and with herself for not being able to help. She had planned on establishing a mental connection with Caval when he visited her on the Sunday before Christmas, or at least talk about how it could be done since she was barred from all energy use.

"You certainly inherited your mothers temper," Horatius mused after telling her the news.

"How could you let him do that?" she seethed. "Caval of all people? He is about as stealthy as a bull in a china shop!"

"We both know better than that Athena. This was mainly his plan and I thought you would be happy we were doing something to help Chance."

"Happy? Really? So now my best friend AND my boyfriend are going to be in those people hands. What part of this is a good idea?" she hissed.

"So he is your boyfriend then. You left that detail out when you told me about your time together," Horatius remarked.

"Really dad? That is what you choose to focus on? Not the fact that Caval will probably get himself killed?" she looked appalled. He father was looking at her with humor in his eyes though, as if this whole situation was funny.

"I forget that you are so young sometimes Athena. You act so much more like an adult most times. All of us are nervous about the plan. Cyrus and Clotho are a wreck. We have just been through situations like this far more often so we tend to keep our heads."

"Dad...I just feel useless here!" she exclaimed. "Caval should have talked to me about this first."

"Well my dear, that is part of the consequences of your rash decision," he explained. "If you had not gone off on your own and assassinated Wisp, Caval would have been able to tell you his idea."

"This sucks," she muttered.

"Welcome to adulthood. Life is rarely ever fair and even less rarely goes the way we plan," he quipped. "He's a smart kid. He knows the dangers. He is also in contact with Cyrus so he will be safe."

"Has he been captured yet?" Athena questioned in a small voice.

"No, but he's only been there a couple days. Cyrus tells me he is planning on 'running away'."

"Makes sense. It'll be easier to get caught and persuaded to go with them if he is a runaway," Athena said thoughtfully.

"That seems to be his plan." Horatius agreed. "I'll make a deal with you," he added suddenly.

"What's that?" she questioned.

"You accept your sentence and don't plan anything stupid like gathering people together to go after Chance prematurely." he stated looking at her very seriously, "And I will let you be a part of the raid to free them when we go."

"Are you being serious?" she asked with doubt in her eyes.

"Very serious. Chance will need to see you before he comes with us anyway. And also you are one hell of a fighter. We can use you.".

"It's a deal," she said with smile.

Harder than it seems

Following the plan, Caval had been on the streets several times. This time he was out for three days. The cold he could deal with; the hunger was not something he was used to. He wondered if the Hunters had a plant in The Social Services Center. It made sense that they would. Kidnapped kids could be registered as adopted out, after energy sensitive people could find and take them. Caval was not certain if his father had thought of this yet but he had.

He was leaking energy like a dripping faucet. So far the Hunters had not found him. He did have to avoid a kind looking woman who was obviously a peripheral or fringe member. She had probably felt the energy he was giving off and had approached Caval and asked if he needed help. It took an hour to convince her he was ok. He went into a small supermarket in China Town. He ate a piece of fruit as he walked around and pocketed other food items, genuinely trying to not get caught. For his plan to work, he could not appear to know how to use energy consciously, but he needed some "accidental" events. He managed to "spill" some energy as he slipped out the door. About ten minutes later he realized he had a tail.

He pretended to not notice and made his way to Central Park, a thirty-minute walk away. He wanted to see if he picked up more followers. He was cold and wished he could use warming energy. The jacket he was wearing was stolen, again one of his attempts to "accidentally" use some energy and get picked up, but it wasn't warm enough. Halfway to the park his tail changed. A youngish woman picked up where the man who was following him turned off. Caval assumed they were already lining his route guessing where he was headed. He kept walking and eating some of his stolen food when he noticed the woman was now walking with a young man. Still tailing him they were trying to tighten a net.

"Dad, I think they are onto me. I need to cut off contact until I know for sure. Wish me luck."

He reached the park as dusk was settling. They pair were still behind him walking and talking casually. He noticed there was no one else in the area which seemed peculiar. He sat down on a bench, cracked open the drink he swiped and proceeded to drink while watching the man and woman walk by him. Out of nowhere a man sat down heavily next to him, smoking a cigarette. He took the last drag, crushed out the stub and pulled out his pack.

"Need a smoke?" he asked casually.

"No thanks, I don't smoke," Caval replied.

"Good for you kid. Don't ever start." He lit a new cigarette and took a long drag.

The man and woman who had been following him were walking toward him again. She had changed her coat and pulled her hair back to look different. Stopping by the smoking man she asked, "Pardon me sir, do you have the time?"

"Sorry, no watch," he responded. He turned to look at Caval. "What about you kid?"

"It's 5:20," Caval told them.

"Shouldn't you be getting home young man?" the woman questioned in a nice calming voice. He could feel her scanning him.

"I'm good thanks. Nowhere to go anyway."

The three Hunters looked around. The park was still clear.

"That was some trick in the Chinese market," the second man announced looking at Caval.

"I don't know what you mean," Caval answered, "but I need to get going." He started to stand when the smoking man put a hand on his shoulder.

"It's cool kid, we're not the cops," He said in a reassuring voice. "We have been watching you for a few days."

"Let go of my shoulder." Caval shrugged off the hand, "And what do you mean you have been watching me?" *If they have been watching me for days, they are better than I thought.*

"Let's just say we recognize talent when we see it," the woman explained with a warm smile. She was pretty, even in the winter coat. Caval understood immediately that her presence was meant to throw him off guard. Attractive young women in their twenties didn't usually talk to teen boys.

"What talent?" he asked feigning confusion.

"Well it's not your thieving abilities!" the man with the cigarette laughed and clapped Caval on the back jovially.

"Don't mind him," the pretty woman laughed. "I'm Allie." She offered her hand.

"Cal," he responded taking her hand. It was very warm even in the cold. "Now do you all want to tell me what this is about or do I scream rape to get the police's attention?"

"You've been on your own for a while," Allie laughed merrily. "We just want to offer you a better life. You have skills you don't know you have." Her voice had taken on a serious note. "With these skills come certain benefits..." she lingered on the last word suggestively.

"Ok, now I know you're just pulling my chain." Caval stated but looked at the woman with what he hoped was desire.

"Let me show you something," she said." She extended her hand and lit the smoking man's latest cigarette with a small flame protruding off of her index finger. Caval pretended to be startled and practically jumped off the park bench, dropping his food and drink in the process.

"Holy shit! What was that?" he exclaimed.

Allie held up her hands like a person trying to sooth a wild animal. "It's ok Cal. Calm down. That was just a small idea of what we can offer you." Her smile was beautiful and full of lies. She took his arm and helped him back to the park bench.

"How did you do that?" Caval asked.

"It's a talent that some of us are born with. Like playing the guitar or painting, only our talent allows us to do amazing things," she explained.

"It's got to be a trick," Caval announced.

"It's no trick." She kneeled before him and looked around to make sure no one was looking, posing with subtle seduction. Allie held her ands apart and electricity sparked between them. Her eyes never left Caval's as he pretended shock and amazement. "You could learn this too Cal, if you come with us."

"When my parents' house burned down, I don't know how it happened. We were fighting and all of a sudden the curtains and lamps were blazing." Caval admitted, hoping these people had his files as he thought they did.

"That was a power leak Cal," Allie explained. "You could not control what you did because you didn't know you could do it. We can teach you to harness that ability. Would you like to come with us?" she again offered a hand.

"What would I need to do?" Caval asked, "Can you teach me that?" putting just the right amount of fear in his voice.

"Just take my hand," she smiled brightly, "We will take you to our training facility. There you will meet others like yourself and learn to control that power inside you. If you don't like it, you can leave at any time." She was still kneeling in front of him. Her eyes spoke volumes about the 'things' he could learn.

Caval hesitated then reached out his hand thinking they were going to teleport when he touched her. Instead Allie smiled and stood up. She held unto his hand, and gave him reassuring squeezes now and again as they walked out of the park to a car that was waiting. The man with the cigarette followed a few steps behind. The second man was behind the wheel. Caval assumed he had gone to fetch it when it looked like things were going their way.

"Just relax Cal," she said as he slid into the back seat with her. "We'll be there soon."

They drove out of the city heading west. Caval was afraid to contact his dad because he did not know if they would detect the contact. Nervous, he didn't have to fake his fear. Allie continued to talk to him in both reassuring and seductive tones about all the things he could learn. She slipped off her jacket complaining that the car was hot. The tight, skimpy shirt she wore confirmed that she defiantly the bait for horny teenage boys. Caval didn't pay too much attention to the words she was speaking, but let his eyes take in her form now and again pretending like he was trying not to look at her. He wondered briefly if they had teams in place for every type; mother figures for the younger kids, attractive teenage boy for the girls, and such. About an hour into the journey, the driver took a freeway access ramp used for utility vehicles. When it was no longer in view of the road an energy gate opened showing a dusty road a stark contrast to the paved on they were driving on and the car went through.

"How did we do that?" Caval exclaimed looking out the window trying to get a bearing on their location.

"It's called a portal," Allie explained squeezing his shoulder. "Our training facility is in a secret location. We get there by teleporting," She smiled at what she thought was his utter amazement. They drove for another fifteen minutes down a long dirt road and approached what looked like a prison. Sensing his tension Allie told him, "We took over an old abandoned prison and turned it into our training facility. The nice thing is all the amenities you could need were here. Beds, a kitchen, a training yard. It's not much to look at but it works well for what we have to teach."

Caval looked at her knowing different. "Oh, well that makes sense I guess." The car pulled into the gates. It was December twenty second. Caval was finally at the Overlords training camp.

"What have you got for us today Radha?" a tallish man asked her.

"New recruit Warden," she replied. "Might be someone good; he seems to have potential." She looked at Caval. "His name is Cal Adams, accidentally killed his parents with wild energy several years ago." Caval was startled at the abrupt change in her demeanor.

"Radha?" Caval asked her, "I thought your name was Allie? And why would you say that about my parents?" he sounded hurt.

"Poor Cal, thought you had an admirer didn't you?" The men in the car laughed and Warden did as well. Warden opened the door and Radha roughly pushed him out of the car. Warden took him by the arms and a couple of guards walked over. "He's all yours, we have another potential in France," Radha said before she closed the car door and it pulled away.

"What the hell do you think you're doing?" Caval yelled. "Let go of me and let me go home. That woman said I can leave any time I want. Well, I think I want to leave now!" He looked around and took in his surroundings. Several kids were looking at him with fear in their eyes and Caval thought he may have just made a big mistake playing his hand so strongly. He did not see Chance. The man called Warden and the guards with him were laughing.

"A strong willed one!" Warden said, "I like that. Take him to the post." Caval was dragged by the two guards to what looked like a piece of a telephone pole, it wasn't until he saw the leather ties on it that re realized what it was. Fighting back in earnest now, his shirt was stripped off his back and he was quickly tied to the post. Everything in him screamed to use what he was taught to prevent this from happening. Then he reminded himself that this was his plan, he could not be Caval. He was Cal, the untrained punk.

"You can't do this to me!" he screamed. Warden took a look at the young man tied to the post. He smiled and let energy whip form in his hand.

"Cal," he spoke loud enough for him to hear, "You belong to us now," and the whip cracked across his back. The pain was like nothing he had ever felt before. Even Chance's steel ball in the leg was nothing compared to this. He grit his teeth trying not to yell. The whip slashed his back again. Already his knees wanted to buckle but he fought against it. A small part of his mind had time to register that the whip being used on him was made of energy. The third slash hit him and he could not help it and let out a grunt of pain.

"Why are you doing this," Caval managed to say.

"To educate you Cal, to educate you."

The whip slashed his back again. Caval had to fight the desire to contact his father. If Cyrus knew he was being whipped, rules or no rules, there would be an explosion in the courtyard in a moment. He closed his eyes and realized he had tears running down his face as the fifth lash hit him. His left knee buckled but he managed to straighten up. The sixth slash hit him and he cried out. His eyes were already clouded with stars. He could feel the cold air on his back as well as the blood running down from each open wound.

"Just four more Cal. You're remarkably strong for someone taking their first lashing." The whip cracked again.

Just let me get through this without losing my cover he thought to himself as the eighth lash struck him. His legs were giving out and he could feel the leather around his wrists biting into them. They held him in an almost standing position. The ninth lash hit, he exhaled strongly fighting to retain consciousness.

"Just one more Cal," Warden teased, "After this maybe you will begin to understand that you belong to us now. No more talk of leaving." The last slash was the hardest and the deepest.

Caval bit his tongue. He tried to stand but his legs didn't work right and he sagged against the pole. He had been just treated like an animal, his emotional state was in chaos but he managed to control his energy.

Thank your teacher for all your lessons. Without them I surely would have lost this mission already.

They took him down from the whipping post and dragged him into another room that looked to be a hospital or clinic. A pretty girl with brown hair was lying face down on a bed with her back being treated. Caval was placed on a similar bed and a man began to treat his back with both energy and salves. He fought to remain conscious. By the time the healer left, Caval was breathing heavy, fighting back the desire to contact his father. He had to have control of himself and hide this before he did.

"First time?" the girl asked suddenly. She had steel in her eyes and a half smirk on her face.

"First hour here..." Caval managed to say. Looking at the girls back he saw a mass of scars as well as new wounds. *Gods, how many times has this girl been whipped?* he thought.

"Customary welcome," she laughed. "I take it you asked to be taken home?"

"Demanded," he managed to say. "The man… Warden… educate me…" He let go at last and the world went black.

When he woke, the girl was looking at him. He didn't have a clue what time it was or where he was at first. The fire on his back quickly reminded him.

"Welcome back," she smiled. "I thought we lost you already."

'I wish you had," he grunted.

"It gets easier," she replied nonchalantly.

"God, I don't want to go through that again," He admitted.

"Pity," she sighed, "You looked like you had more backbone. I guess you are just going to give in quickly like most do."

"Oh, I am not giving in," he retorted, "I said I don't want to go through it again, not that I wouldn't."

"That's the spirit. Piss on them." She smiled.

"I'm Cal," he said "Good to meet you."

"Mouse," she told him. "I don't know if it's good to meet you yet."

"You're honest and blunt." He laughed, and cringed it triggered a wave of pain. "You remind me of an old friend of mine." Gritting his teeth pretending it was the pain he realized he said too much. This girl could be just another carrot like Radha.

"When you're here long enough you tend to get this way," she replied. "Well that's not true. Most are broken so they are more polite then me."

He looked at her intently and realized that she noticed.

"What is it?" she asked.

"I am trying to figure out if you are another trap like that Radha woman," he admitted.

"That bitch? No she helped capture my friend Spark too."

"Spark, Mouse...you all have some different names."

"Fighting names. You'll get one soon enough if the training doesn't completely break you." She smiled as she said this but not in a viscous way. She looked like she pitied him. He was afraid to reach out with his energy but wanted to know more about her.

"Fighting names? Just where the hell did I wind up?" he questioned.

"Welcome to the Overlords Army Camp." She said, spitting each word out with venom. "That's what we're all being trained for, to be some kind of army."

"Great, and here I thought I was just going to learn magic powers," he gambled.

"It's not magic Cal, not at all. We manipulate the energy in the world to do our bidding," she scoffed.

"Are you sure you are not another plant? You're talking very freely with someone you just met."

She rolled her eyes at him. "Yes, I had myself whipped within an inch of my life so I could spy on the new guy." She sounded bitter.

"Sorry. That was a dumb thing to say..." he admitted.

"Plus I got a good read off you when you were out cold." She declared, "You have a good heart." She laughed and so did he at the ridiculousness of the situation. They were hurt and bleeding but Caval felt a kinship with the girl.

"Now I really don't trust you," he smirked causing them both to laugh more. The healer walked in then and they quieted down.

"I have been instructed to heal both of you in the next two days so you can attend Chance's fight." The healer announced. He grabbed Caval's hand and shot something with a medical tool into his wrist.

"Ouch," he complained, "what the hell was that?"

"Your ID chip," the man replied. He looked at Mouse added, "You can explain it to him when I leave."

"Wait, we're attending his fight?" Mouse asked ignoring the RFID chip for now.

"Who's Chance," Caval asked trying to keep the surprise out of his voice. His mind screamed, *Chance has a fight on Christmas Eve!!!*

"Harbinger has decreed that all members of the camp over thirteen be at the fight as it will be between Chance and the guard Inferno." The healer's smile was not pleasant. "He wants you all to learn your lessons from this battle." After applying some more salve to both of their backs the healer left.

"Holy shit," Mouse breathed.

"What's this fight and who is Chance?" Caval almost demanded. Scared to death for Chance, his mind raced.

"Chance is my friend," Mouse confided. "We knew the fight was coming up but prisoners like us are never allowed to attend. Only those who have proven their loyalty and graduated out of camp can go."

"So they what? Box?" Caval questioned feigning ignorance.

"No Cal. When we fight it's to the death." Mouse's voice was sad. "Chance has turned the camp on end. A lot of kids see him as a leader in some ways. If they want us to watch this fight, Harbinger must be almost certain Inferno will win."

"Why did I get in that car?" Caval swore.

"Well, you're here now, and Chance is your best opportunity to get out." Mouse assured.

Caval thought about that and did not answer. He felt bad lying to Mouse. Little did she know Chance's best bet at getting out way lying in front of her bleeding. While thinking of this Mouse explained how to use his ID Chip.

Tempest

Christmas Eve Morning Chance was not just scared, he was terrified. Although he had fought before and killed before, each time had been a surprise and a reaction. This time he had the opportunity to think about what was coming. Knowing he was going into a fight where the outcome would be life and death was almost overwhelming. He had taken the last three days off to rest and hoped he could just relax and talk to his two new friends.

Mouse unfortunately had reminded the History of Combat teacher that she was much stronger than him. During his lecture on power versus cunning in battle, Mouse started laughing. When the teacher asked her if she had anything useful to add, she started cooling the air around him. He tried to fight off her energy but she overcame his defenses with raw force and his fingers started to freeze. She then proceeded to ask him if his cunning and battle savvy could save him from an obviously superior opponent. The guards came in and stunned her before any real damage could be done. While being punished, she told Chance that she knew the teacher was actually correct, but she could not help wiping that superior look off his face. He was hoping she would be out in time for him to say goodbye in person but that was not the case. When Warden came for him he was sad to realize he would not get the opportunity to say goodbye mentally either.

"Good Morning Dale!" Warden said cheerfully. "Are you ready to be taken to the arena?" Many of the kids and teens in the barracks were watching the exchange with wary and confused eyes.

"It's eight in the morning," Chance stated. "What time is the fight? I thought it was this evening." He did not allow the name Dale to affect him. It may or may not be his real name, and at this point he needed to survive before he could ever find out.

"We take fighters to be sequestered the day of their battle to mentally prepare themselves." Warden smiled. "As far as the time it will be eight this evening. We don't follow Forum precepts of one o'clock fights here. Are you ready?"

"I would like to shower and eat first if you don't mind," Chance gambled. Spark looked at him and shook his head.

"Food and amenities will be provided for you in the battle quarters." Warden informed him. Everyone in the room knew what Warden was telling Chance was a lie. Normally kids who were going to fight stayed at camp until they were taken to the fight. Then they returned to camp, the healing room, or a grave.

"Well then, I guess I am ready." Chance shrugged. He looked at Spark and quickly added. "Tell Mouse to wish me luck and that I hope she will be on her feet soon." Warden led him away to a waiting car.

Warden could see the boy was scared and subtly tried to increase it. "Big day for you Chance, I know Inferno has been looking forward to this fight." Warden knew the more afraid he was, the sloppier he would fight.

"I am looking forward to seeing him too," Chance intoned, suddenly serious. His mind went back to the man blasting Athena at their first training camp. Getting into the back seat of the car he allowed himself to remember what the cabin looked like. No one could have survived that initial blast. Suddenly he was more anxious than afraid to meet Inferno in combat. He noticed Warden was studying him for a reaction, hoping for fear. Chance smiled a little, happy to disappoint the man.

Athena had told him she loved the rush of the arena, and the adrenalin shot from going into battle. He had thought it was kind of sick when she first told him. Those thoughts changed a bit after the field and spending time with her. He began to understand some of what she meant even if he never wanted it for himself. But in several hours he would be fighting the man who killed her. He would win, he had to.

They took him to a room in the cavernous underground of a facility where the arena was. Clotho had explained how they were built and he assumed this one was the same. Water, cement, and steel, he understood the need for it better than ever before. He was surprised to find a wall full of clothes all in his size, in styles ranging from t-shirts and jeans to flowing monk's robes. From the looks of it they did not know what clothes he would want to fight in so they gave him a little of everything. Shoes were a problem. There were combat boots, sneakers, thigh high boots, even cowboy boots. Chance didn't know what the floor was made of. It could be stone, wood, or even dirt.

Next to the clothes, and array of weapons hung on the wall. Looking at them he realized he had not practiced with a weapon in years. Picking out a well-balanced long sword he was not concerned, he figured the fight would be with energy. Breakfast was served, eggs, bacon, toast and coffee. He was not hungry but ate it all because he knew his body would need the fuel. Looking over the clothes he decided to stay with his usual clothes, jeans, a t-shirt and sneakers. He decided if the floor was sandy he could kick the shoes off quickly.

He bided his time and rested a bit, but it was tough to relax. The determination he felt when speaking to Warden waned as time passed and nerves tested. The woman who criticized his kinetic use walked in with a tray containing his lunch.

"Hello Chance," she smiled. "I brought you something to eat."

"Hello 'No One'," he retorted. "Thanks for the food?" She walked in the room and set the tray down. He noticed that there were two plates of food on it as well as a carafe of coffee and two cups.

"Please, join me." Melaniya gestured to the chair opposite the one she was sitting in. Chance cautiously sat down and watched the woman with curious eyes. The food on the plates was pork chops, potatoes and broccoli. She proceeded to cut a small piece of meat and fork it into her mouth watching him.

"So, are you going to tell me who you are?" Chance asked pouring them both a cup of coffee.

"I can't do that," she responded. "I am not supposed to be here." Chance started to eat watching the woman again curious as to who she was. She was dressed conservatively so she was not here to try to seduce him he concluded.

"So, why are you here?" he posed.

"I don't agree with this fight," she admitted. "I think it's a mistake. You are far too valuable to our leaders to lose against such a petty man like Inferno."

"Great thing to tell me six hours before I face him," Chance spat.

"Oh don't get me wrong, I think you can win," she said lightly. "You definitely have a chance." She smiled at the pun.

"Then again, why are you here?" he demanded.

"To feed you and warn you," her smile was tight and surprisingly full of concern. "Inferno hates you more than you know. He will try to play with you and hurt you very badly before he kills you."

"I know why I hate him," Chance said darkly, "But why does he hate me?"

"Chance, you did two things no one has ever done to the Overlords. The first was your escape, which was quite brilliant by the way."

"Thanks," he quipped. "And the second?"

"You evaded capture for close to three years." She responded bluntly. "No one has ever evaded us for more than a few weeks. Inferno was the man in charge of your hunt. So you embarrassed him and got him demoted from Hunter to Guard."

"Well he should have been better at his job then," Chance practically yelled. "If he was, maybe Athena would still be alive!" He was in a rage; energy was flowing around him and he was having a hard time bringing it down. Melaniya stood up and backed away from him.

"Then make him pay," she told him. "Don't let him get away with it. Live to try to take your revenge on us all." Chance stared at her as she calmly walked to the door and left.

Chance entered the arena, sword in hand, focused for combat. He didn't understand why the strange woman showed up to give him his lunch and a pep talk and he didn't care anymore. He looked around the arena. The floor was made of marble so his choice of shoes was fine. He could see rows of seats behind glass that he assumed was shatter proof, as Clotho had described. The walls were lined with dark wood which surprised him. The lighting here was not as good as the Manor. Chance thought it must be for effect. Everything about the room screamed evil, including the day they chose for his fight. Behind him the door slid down with a crash and he heard water filling the chamber. *So that's how it's done* he thought.

He was startled when he realized Inferno had entered from the other side while he was looking around. *Have to be more observant than that* he scolded himself. A man whose face he could not see from somewhere high in the arena, stood to announce the fight.

"Welcome Overlords and guests." His voice was quiet but could be heard eerily throughout the room. "Tonight we witness combat to the death between Inferno, a man known to many of you" A slight cheer rose from the crowd. Chance was not reassured to hear he had a following. "And Chance, the rebellious child who escaped us some three years ago"

The stands reverberated with booing, but he clearly heard Mouse yell, "Give him hell Chance!" above the noise.

"There will be no quarter given," the man continued. "Gentlemen...fight."

• •

With the kinetic energy barrier around him Inferno charged. Chance was surprised at the ferocity of the first attack. He only just raised his weapon in time to block the slash.

Inferno's scimitar was heavy but balanced. The shield he had been taught was working, kinetic energy was being dissipated before it could do any harm. His next attack pushed Chance a couple of steps back. He smiled; the boy was not able to keep up with him. He slashed a third time but changed the angle of attack at the last second. Chance could not react in time and the sword bit his shoulder causing him to cry out and retreat to the left. Inferno knew he outclassed the teen in swordplay, and was still countering his kinetic energy. As Chance retreated Inferno sent out a blast of heat that was blocked by an energy shield. *Good. You can block some energy so I can still have fun cutting you to ribbons,* he thought pressing his attack once more. *"Let's see how long that shield lasts when you're hurt and bleeding."* He scored two more hits, light wounds before Chance even tried to swing. Inferno parried the attack easy and gave a viscous downward slash with his scimitar.

Chance had not expected Inferno to charge physically. When the large curved sword was almost on top of him, he quickly sent out a kinetic burst to knock the man backward. He raised his own weapon and parried the attack but the vibration of the two swords hitting at such force sent a shock up his arm that he didn't expect. He tried to blow the marble up under Inferno's feet with a blast and again nothing happened. *"What the hell?"* he thought trying to block the weapon coming for his face. He retreated back and could not gain his bearings for a counter attack. Inferno was much better than him. *"Why is my energy not working?!"* Chance thought furiously. He missed an attack and his shoulder was sliced open. Shifting away again he staunched the bleeding with the technique he learned from the healer as a fire blast came at him. His shield deflected it easy and he was happy to know some of his energy was working. He concentrated on the blade as he tried to defend against the attacks. He was sliced across the top of the thigh and again on his arm when he realized all his attempts to melt the blade like he did the stove were failing. Attacking back proved fruitless and Chance dove out of the way as an overhead strike came down. Rolling across the hard marble floor he jammed his left shoulder and his fingers went numb. Knowing teleports were allowed in the arena he tried to port across the room as he rolled to his feet, but instead he was slashed across the chest. The pain was intense; his port had failed. His left arm was still not moving very well and he could get cut pretty much at will. The blast of wind energy that was sent at him was countered by his shield just like the fire. He was grateful that something was working. *"I am going to be in serious trouble soon, maybe if I draw him in."*

Inferno was enjoying himself immensely. Chance had so far evaded any killing blows but he was sustaining injuries at a quick pace. All of his energy attacks were being deflected but that could not last forever. He attacked again in a series of sword blows. Chance had turned his body to the side and was using his sword with one hand. The change in style made Inferno pause for a moment, wondering what the boy had planned. He sent out his shockwave attack and was mildly frustrated that it did no good. When he attacked again, Chance retreated and got lucky with a couple of blocks. Inferno charged a static burst and watched as Chance caught it. Still attacking with the scimitar he was given a shock when Chance stepped *into* a wide swing and not away from it. The hilt of his weapon caught Chance on the shoulder as an elbow crashed into his chin. It knocked him backwards and he saw stars for a moment. He used hyper acceleration to retreat to the other side of the room to shake off the lucky hit.

Watching the fight from the stands Caval was ready to jump out of his skin. Chance was at the mercy of Inferno. He could plainly read the energy surrounding the two. Everything Chance sent at Inferno disappeared before it could so much as puff air. The concentrated line of energy sent at Inferno's sword, probably intended to melt or freeze it, never touched it. He wondered what was wrong with him. This was not the crazy powerful style of fighting he faced off against.

"He's getting killed out there," Spark cried out when Chance was slashed across the chest.

"He's not bleeding from any of his wounds," Mouse remarked calmly. "His time with the healer was well spent."

"That won't matter when Inferno takes his head!" Spark retorted. "Why isn't he attacking with energy?"

"Keep calm. He won't let Inferno beat him, not after the man killed his girlfriend." Mouse assured.

"Killed his girlfriend?" Caval asked in a surprised voice. "What do you mean?"

"When inferno captured him he was staying at a cabin with his girlfriend," Mouse explained. "She didn't make it."

Caval went pale. "I know it's terrible, he won't let that man live. He owes him for Athena." Mouse finished.

Caval's mind raced as he realized that for the last three weeks at least Chance thought Athena was dead. Then he was impressed as they watched Inferno almost get knocked out.

"How the hell did he do that?" Spark shouted.

"No trained sword fighter would have expected that attack. It was totally insane and dangerous," Caval stated. Spark and Mouse stared at him, too surprised to realize he was giving some of what he knew away, "Only Chance could have pulled off something like that!" he laughed. With Mouse and Spark still trying to figure out how 'Cal' could know something like that, he thought, *Chance you have to make it man just so I can tell you Athena is alive!*

Catching his breath as Inferno retreated the length of the arena, Chance could not believe his good fortune. *I thought I would have taken a bad shoulder wound to pull off that move!* The healing energy flowing through his left arm was working and he was getting solid movement back. Trying to attack once again he was frustrated when it failed again. *How is he stopping everything?!* Taking the sword in both hands he prepared for another assault. He saw the blur of movement and unconsciously countered it with the wrap around electric power he learned from Spark. Inferno showed no emotion as he retreated away. Watching the man tilt his head to consider his next assault Chance swallowed hard. He was glad he did all the training keeping a constant energy flow. His body was in bad shape. The sword wounds were not bleeding much but he was beginning to feel shaky because of the damage to his muscles. This fight had already lasted longer than his battle with Caval or the one at the cabin. Thinking of the cabin his hands gripped his sword again and this time he charged.

Surprised to see Chance charging at him Inferno threw a wall of fire up across the arena. He could see through the flames that Chance stopped short and held his arm out to try to counter attack. Of course the kinetic barrier was still doing its work and the boy had to be getting weaker by now. He saw Chance drop to one knee with the sword point in the floor. Laughing, he could not help himself, he had to gloat a little. "You don't understand why you can't attack me do your boy?" he yelled.

"The thought had crossed my mind," Chance countered breathing heavy. Inferno just laughed harder at this.

"There is nothing your kinetic energy can do to me Chance," Inferno continued to laugh. "Joule taught me well. I have a counter for anything you can produce." His voice became whimsical. "You will die knowing that your little fireball is cursing you from whatever hell I sent her to." He was still taunting Chance when the fire went out.

• •

Chance dropped the sword to the floor and stood up. At the mention of Athena his mind seemed to reach a level of clarity he did not know existed. Cold anger surged through him as he reached out and cut off the fire at its source. Shaking his head slightly he asked "Why does everyone think I'm a Kinetic?" With his eye locked on Inferno he sent a wave of energy into the floor that cracked it down to the metal beneath. "I was wondering why everything I was using was failing." Reaching out with a pulse of magnetism he ripped open a hole in the steel plates. "Thanks' for clarifying that for me." The concrete above the water dissolved into a powder from the sound burst that hit it. "Her name was Athena." Fine mist started pouring out of the hole in the floor Chance had created. Inferno moved to attack and ran into an invisible wall of pure force. "You don't want to miss this Inferno." Mist filled the room at an alarming speed, obscuring the two combatants from sight. Air began to move in a circular direction. Chance stood in the middle of the space, perfectly dry, as clouds coalesced near the ceiling blotting out the lights.

Inferno felt like he was standing in a thunderstorm. He could not see where Chance was and his energy was all over the room so he could not pinpoint the boy's location. He had to have moved, there was no way he would just stand there. He experienced a moment of surprise at the level of power being displayed. Inferno realized he had made a mistake thinking Chance used kinetic energy almost exclusively. He assumed the boy could use other types of energy, but would stick to his main. Consequently, he was not prepared for what he was seeing. The fight had turned and rain was falling from the ceiling. It was as dark as when clouds block out the sun.

Inferno stated to move around the edges of the combat space. He radiated heat to keep the rain off him, unaware that he was helping to feed the storm. He needed to keep calm and strike the boy down as soon as he saw him again. He had watched Chance drop his sword so he knew he was unarmed. *"Where did the boy learn to do this and how can he have this much energy at his age?"* he was thinking as the wind picked up even more. The rain was starting to fall at an angle and the wind grew stronger and stronger. When lightening started flashing in the air he suffered the first taste of true fear in his life.

To those watching the battle, the arena was blacked out. The last thing they had witnessed was Chance starting the insanity before them. The most energy sensitive of them were struggling to find the two combatants through the gale that was forming. Now and again they were able to pinpoint

Inferno as he strained against the winds that were reaching higher and higher speeds. Of Chance, no one could see a thing. His energy was so vast; it was as if he himself was the room. Thunder boomed in the arena and lighting flashed across what passed for the sky. The fog had cleared as sheets of rain whipped the glass they watched through.

The leader of the Overlords stood in his box smiling. Harbinger and Melaniya sat in stunned silence at the spectacle before them. Mouse and Spark who had been trying to get answers from "Cal" were also silent watching in disbelief at what their friend was doing. Caval sat back with a smile, wondering if he should be preparing to shield the teens on this side of the arena. No one knew how far this was going to go. Displays like this had only seen from the Queen and Phantom, two of the most powerful energy users ever known to have existed.

Pushing his energy to its limits, it was not enough yet. Chance closed his eyes and dug deeper adding to the swirling madness around him. Standing in the eye of the hurricane he had created he could feel the fear and panic coming from Inferno. Chance smiled. Lightning strikes chased Inferno who was running in the same direction as the wind, hardly able to keep his feet. Chance picked up the sword that was at his feet and tossed it into the swirling winds. *Just another thing for Inferno to avoid.* He smiled darkly. *Any minute now and he will be swept away.*

The glass around the arena floor started to rattle from the intense pressure. Chance silently thanked Inferno for adding so much heat to the room and helping him create the hurricane. He felt the moment that Inferno was swept off his feet. The fear was like a smell in the air. The man's screams were lost in the sound of the howling wind. Suddenly, the glass around the room shattered from the vibration. A collective yell of surprise went up in the strands as rain; lighting and glass assaulted the audience. Inferno was shredded with glass pieces and his lifeless body was tossed against the shield the leaders had raised in the leadership box. Chance felt his body swaying and smiled knowing he had won. He had used far too much energy and he was struggling to stay awake. "For you Athena," he whispered before passing out.

The stands were in complete chaos. Glass was everywhere. Many people were injured from lighting flashes or cuts. Almost everyone was soaked; water was still running down the walls to the arena floor where it disappeared through the hole Chance had made. The only group untouched was the teens. Someone had erected a shield that protected them all. Most of the ceiling lights were out, the rest were flickering.

Mouse jumped down into the arena not caring who saw her and ran over to Chance who was in danger of drowning in the aftermath of his own storm. In the leadership box, a man stood up and started clapping lightly and uttered two words.

"Winner, Tempest!"

Confessions

Caval waited patiently in the barracks for Mouse to return. She had insisted on helping take Chance to the healing room. Spark was still giving him dirty looks and the room was abuzz with discussion of the fight. Caval found more than a few looks tossed his way as well. Not everyone, but a few had seen him put up the barrier that protected them from Chance's power. Spark and Caval had convinced them to keep their mouths shut but he was not sure how long it would last. Caval only hoped the adults had been too busy to notice. The battle had had the opposite effect Warden had hoped. Chance was their hero; he had taken on a guard and won spectacularly. Most of the teens thought Chance had shielded them as well as shattering the glass. Even most of Eliza's group had come around realizing there was no way he had sided with the Overlords, who were again being referred to as their captors.

"So...'Cal'," Spark began when they were alone. "Do you want to tell me who or what you really are?"

"Umm, a teenager?" he responded.

"How the hell did you erect a shield that strong that fast?!" Spark hissed, "This is your second day here and you are supposed to be a nobody! When Mouse asked you to sit with us I thought ok take pity on the new guy, then you do something like that!" he sputtered.

"Can we wait for Mouse?" Caval whispered.

"Fine. She knows you are more than you pretend to be as well." Spark warned. They sat there in an uncomfortable silence listening to the kids in the room talk. Spark continued to throw accusatory glares at him. Twenty minutes later Mouse walked in and headed straight towards the pair, looking serious. Caval knew twenty questions was going to start as soon as she gave them an update on Chance.

"He's going to be fine," she stated first. "Some woman named Raeya showed up with a personal healer and informed our healer to take a hike." Mouse shook her head. "Mostly he is just exhausted." She looked up to see they had an audience. "He's fine and I need to talk to my friends. Scram!" she shouted. They were left alone quickly.

"So his sword wounds will be ok?" Spark questioned.

"Scars, nothing more," Mouse assured. Caval cringed at the withering look she gave him. "You on the other hand are going to have a lot more then scars if you don't tell me who the hell you are 'Cal.'" Her voice was cold and the temperature of the area around them had dropped a few degrees.

"How about you try not to freeze me to death and I don't destroy half the room defending myself?" Caval warned. Mouse sat on the edge of the bed and glared at him. She had pretty eyes he thought. He also realized she was the only girl in this side of the barracks.

"Fine. I get the idea that you're not kidding when you say something like that." Mouse agreed.

"Why are you the only woman here?" he asked suddenly.

"Mouse sleeps where she wants to. The guards learned that her fist month here." Spark responded exasperated. "Now answer her question."

"Oh. Sorry, just weird." He remarked. "How much did Chance tell you about Athena?"

"Enough to know he loved her," Mouse filled in.

"Did he tell you about his fight with her friend?"

"No, he was pretty closed off about the whole situation," Spark chimed in. Caval frowned at this, thinking it would be much harder to convince them now.

"Damnit," he swore. "I was hoping he would be here when I spoke about this but I have no choice after his fight." Thinking over his options he decided on honesty.

"When you spoke about what?" Mouse demanded. Looking around and wrapping a minor cone of silence around them he began.

"I was captured on purpose to rescue him." Caval whispered. Mouse raised an eyebrow looking at him.

"You really don't expect us to believe that do you?" she smirked. Caval sighed heavily.

"I know it sounds like a load of bull but it's true. How else could I have created that barrier?" he asked looking directly at Mouse.

"If you're telling the truth, who sent you?" she challenged.

"Athena's dad," He stated simply. Spark and Mouse looked at him in disbelief. "I was supposed to contact MY dad with a location when I got here. I didn't expect to get whipped half to death when I first arrived," he snapped.

"How are you supposed to contact him?" Spark scoffed.

"Mentally of course," he responded as if that was the obvious answer.

"That's not possible," Mouse countered. "You're not close enough for a mental conversation."

"He could be on the other side of the globe and I could contact my dad," Caval responded. "Distance is only in your head, just like teleporting." Mouse was looking at him with critical eyes.

"Say we believe you," she consented. "How would you get him out?"

"Well we can't until the after the New Year at least," Caval confessed, "The restrictions on battle and raids are in place till then."

"What restrictions?" Spark questioned.

"I can explain that part later. For now, just understand that I am highly trained and here to help." Caval swore.

"That's why you knew about that sword move?" Spark countered.

"You let yourself get whipped to save him," Mouse said in awe looking at him with a new respect.

"Athena would kill me herself if I didn't do everything I can to get him out." He smiled back.

"Wait. She's still alive?" Spark stammered.

"Yes, one of the many things Chance needs to know. She went for a walk that morning. One of Inferno's men knocked her out and left her to freeze to death. Horatius, her father, found her and brought her home."

"I still don't get how you plan to rescue him," Mouse put in.

"Well, we're going to rescue the whole camp now," Caval said with conviction. "My father and his friends are very powerful. I just need to get a lay of the camp, how many guards, and things like that." He could see they were still skeptical. "Chance knows who I am. When he gets out of the infirmary we can all sit down and he will tell you." He looked around and found a pen and some paper and wrote something down. "When we see him, he will call me this name. Don't open the paper till then so you know I am telling you the truth." Mouse took the paper and slipped it into her pocket.

"If you're trying to double cross us, I'll make sure even your ashes don't remain," Mouse said seriously.

"Of that I have no doubt." Caval smiled back and lay down on a bunk. Spark and Mouse lay down on bunks close to him. The rest of the teens in the room slept a little bit away from the trio because of Mouse's outburst.

• •

When word finally came from Caval about how things were going it was Christmas morning. Cyrus considered this the best present he could have gotten. Clotho and he were worried from the three days of silence since he had let them know he was about to be captured. Cyrus was disturbed when he heard Chance had a fight with Inferno the night before. Apparently, these Overlords did not believe in the precepts everyone else followed. He seriously considered launching a raid early because of that. However, he abandoned the plan because he felt strongly that they were stewards of the law. If they broke them, everyone else would too. Sitting in a meeting room Christmas morning the fifteen leaders discussed what Cyrus had been told.

"That was Chance?!" Meteo exclaimed.

"You knew there was a fight last night?" Ares questioned.

"Joule told me she was invited to watch an unofficial 'challenge' because she paid back a debt by training someone. I can only assume it was Inferno because it was his fight."

"Good Gods." Cyrus shook his head. "She trained Inferno to kill Chance while we've been desperately trying to save the boy."

"Did she go?" Hera questioned.

"No, but another friend of hers did. Said he was nearly speared by a sword when the glass in the arena shattered," Meteo replied.

"Joule needs to pick better friends," Gerrod declared.

"People, all that is secondary," Cyrus spoke thinking all the while that Chance was stronger than even Caval had thought. "He has some help. A couple of stronger teens and the camp seem to be on his side. I think the Overlords are regretting ever re-capturing him."

"What's our next move?" Ares asked.

"Well, we know he's alive, defiant and strong," Cyrus continued. "Caval will be able to fill in more details in a few days. The group is located in eastern Georgia close to the

South Carolina boarder. Their base of operations, like most of ours, is off the grid.”

“In the States?” Hera asked shocked. “I thought they were overseas somewhere.”

“We all did,” he agreed. “As soon as I have a location pinned down a hundred percent I’ll share with the rest of you. In the meantime, prepare your raiding parties. We will attack as soon as we can.”

“Athena is going,” Horatius added. “I promised her that she could. We don’t know what mental state he will be in and we will need her.” He looked at Ares as if daring him to question the decision. Ares just nodded in consent and understanding.

“Enjoy your Christmas everybody. We will meet in a few days to discuss attack details.” Cyrus finished.

• •

Warden was not about to allow Chance to join the rest of the teens. He was too popular now and too much of an influence. Mouse and Spark were waiting for his return. The new teen Cal had taken to hanging around with them as well. He would need to break him of that quickly. Eliza had reported that most of her group excluding Bevan had deserted her. The talk around the camp had become ‘us versus them’ again.

“I don’t know how you did that Tempest, but you will learn your place.” Warden spat Christmas morning. Tempest had been healed by Lady Raeya’s personal healer for some reason and was already sitting up in his cell.

“If you don’t let me out there, they will do the damage themselves,” Chance told him.

"Why do you think that?" he asked.

"Well, you all set up the rivalry and everything. If they see, I am rewarded for winning by being put in solitary confinement they may rebel on their own."

Warden thought about what the boy said and realized he was probably right. This was disastrous. "You may have a point Tempest." Warden admitted, "But I can't trust you out there with them."

"First, why are you calling me Tempest?"

"That's the name our Leader gave you after your fight with Inferno." Warden grimaced.

"Fantastic," he said sarcastically "well you can trust me because I still don't want innocent kids to die. And although Eliza hates me, I don't want her to die either."

"What else?" Warden frowned sensing there was more.

"Stop whipping Mouse. I won't cause trouble," Chance declared, "but I'll never be one of your soldiers." He took a sip of water and looked Warden in the eyes.

"Very well, but one wrong move and I will have you shot." Warden warned. "Let's see how well your shields hold up to that."

• •

Chance walked out to the yard looking for Mouse and Spark. He knew that Warden's words were an empty threat. Something changed in the arena last night. What he didn't let on was that he was so drained he could not even contact his friends mentally. He had nothing left and was scared he might not again. The memories of last night were perfectly clear however, but he had no idea how he had pushed out that much energy. He shuddered thinking about how cold and calculating he was in battle, even though a hurricane inside the arena was damned cool. When he spied the pair he was looking for he stopped dead in his tracks. They were talking to a young man whose face he would never forget. *How the hell did he get here?*

Mouse saw him looking and just walked towards him, the two boys in tow.

"Chance! You're up!" she said happily and gave him a hug.

"Hey Mouse, good to see you," he smiled looking at Caval. "I had a good healer; still feel a little sore though." He shook hands with Spark who was looking pleased that Chance was standing.

"This is our new friend Cal," Spark stated. "He was in the healing room with Mouse after being 'educated' by Warden."

"Cal is it?" Chance questioned extending his hand.

"Good to meet you Chance," Caval responded taking his hand. "That was one hell of a power display last night." He smiled.

"Let's go sit somewhere and talk," Mouse said cheerily. "You must still want to be off your feet as much as possible," she finished.

"Great idea. I am feeling a little run down still." He tried to contact them mentally but didn't have access to it yet. They walked to a picnic table near one of the fences. The guards watched them a bit but made no further move. When they sat Caval looked at him and laughed.

"You can tell them who I am," he stated. "I already tried to explain everything."

"Caval," he whispered, "What are you doing here?" Mouse pulled out a piece of paper and looked at it, and then nodded to Spark as she handed it to Chance. It read 'I am Caval'.

"Ok, you were telling the truth," she said to Caval.

"Again, what are you doing here?" he realized he had been asking that question of a lot of people the last couple of days.

"Athena's dad sent me," Caval explained, "I need you to be very calm when I tell you this. Don't make a scene. But he saved her from freezing to death in the forest." He said it quickly, hoping Chance would not draw the guard's attention.

"Athena is alive?" he asked in a voice barely above a whisper. The shock of hearing that made it very hard to keep a poker face during this conversation.

"Yes, very much so. Just keep calm and don't show your emotions." Caval smiled, "She had to spend a day in the Tank to fight off some frostbite but she is ok." Chance closed his eyes in disbelief and joy, rubbing them feigning exhaustion to cover his emotions.

"Does she know you're here?" he questioned.

"She kind of got into some trouble before I left. Nothing major and she is off house arrest today in fact." Caval explained. "But her dad was supposed to tell her about my plan after I was gone."

"Why couldn't I contact Athena at the Cabin?" Chance challenged, feeling like this was all too good to be true.

"Athena was out cold. Horatius said he had to actually find her soul to locate her." Caval supplied not at all put out by the accusatory tone in the question.

"I can't reach you right now," Mouse added, "We tried this morning and thought it was because you were in a null-room or something."

"About that," Chance laughed and proceeded to tell them about his meeting with Warden and how he could not tap into energy. They were not at all surprised that Warden had threatened to keep him apart from the others.

"What you did last night Chance has not been seen in twenty years," Caval told him. "Your energy is just run down. My teacher had me do that to myself on purpose several times so I know what it feels like."

"What is your plan?" Chance asked.

For the next few hours the four spoke, pretending to laugh at jokes and having Chance show his new scars. Caval explained what he could about the events starting with the betrayal and ending with exposing his abilities to save the teens and how he had to explain it to Mouse and Spark. Chance was grateful that Caval had been able to shield the teens; he had not been told they were going to be there. He remembered hearing Mouse cheer him on but was so far gone during the fight he didn't take into account he could have hurt them.

"Now we wait," Caval finished. "My father is getting a small army ready to raid this place as soon as they are allowed."

"Well," Chance smiled. "At least I know why they are afraid of me." He was laughing now feeling like maybe there was hope.

Preparation

The five days following Christmas were a flurry of activity. Each organization contacted their strongest members for the raid. Cyrus had been in contact with Caval as much as possible to get details about the camp and the guards. They had learned that twenty guards were on the grounds at all times. The man called Warden was always there. Cyrus detected an odd mental sensation from Caval when he mentioned him. Most of the kids and teens at the camp now looked up to Chance as a leader and mentor. Caval had played off trying to learn how to manipulate energy on purpose, but kept a low profile. The worst thing that happened was a close call while communicating with Cyrus. Caval had been so deep in it, that he did not see the guard approach him.

Mouse had saved the day when she grabbed his face and kissed him, then said, "Yes, you did it! Great job I heard you in my head! And of course I'll be your girlfriend!"

The guard had turned away and Cyrus was treated to some rather inappropriate thoughts before Caval cut off the connection. Athena had learned all this by sitting in the planning meetings. The adults had a fun laugh about whether Mouse would keep up the act and how Caval would have to play along. Secretly Athena hoped something was really starting to happen there. Her best friend was like her, too picky for his own good and alone for too long. Using the

"Hey, I've never had a girlfriend before. I'm enjoying the attention and the learning curve," Caval answered with a grin. Mouse punched him in the arm for that comment.

"Don't listen to him. He knows we felt a connection right from the time we were both lying face down with our backs flayed open," she teased.

"I have to say, that's the strangest way I ever heard of people meeting," Chance mused out loud.

"So are we ready?" Spark asked, cutting off all conversation about the budding relationship.

New Year's was in two days and Chance was trying to make sure all the details were in place. They still did not know exactly what their part would be other than to take out guards if they could. It was someone else's job to get the kids out. He had not met the two women who would be doing that but Caval assured him they had motherly natures and the kids would follow them. Chance just wanted Harbinger. The man was behind all of this and he needed to pay. Caval promised Mouse she would have a shot at Warden. The adults wanted to capture the two for information but the four teens agreed that they needed to die.

"As ready as we can be." Chance said. They all knew the plan, but he went over it again. "I will port Mouse and myself into Wardens quarters as soon as the lock is down. I imagine that's where Harbinger will arrive as well."

"Don't forget, Athena will be here," Caval reminded.

"You better not be lying to me about that Cal. I can't take losing her twice." Chance countered still using Caval's fake name.

"He would not have said it if it was not true," Mouse defended her possible boyfriend. They still were not exactly sure if this was a real thing or not.

"Are you sure you want to take out Harbinger?" Caval questioned.

"I thought when I killed Inferno it would be over," Chance explained, "But I know now that Inferno was a symptom. Harbinger is the cause of all this. It ends with him."

"Well then I'll support your decision. I trust you after everything you did for Athy," Caval said seriously. "However, the leaders coming to the raid might see otherwise."

"They're not my leaders yet," Chance clarified. "I don't have to take orders from them unless I decide to join."

"Let's not start second guessing ourselves now," Mouse spoke up. "We have our plan. Just stick to it."

"Well then, we just need to wait for the raid to start, and not get dead between now and then," Chance said with mock confidence.

Two days later the four were sitting in the barracks, the sense of anticipation all around. They had enjoyed a good show of lights and illusions. A radio had been brought in and everyone was listening to the music. Guards were making their usual rounds but some of them had bottles in their hands. Eliza had her circle of friends around her. Bevan as always by her side. Over all, the atmosphere was one of excitement.

At twelve midnight, the ball dropped on New Year's Eve...and all hell broke loose at camp.

Liberation

When the attack started the camp guards were taken completely by surprise. Two of the teleport lockers were taken out in the first few seconds. The Overlords had not considered that teleport locks could stop people from teleporting out, but could not stop someone from teleporting in. The shock of an overwhelming force of fighters arriving both in and out of camp was too much for the slightly inebriated guards. Athena arrived in the middle of the barracks with the team as promised. A collective scream rose up from the kids who were frightened by the arrival of such a fighting force. Clotho and Illyria had tagged along with this team as it would be the best place to set up the gates to free the kids. When one of the teleport lockers fought back against a raider, they created an explosion of energy in the yard which killed them both. When two of the remaining three went down, Chance felt access to teleport energy return.

"Mouse!" he yelled. "It's time!"

Taking his hand, Mouse prepared for the port, when Bevan attacked Chance from behind, slashing him from shoulder to hip. Eliza who was standing next to Bevan stabbed Mouse in the side with a katar a dagger with an h-shaped horizontal hand grip which results in the blade sitting above the user's knuckles to deliver a punching blow. Chance registered the pain of the attack that disrupted his concentration and did not manage to port. Turning he struck

Bevan full in the chest with energy gleaming in his hand. The resulting blow caved in the young man's ribs killing him instantly. Mouse gathered her energy and blasted Eliza with a full discharge of ice. The girl screamed and grabbed the side of her face backing away from the enraged young woman. Chance could already see the damage caused would blind her in one eye and disfigure her.

"I won't forget this Chance," Eliza managed to say before she teleported out, surprising them both.

"Mouse!" Caval yelled and put his hands on either side of the wound in her side. "This will hurt like hell!" he exclaimed and cauterized it with a blast of fire. She screamed in pain and slumped to the floor. Around them the room was filled with the sounds of crying kids, shocked teens and raiders. It was now twenty seconds into the New Year.

• •

The plan was going well. They had lost a man taking out the teleport lockers but all four were dead now. Cyrus could not think about the loss at the moment, there would be time to add up losses later. Clotho had contacted him briefly to let him know a gate was already open and kids were being sent through to the waiting medical teams. Perion and Hippocrates would have their hands full.

In the yard, a guard rushed out of a building with a machine gun. It startled Cyrus for a moment to see a man with a gun, but he recovered and took the man out with a power ball. Behind him his team scanned for more energy signatures and reported there were twenty inside. Cyrus knew that at least a few would be nursemaids. He didn't want to hurt the caregivers if he could spare them. One of his men opened the door and Menelaus went in first. The sounds of a battle started immediately. They rushed in and found him crouched over a crib protecting the infant inside. There was a whole in his back that Cyrus knew immediately would be fatal. The woman who tried to kill the infant as a distraction was currently turning to stone. The cells in her body were solidifying from the energy Menelaus had fired at her as he protected the baby.

"She tried to kill the kids as soon as I entered," he breathed. Cyrus could only look at his friend and fellow leader as he died. Around the room he could hear people saying that the room was secure. They took two women and one-man hostage. Cyrus contacted Illyria to let her know the location of the younger children's room so she could open a gate here and get them to safety. Picking his friend gingerly off the crib he sent his body to the specified location at headquarters for losses. He could not fathom the evil of this group using guns and targeting infants. The woman who was now a statue had attacked the baby as a distraction. Cyrus walked over and delivered a viscous punch to what remained destroying the stone.

"Let's get these little ones out of here," Cyrus informed Illyria who had just arrived. "I'll leave a detail here to make sure you're safe until the room is empty." He shook his head in anger and sadness. "We lost Menelaus," he informed her then walked out to the courtyard area to wait for the Overlords to arrive. He knew that reinforcements would be coming and now he was looking forward to it.

• •

Athena had just turned in the direction of a familiar feeling energy in time to see Chance slashed across the back. Everything happened so fast that she had hardly moved when the young woman who must be Mouse fell to the floor.

Caval was picking the woman up and his eyes locked on hers as another boy flashed across the room and killed a guard who had just walked in to check on the commotion. The man's body shook from a blast of electricity that left a fine ozone smell and less fine burned smell in the air. Running across the room in her direction, Caval and Chance almost collided with her before stopping. Chance grabbed her in a fierce embrace which she gladly retuned. The chaos in the room around them with raiders moving out and children screaming made the reunion feel surreal.

"My god you are alive," he whispered holding her a moment longer.

"Athena! I need you to take Mouse to Clotho now!" Caval yelled pointing at his mother. She had never seen her best friend look so frantic before. It took her a second to realize that the young woman was in trouble.

"What about you?" she asked taking Mouse as Chance let her go.

"I have someone to take care of." He said in a deadly voice looking at Chance.

"We will be right back," Chance assured Athena, kissing the top of her head. "Get her to Clotho." Putting his hand on Caval's shoulder they teleported out.

"Damnit!" she thought, realizing they had left her behind. She had Chance's blood on her arms and hands from his wound, but she had to take this girl to Clotho and the gate. Thinking of the wound Mouse sustained and briefly wondering who the young woman was who had teleported out, she carried the girl in her arms to the waiting gate.

"Athena?" Clotho asked startled seeing the injured girl in her arms. "What happened?" The gate was open and Athena could see the infirmary at the Forum house on the other side.

"No time, I need you to take this girl through."

"I can't leave the gate," Clotho said. "Cyrus found the younger kids in a separate place. Illyria has a gate opened there."

If I take her through I can't get back Athena thought to herself remembering Cyrus's orders "If you must leave the field of battle, do not return under any circumstances." As much as she wanted to stay and fight, she had promised Caval to get Mouse to a healer. "If you see Chance, tell him I am taking care of his friend," she told Clotho and stepped through into the insanity beyond.

It was almost more chaotic there than it was back in the barracks. Kids were crying. Teams of adults were running around finding them beds to sit on, and healers from the group called the Physicians who were being paid a crazy amount of money were tending them.

Spotting Perion talking to an older boy, Athena screamed for her. "Perion I need your help here!"

The senior healer at the Forum looked over eyes going wide. "What happened?" she asked in a professional manner. Athena described the scene she witnessed in as much detail as she could.

"This girl needs a Tank if she is to survive," she stated simply. She touched Athena and Mouse and the three women phased to a new room. "Gyro!" she hollered. "Prep a new Tank. We will have a DNA sample in a moment."

"Will she be ok?" Athena asked. "Caval is really worried about her."

"I don't know yet," Perion said truthfully, "He acted quickly but there is still internal bleeding and she will probably need blood. I need to type match her and get her in a tank STAT!" She had grabbed a pair of scissors and started cutting the young woman's clothes off. The two women were shocked when they saw the scaring and fresh wounds on Mouse's back.

"What can I do?" Athena asked.

"We have your blood type on file; if you're a match you can give her some. We have more in our bank but I am assuming there will be many injuries tonight and every little bit will count."

Athena rolled her sleeve up and wondered how things had changed so dramatically for her in the span of ten minutes. Instead of fighting side by side with Chance as she hoped, she was fighting to help save the life of a girl she didn't know for her best friend. Looking at Mouse's back she realized this young woman had been through more than she could imagine.

"Take what you need, she can't die." Athena said seriously. A technician came into the room announcing the Tank was prepped and the girl's blood type was AB positive.

"Great," Perion affirmed, "She is a universal receiver. We can use you, now let's go." Athena followed watching healers get in place around a tank with liquid being pumped in infused with Mouse's DNA. They put her inside and placed the oxygen mask on her face. A needle was inserted into her arm leading to a saline solution and an empty bottle. Athena sat on an elevated chair above the Tank. They put a needle in her arm which immediately started filling the bottle with her blood.

This is going to be a long night, Athena thought looking at the girl in the now filling Tank. "Happy New Year." she said sarcastically, wondering how things were with the raid.

• •

They arrived just outside of Warden's office. Caval winced at the teleport and realized that Mouse who had never ported before might have been put out of commission by the mode of transportation. He filed that away to think about another time. For now, he was going to fulfill Mouse's wish and take out Warden. Chance was more focused now that he had seen Athena. Hopefully, Athena had gotten Mouse to the infirmary. They would take care of her. He was having trouble containing his energy. They could feel Warden inside; the man was charging for a fight. Chance blasted the door off with a kinetic ball and they both stood aside.

"Boys," came from an unexpected voice. "Why don't you come in and we will face off like men." Harbinger laughed.

"Uh...we're good out here, thanks." Caval responded. Chance laughed nervously. Two blasts of pen thin energy went through the wall next to each of the boy's heads.

"You realize I can see you?" Harbinger announced with light laughter still in his voice.

"We should go in," Chance said suddenly. "It's only fair after all."

Caval looked at him like he was crazy, but nodding his ascent, entered first. He was not surprised to see Warden and Harbinger, but there was a woman with them standing towards the back of the office.

"Well, isn't this nice!" Harbinger said. "All of us together as my camp is being destroyed." His voice became much darker. "Was it you who brought them here?"

"Well, I didn't bring them here, but I did let them know where you were," Caval answered smugly.

"I helped," Chance smiled.

"Your girlfriend is dead by the way," Caval announced hoping to throw off the man in front of him.

"Ahh, Wisp. We thought as much," Harbinger responded. "She was nothing more than a useful tool. I hope she took a few of you out with her."

"Nope. My girlfriend killed her," Chance said happily. Caval could feel his friend charging up for a powerful attack.

"I am going to enjoy flaying the skin off you both," Warden declared. His energy whip cracked with more power than Caval had ever seen it. Warden slashed it and the table in the office fell in two.

Much stronger version of the man's favorite energy apparently he thought. "That's only possible when someone sits there and lets you whip them," Caval stated darkly. His mind went to the scarred back of Mouse and his power flared up higher.

"I think this boy wants to kill you Warden," Harbinger said lightly. "You can take him. I want Tempest."

"Do you have this?" Chance thought to Caval.

"Warden will be toast. But we need to watch the woman. Three on two is not the best odds even for people like us," Caval responded.

"That's the woman who gave me advice on how to fight Inferno. I don't think she will join the battle." Chance told him.

"Well, let's hope you're right. I need more space to kill this asshole. Good luck and don't die!" Caval flashed across the room and collided with Warden, knocking him through the wall into the open yard behind. They came to a stop about twenty feet away from the building.

Warden's whip slashed down and caught him across the back of his left calf. Screaming out in pain, Caval flashed away from his opponent. Facing off against the man, he brought all his anger and training to the forefront of his mind. Quickly he erected a shield with multiple facets like a diamond that he hoped would deflect the whip and attacked. The ground beneath Warden's feet softened and started pulling him in. Warden flew out with an explosion of sand, his energy whip slashing out and crossing the ten-foot distance easily. Caval's shield deflected the blow and he countered with a thin beam of force that punched a hole in Warden's left arm. Turning the bursting sands into hands, he tried to grab Warden to throw him to the ground. An unexpected flash of light blinded him temporarily.

A slash of Warden's whip made it partially through his deflection shield and flayed open his cheek. Caval kept his concentration and used the blind fighting techniques his teacher had drilled into him. He heard Warden land on the ground not far to his left. Turning quickly, he stomped on the ground and infused the earth with heat which created a magma wave to engulf Warden. The man's shields held for a moment then Caval heard the muffled scream and felt the man's energy cease. Caval sat on the ground hoping no one was near trying to clear his eyes. He was afraid to reach out for Chance for fear of distracting him if he was fighting Harbinger. Instead he reached out for Horatius.

••

When the Overlord reinforcements arrived, Cyrus relished the coming battle. He had been in more battles than any other person on the planet with possibly the exception of Typhoonus. The pair never felt the need to compare notes. The first three to enter the courtyard were crushed by a disembodied hand of energy created by Cyrus. Ares and Gabriel worked in combination to cut down five more with swords that moved faster than the eye could see. When Cyrus's people raided the compound they had not been expected and the enemy was not prepared. The reinforcements, however, were prepared.

Cyrus' forces were ready to annihilate anyone porting in. They had been instructed to stay away from the field and not come back if for some reason they had to leave. Otherwise, they would have been killed before anyone realized they were not the enemy. His team had taken damage, there were several injuries and one woman had lost her hand. However aside from the two deaths he knew of, they had not sustained anything worse. Cyrus recognized this would be over soon and started looking for his son.

••

Athena heard the yell of a young man coming from the next room, demanding to know where Mouse was. It had been almost twenty minutes since they put Mouse in the Tank and she was doing better already. It was not a guarantee that she would be ok but Athena had seen people in worse shape survive. Leaving her chair, she found the door to the main room in the infirmary where the camp kids were being kept. When she stepped in she saw the chaos had been put under some sort of control. Most of the kids seemed to be content with meals on their laps or drinks in their hands. The young man causing trouble was the one she had witnessed kill the guard. She hoped she was correct in her assumption that this was Spark.

"Spark!" she called out across the room. The young man looked her direction but did not see her. Waving her hand, she yelled his name again. "Spark!" He wrapped himself in what looked like lightening and was next to her the next instant. There was a collective scream from some of the kids who were just getting settled.

"Who are you?" Spark demanded. "Where is Mouse?" Athena reached out with her energy and shut off Spark's power. He was surprised to say the least.

"I'm Athena," she said in a clipped voice. "I assume you're Spark. If you would calm the hell down and stop scaring these kids I'll tell you what you want to know!"

"How did you do that?" Spark asked, shocked.

"My father taught me a lot of things," Athena said. "It's considered poor manners to use energy like that in a healing ward!" she scolded.

"Sorry," he said, blushing. "Chance talks about you a lot. It's a pleasure to meet you." He held out a hand. "Is Mouse alive?" he asked with his hand still extended.

"She is. I brought her here." Athena took his hand. "It's good to meet you too Spark. She was in bad shape, but she's being treated by the healers."

"Will she be ok? She's my best friend. I don't know what I would do if she were gone."

"We have the best healers in the world here." Athena informed him. "I can take you to see her but I have to warn you, we heal people naked. Is that ok with you?"

"That doesn't bother me. We treated each other's wounds enough that I'm used to her at least partially undressed."

The two went into the next room so Spark could check on his friend. Athena had the feeling she was going to be needed in the main room soon. Some of those children had such hollow looks in their eyes it frightened her.

• •

Chance faced off against Harbinger with more fear than he had against Inferno. This was the man who was the cause of all his sorrow. When he gave the order to kill either Jim or Eliza it has caused an irreparable rift that led to Eliza trying to kill him and Mouse. His back was still injured. The healing energy he had been using was only enough to stop the bleeding and lightly scab the wound. He had not let Caval know that energy alone was holding him on his feet. Setting aside thoughts of spinal damage, he squared off against Harbinger. The man was calm, collected and looked almost bored. In comparison Chance felt enraged and ready to kill. An outsider coming into the room would think Chance was the bad guy.

He struck first sending pieces of the desk and wall flying at Harbinger. The man simply waved his hand and the pieces fell to the floor. Another flash of laser thin energy just missed his heart and burned his shoulder. Chance used Sparks' power to try and attack Harbinger up close. Flashing across the room his fist was caught and Harbinger punched him in the face with power in his own fist. Chance's shield absorbed a lot but not all the energy and the resulting blow cracked his cheek and made his eye swell shut. Retreating from his opponent he pulled electricity out of the lights and shot it at Harbinger. This at least caused some damage as it burned holed in the man's suit and cause him to change his shielding to deflect 'natural' energy. Pressing his attack Chance tried to intensify the heat from the burns caused by the electricity. Still moving as, he attacked, the wall behind Chance exploded. Wires reached out with a life of their own and grabbed him, wrenching his arm out of socket in his attempt to escape. Harbinger smiled at him and sent another beam of concentrated light at his head. Chance used a variation of Warden's whip to cut the wires and managed to dodge the light. Giving the air a life of its own, Chance made it attack Harbinger like a living being. Harbinger was forced to step back and opened some kind of small hole that sucked up the wind entity. Using the stored up energy he had been building Chance fired what looked like a beam of silvery power from his hand. It caught Harbinger in the chest and lifted him to the wall, injuring the man. Just when he thought we was winning a crushing force pushed Chance to the floor. He lost concentration on his energy as he threw everything he had into his shield. No matter how hard he pushed it did not help. He felt himself being crushed under an unbearable weight. He could not believe the strength of the energy pushing him down. Harbinger smiled at him as cracks started forming in his shield.

• •

Communication from Caval was the last thing Horatius expected to hear tonight. He had just finished clearing a section of the camp with his team when the young man contacted him. In a series of flashes, less like communication and more like visions, Caval brought him up to speed on what had gone on. He was surprised to learn Athena was no longer at the camp fighting having chosen to take the girl Mouse through the gate. He was also angry to learn of the plan to kill two most wanted men in camp but could not blame the teens after what they had been through.

Horatius instructed his second in command to finish the sweep and then teleported into the hall of Wardens office. The energy he felt coming from the room was extreme. There was a strong shield surrounding the area and he could not get in. Every shield had a weak point and he started searching for one, desperate to get through to enter the room. The sounds of battle were intense and the waves of energy he felt were even more intense. While he was searching for a weakness he heard a woman's voice say.

"No! Harbinger! He's wanted alive!" Looking in the door he could see Chance on the floor fighting off some kind of energy that was pushing him down. The man called Harbinger was looking at Chance intently pushing more power into his attack.

"This brat 'Tempest' has caused too much trouble as it is!" Harbinger told the woman. "We can say he was killed by someone else during the attack."

"Stop!" she demanded again. "We will not be forgiven. They'll know!"

When she spoke, the shield weakened and Horatius realized she was shielding the area as Harbinger attacked. Looking at her intently he got a good read on her energy and was able to find the chink in her shield. He took it down and stepped into the room, then blasted the two with a wave of force. The woman was tossed backwards into the wall. Looking up at him she disappeared. Harbinger was knocked away from Chance and his attack on him lessened. Horatius quickly tossed up a teleport lock to prevent the man from escaping as the woman had.

"We're supposed to capture you alive and find out more about the Overlords," he said. "However, I find myself feeling in a vengeful mood over my daughter and her boyfriend."

Harbinger tried to switch his attack from the nearly unconscious Chance to Horatius. "Don't bother. I analyzed your attack in the hall. It won't work on me," he finished.

The man at least looked a little frightened. A beam of concentrated light energy shot at Horatius hitting him on the right side of his body and exiting from his back. Chance cried out thinking Harbinger had just killed him. Closing the wound Horatius smiled and reached out with an unconventional attack.

"What are you doing?" Harbinger asked in alarm.

"If you knew, you would be more afraid than you are now!" Horatius answered. He used his power to pull the living energy out of Harbinger and transferred it to himself.

By the time Harbinger realized what was happening to him, it was too late. Horatius seemed to become younger, age lines disappeared and his gray hair faded.

"You think this ends with me?" Harbinger laughed as his body started to collapse in on itself. "I'm just a General!" When the energy finally ceased, Harbinger dropped to the ground a dried dead husk and Horatius looked a vibrant late twenties.

"What the hell power was that?" Chance whispered staring at Horatius. Both men also wondered what Harbinger final words meant.

"So, you're the young man who stole my daughter's heart," he said with a smile. "I have to say I expected more after hearing about your fight with Inferno," he joked, feeling tired.

"Sorry Sir," Chance responded in a voice barely above a whisper. "I promise to do better next time."

Horatius laughed and helped the young man to his feet. "Let's get you to a healer shall we? That's a nasty wound on your back."

Epilogue

In the weeks that followed the liberation of the Overlords' recruitment camp, Chance had time to try to heal and adjust to his new life. After five days in the Tank to repair damage to his back (some of the healing supplied by Caval's enigmatic teacher) he met with Athena, Caval, Mouse and Spark to discuss the aftermath of the raid. Seventy-four teenagers, forty-two kids aged five to twelve, and sixteen children ranging from infants to four year olds, had been liberated. All told, one hundred and thirty-two children needed homes and training. During the raid, eighteen of twenty guards on duty and two loyal teens had been killed, as had Warden. Counting Harbinger and his reinforcements, an additional thirty-seven people had died.

Cyrus had assumed that someone in charge realized their people were basically cannon fodder and stopped any attempts at salvaging the camp. Seven teens including Eliza had fled either on foot, by teleport, or the car. They were all still at large. The raiding unit had lost four members which included one leader. There were scores of injuries, the worst being a woman losing her hand and one man losing his right leg above the knee. All in all, it was considered a textbook raid.

Spouses and children were told about their lost loved ones by Cyrus, Michael and Ares personally as they were the three main leaders in charge. The lost ones were considered heroes for the liberation of so many captive children but the grief remained.

Mouse had gone into cardiac arrest in the Tank and was revived by Athena who happened to be in the room at the time. Caval refused a Tank for healing as he wanted to have a scar from his battle with Warden to offset the ones he now had on his back.

"What do we do now?" Chance asked Athena. Sitting down at a picnic table in a secluded area he was still finding it hard to believe he no longer had to run.

"Now we heal and enjoy ourselves for a little while." She replied looking tired. The ordeal in the infirmary had taken a toll on her. She had helped provide comfort to many of the rescued kids. Learning about Chances life didn't prepare her to see so many kids living in the same conditions he had.

"I for one want to take few weeks off training," Caval stated surprising everyone.

"You?" Mouse asked. "And what will you do with all your time?"

"Help dad finish Sanctuary." He waved at the small town community under construction, not far from them. "If it had been ready, Chance would have been able to just go there instead of running for all those years. Most of this could have been avoided."

"And what about me?" she smiled.

"You can help. I'm not going to let you out of my sight for a while anyway," he promised giving her a gentle squeeze.

"I need to decide which group if any I want to be a part of" Chance declared. "And there are so many kids from camp that need homes, I think after we rest a bit we might want to help place them.”

“I chose the Seraphs already,” Spark mentioned. “Raphael offered to let me stay with him and his wife.”

“I didn’t know that!” Athena exclaimed. “Uncle Raph is a great guy.”

“They are still looking for Cinder,” Caval told Chance. “They hope he will agree to train you. He was one of Phantom’s teachers before he fled the Queen,” he added.

“I’ll think about that later,” Chance answered. “After what we have been through I agree with Athena; I think we all deserve a rest.” The five friends agreed not knowing what the future held but knowing for now they were safe and had each other.

Chance’s story will continue...